the
Connemara
Connection

by Nancy Bradley

Order this book online at www.trafford.com
or email orders@trafford.com

Most Trafford titles are also available at major online book retailers.

Printed in the United States of America.

ISBN: 978-1-4269-6894-5 (sc)
ISBN: 978-1-4269-6896-9 (hc)
ISBN: 978-1-4269-6895-2 (e)

Trafford rev. 05/06/2011

 www.trafford.com

North America & International
toll-free: 1 888 232 4444 (USA & Canada)
phone: 250 383 6864 ♦ fax: 812 355 4082

CHAPTER ONE

The dying sun, reflecting off the high corrugated metal wall, sent a dull gold light through the window. Sheila pushed the curtain aside to watch down the street. A cigarette butt smoldered in a rusty lid on the windowsill. "Damn," she muttered, "Damn them -" She took the last cigarette from her pocket and lit it, cupping her hands around the warmth of the match. She had been waiting since five o'clock and no word from any of them. "Damn," she said again and pulled the curtain back over the window and a cold greyness settled over everything in the room.

Grey like my mind she thought, grey and dull. The lads should have been done with it by now, and back. She was too

1

tired to worry properly; she had worried too many times and what good had it ever been? Still it went on, still they fought and still they died. And still their land lay under the hand of the bloody English, did it not? Sure, her Wolfe had the desire for freedom like a faith in him, more real, she thought, than his faith in the Blessed Virgin. Her hand made the sign of the cross, all independent of her mind, and she knew it was a prayer for him and her brother she was making. So tired she was; it was one of those days when she knew it would never end. The great wall would always cut Belfast in half just the way her life was cut in half by the endless fighting. Not that she wasn't a fighter herself; what else had she ever known? Her Da was dead in the first troubles, twenty years since. All she remembered of him was strong arms and the smell of Old Bush in her face when he held her and said, "I'm coming back, luv, never doubt it, and bring ye a dolly to play with -" Then it was only Mum, always crying, her face drawn and thin, her tired arms lifting the baby to wash him, and always the men at night in the back, talking, planning.

The baby - her little brother - now the man, Sean, who was feared by them all; so mean he was, so hard, driving them all on, just as though he believed that by the sheer force of their hate they could rid themselves, one fine day, of the Brits and their filthy RUC forever.

Wolfe said they would, but, then, Wolfe always hoped, even in the darkest times, and when he smiled in his dream, it was like the warmth of sunshine. Ah, Wolfe, my luv, she thought, pray God you get your wish, pray God you live this night and always. At least this night, and your arms around me and the bed warm with our love -

Darkness fell before she left the window and her heart was lead in her breast. Then the sound of guns fired behind the wall. It's always the same, she thought, always the hate and the fighting. Standing by the sink she heard a sound at the door; a wee sound, surely not Wolfe or Sean. "Who is it?" Her voice was like a knife cutting the air.

"It's me, Willy -" a small whisper on the stoop. "Let me in, Sheila -"

She pulled the tiny lad into the room. "Child, what are you doing out alone? Cum in -"

"Wolfe sent me," he said. "They daren't cum here. I'm to tell ye where they are." Eight years old, maybe, Willy was thin as a string bean and his white skin was grey with the kind of grime only a little boy can find and cover himself with. He should be playing in the streets with his mates, kicking a football for sport, not running their dangerous errands in the night.

Kneeling beside him, she put her arms around his skinny shoulders. "Does your Mum know you're out?" she asked him, and even as she said it she knew that Maggie would risk her life or her child's, if it would help the cause. She was Wolfe's sister, and as strong as he to fight, but without the gentleness he had with him, and without the sorrow and the pain. The child had Wolfe's eyes; it was eerie to see the same light in them, the blue of the sky shining through the dark. He would be another one, sure, another heir to the struggle, another Wolfe Tone fighting to drive the enemy from the land. She wondered if her Wolfe had been different if they hadn't named him that - Wolfe Tone Morrison,

3

like a mantle on his shoulders.

"Sure she knows," Willy said. "And who else would they send? No one knows how I go through the streets. And who would be caring?" The matter-of-fact little speech was so much an echo of Wolfe that she could cry. Of course they'd send Willy; as he said, who'd be caring if a little lad ran through the street at night.

"Are they all right?" she finally asked. The question had been on the back of her tongue since she opened the door; she was cold afraid to hear the answer.

"Billy's been hit." He dropped his eyes from her for a moment. "The bloody RUC saw him. He'd not got the bum lit right and had to go back -" He bit his lip. "I saw him fall, Sheila, and he was bleedin' - I think he's dead." It was a whisper now. "Wolfe and Sean got away, but they'd been seen; that's why they couldn't come, not here, and be followed -"

So Billy was dead, the wild one, the lad who would go anywhere, do anything; he was gone. There were no tears in her heart for him, just a red rage that burned her like a fire. "You must stay here, Willy. Keep locked and don't answer if anyone cums. I'm going to them."

"Aye, they said you must," Willy nodded. "They've got news, they said. They're at O'Shaunessy's, in back the pub. You'll not want to go straight though - I'll tell ye how." His knowledge of the streets that crossed the wounded city was encyclopedic. She couldn't help thinking that in a day when children played and laughed in the streets he would have been a great one at hide and seek; there was no alley, no hidden doorway he hadn't found. She

4

memorized his instructions while he chewed greedily on a cold sausage sandwich. "You're our bravest, best lad," she said. "Go to bed now. Mum will get you tomorrow."

The streets were dark, but still noisy. In an alley she heard voices and hurried past. A dark shawl covered her head and shoulders and hid the small 45 caliber gun she had tucked in the waist of her skirt. Even on this side of the wall a woman, or a man, was not safe. Here and there a solitary figure hurried through the dark and gunfire punctuated the night with its sharp staccato song. If they had gotten Wolfe or Sean she would have killed them. She laid her hand on the cold hard metal that pressed into her side and prayed for a chance to use it on them. She was proud of the hate in her soul; she carried it like a banner with her through the awful days and endless nights. Her cheeks were hot and her eyes glistened. Ourselves alone, she thought, only our own selves to throw off the bonds of slavery - the filthy prods! The Brits with their paid gunmen! Constabulary, they call them. Hired killers, if you ask me!

She slipped down the last alley. A big tom-cat, offended by the interruption of his nightly prowl, snarled in the corner of a doorway. She stiffened at the sound and her hand flew again to the gun at her side. The cat, perhaps feeling remorse, spoke in a mild miaow, and she laughed. Lord help me, she thought, must I jump at every sound I hear? Sure I near shot the poor old cat for his troubles. "Sorry, Tommy," she whispered and leaned to give him a pat. He spat at her for her efforts and went his way.

She felt her own way down the dark alley, counting the doorways by touch; like a blind man, she thought. In this poor land perhaps the blind were the lucky ones; they couldn't see their lovely city torn in half, nor see the hungry children on the street and the jobless men drinking their despair in dirty corners until blessed oblivion covered their shame. Sure, Wolfe would be having his and Sean, too, and could she blame them? Billy most likely dead, and they barely escaped alive themselves. She could feel the beat of her heart; her breathe came in quick stabs and burnt her throat. Wolfe was alive! and Sean, and they HAD done it. Willy said it was a good one; they had brought ambulances, and black smoke had come out the windows. Five engines from the Fire Force had come. Sirens had screamed, police had run around like sheep got loose. Willy had been sure there was trouble from it. How many did it kill, and how many were dead? That's what mattered.

Then she was in Wolfe's arms and all the hate was gone. Fool I am, she told herself, to go all soft inside just because this man holds me to him and I can smell his skin and feel the rough of his cheek against mine. "Lass," he said. "Lass, we've got news to make the stones rise up and dance a jig for ye." He held her at arm's length. "My luvly lass," he said, "Thank God you're safe -"

He pulled her down beside him where they were sitting in the corner of the room. Through the half-open door she heard the rise and fall of voices; students drinking and laughing, the telly blaring a football game and old men telling stories of the time before the troubles while the drink made their voices mellow and made their eyes grow dim and rheumy. She could see the cold blue light of the telly and it puzzled her that the kids in there were

6

able to make the damn football into a cause to care for, while real men were dying for their freedom not ten blocks away. She felt Wolfe's body, warm against hers and his hand on her thigh and she let herself be happy, really happy, just for a moment of time. Was there some place, she wondered, some place in the world where a woman could love her man and be loved and never fear -? It wasn't Belfast, that she knew.

"What is it, then," she said. "What's the wonderful news you have?"

"How would you like it, my luv, if we should kidnap the Queen?"

"And how should I like it if the cows had wings and could fly? You daft man, you've been at the drink too long-" She turned to her brother. "Sean, lad, you mustn't let him -"

"Shut up, Sis," Sean snapped. Oh, he was mean, he was. Never a little laugh from him, only the cold, hard words. Sure, if she couldn't laugh now and then she would die; the hate would eat her right up, from the inside out. "Listen to Ben - he's back from the coast, just."

Then she saw that from across the table a stranger was staring at her. Against her will she raised her hand to smooth her hair; it was that kind of look he was giving her. "Yes, luv, listen," Wolfe whispered.

The man swallowed about two fingers of whiskey and poured some more in his glass. "She'll be in Connemara," he said. "Next munth. When we're coming up from Carna, she'll be there."

"No," Sheila breathed. "She doesn't cum to Ireland. She'd

never dare."

    "I found it out," Ben said. "For sure. My cousin Annie as does linens at the Ussher, she told me. She can read, may God rest her soul, and she saw it in a letter." He looked around the table. Five heads bent close and his voice was a whisper. "Each year the Duke cums for the fishin' - he stays there a week with a bunch of his buddies. Great sportsman he is, they say." A smile went round the table. Dukes fished by the mercy of their guides and caught what their guides showed to them. Ould Ian at Ussher knew the name and life history of every fish in the lake and if the Duke caught the big ones it was because Ian took him where they were. "Great sportsman, I said," Ben went on. "Well, lads, Annie saw this letter when she was taking the linens in and no one was there. She couldn't help but her eyes fell on it. The gold seal was shinin' like the sun, she said.   AND it was from Lady Somebody-Fine-and-Fancy makin' sure that when the royal person, it said, come with the Duke, there should be complete privacy and absolute secrecy. The very words, Annie said, and she has the memory of a elephant, Annie does."

    "You're all daft!" Sheila said. "I suppose you just walk in and say, Your Majesty, my luv, cum take a little walk with us, and she cums - then you say to the Duke, you can have her back if you just give Ireland back to us and take the all the protestants and all the RUC back to your bloody land and be gone with you! And then he signs a letter, WITH a gold seal shinin' like the sun and we're all free! F--- you all!" She said and felt hot tears in her eyes and her hand shook so much she had to put her glass down to hide the shaking from them. "You can keep your silly jokes -"

8

She turned on Wolfe. "You sent poor wee Willy all that way to get me just to make fun? Ah, Wolfe, luv, you know me better than that -"

"It's no joking, Sheila. It's God's truth, and by the Holy Mother of God, I tell you, luv, we'll do it -" He put an arm over her shoulder and smiled down at her and she knew it was true. He would find a way.

Sean slammed his mug down on the table. "Kill her," he said, "Blow the lot of them into Hell -" His eyes were black with the rage in him, the hate Sheila had seen there even when he was a wee lad, the little brother she had taught to tie his shoes and blow his nose, those long years ago. "F--- you, Sis," he would say to her then. "Take your bloody hands off me-" And she would tell Mum and Mum would cry. Ah, Sean, why do you hate yourself so? she thought. Sometimes Wolfe could reason with him, he could, just as though he never saw how the fires of hell looked out of those wounded eyes; he seemed to pity Sean for the fear that tore at his gut and filled him with the madness to hate and kill.

"Lad, if we can't give her back, what will be getting for it? She'll be our price - the price of our freedom." The radiance in his face was a torch in the dark and Sean was silent again.

They carried Billy to his home that night. His weeping wife and children sat by the body, then, staring at the blood-stained sheet that covered it. Wolfe and Sheila held her hands and wept with her. The tears ran down her cheeks

9

unstopping; she made no effort to dry her eyes. Now and then a small sound came from her mouth, like the cry of a wounded rabbit. She seemed not to notice the sobbing children clinging to her side; her eyes never moved from the lighted circle in the center of the room, where all that remained of her husband lay in a pool of blood on the table, cold and still forever.

When at last they fell into bed, day was breaking over the ugly wall. Wolfe pulled the curtain across the window and turned to Sheila. She felt the warmth of his body against her and she held him close to warm away the cold that shook her. The chill that trembled through her was not for Billy's death only; it was for knowing now what it would be like for her when Wolfe should die.

Their love, then, was wild and strong and filled with their sorrow. "Death be damned-" Wolfe breathed when at last they lay quiet in each other's arms. "Be damned to Hell!"

CHAPTER TWO

A thin, pale light was beginning to fill the black square of the window; daybreak was rushing towards them high over the ocean. It wasn't fair; the movie had just ended and there was the sun, telling him it was time for breakfast. In less than an hour the lovely green of Ireland would be beneath them and when the plane touched down in Shannon the day would be fairly begun. Charley Gibson closed his eyes, firmly. He needed sleep more than he did breakfast.

But sleep wouldn't come to him. His mind kept running on, planning, thinking. He decided he'd dash into the terminal while they were on the ground in Shannon and give Harry a call in Dublin. Maybe they'd send a car when he got there; it wouldn't

11

hurt to give it a try. It really was the least they could do to make up for ruining his weekend on three hour's notice.

He should have been spending it with Sally in Upperville instead of here, crammed into the window seat of the 747, wedged in by a three-hundred pound Goliath who snored and snuffled in his fitful sleep. The Agency had no consideration for a man's happiness, none whatever.

Of course he'd never expected an assignment like this so soon, not after just over a year with the agency. Bill Hayward had called him into his office right after lunch to brief him. A map of the British Isles lay on his desk.   He pointed to one of the jagged points of land that Ireland flings out into the stormy waters of the North Atlantic. "You've been there, Charley," he said. "Didn't you spend some time out there in Connemara when you were a kid?"

"It was a long time ago," Charley said. "With Mom, that time, and Jamey."

"Well, we think that's where they're bringing the stuff in," Bill said.   "They're getting it from Qadaffi, and the Brits think it's with money going through that girl from Boston. That's why they want us over there -" He paused. "What can you remember about the place, Connemara, I mean? Find your way around, you think?"

What DID he remember? He remembered, for one thing, that fifteen years ago he had been too excited to resent how inconsiderately the sun ate up the comfortable blackness of the night, pushing it back across the Atlantic and forcing him into a new day while the softness of sleep was still upon him. He had sat up very straight then; sleep was unthinkable. He hoped he looked older than thirteen. The stewardess, he remembered thinking, was quite a dish, and he had spent the night convincing himself the she must believe he was sixteen or seventeen; he didn't look like a child. He was, after all, escorting his widowed mother on a long journey; he was the man of the family.

He remembered that other plane beginning to lose altitude, beginning its descent into Shannon. He saw Mom still awake, looking out the window, her face illuminated harshly in the cold, early light. She looked so sad he wanted to say something to her, but he didn't know what. There was a sort of wounded look around her eyes that he sometimes noticed whenever she didn't think anyone was looking. Everyone said how brave she had been when Dad was killed (the words, "Dad was killed," still hadn't seemed real to him then). They said she was wonderful to go on with her life the way she was doing. What did they think she'd do? Die? Not Mom, not ever.

Instead, six weeks later she and Charley were on the plane going back to Ireland, and they were going to take the pony trek Dad had promised them. "Peggy," he had said, "You and Charley would have a great time. Why don't you take a couple weeks off and do it?" That was the day before it happened. The day before the crashing glass, the sharp sound of gunfire, heard, somehow, after the breaking glass. Then the blood and his mother's scream. The blood ran down his father's face; it was very bright red and ran in slow motion over his open eyes. Sirens howled outside but

13

in the limo there was silence, time frozen, himself frozen, while his father's body sank sideways onto his mother's lap.

At the Embassy it was supposed that they had thought Henry Gibson was British and it was just another incident in the long catalog of resistance; another chapter in the bloody battle for the soul of the six counties that make up the torn and battered body of Northern Ireland, where, in cottages and pubs and churches men and women still plot to rid their land of the tyranny they hate and fear. His father had been just one more in the list of senseless victims of a war that brought neither freedom nor happiness to those who waged it.

And then there was the day at Arlington and his mother holding the triangle of the folded flag against herself as the guns echoed through the hazy, hot summer air, and later, alone at the farm she had said, "Let's just go on back and go to Connemara like Dad wanted us too -" And so they had gone; the tall, skinny thirteen year-old boy and the slender woman, carrying their sorrow with pride, sharing the unseen burden of their grief.

In Shannon they had rented a car and Mom drove it to Clifden, where, on a morning of glowing mists and tattered clouds, they were taken to land's end. The ocean beat in upon the cliffy shore and the wind whipped the waves to frothy white. A man stood in shirt sleeves by the stone wall, laughing into the gale; a girl stood by his side. Two older boys were roaming the rocky field - "If you could call it a field," Mom had said - chasing horses and ponies through boggy paths between the boulders.

That day was the beginning of healing for Charley, and maybe for Peggy, as well. It was a magical two weeks they

14

spent, following Jamey Leary and his daughter, Megan, over the rockbound hills and haunted valleys of Connemara. It seemed as though the land itself was steeped in a kind of warmth that felt to them like love and they were comforted by it. The days were long and their minds were washed and cleansed in the wind that blew over the barren hills and their hearts were made whole in them while their bodies were toughened by long hours in the saddle.

They rode most of each day and at night they stayed in hunting lodges and inns; they didn't see a town, a real town with shops, for five days. The ride belonged to Jamey Leary and he managed both riders and horses with cheerful disregard for life and limb. Huntsman of the Galway Blazers from September to March, the rest of the year he hired his horses, ponies, children and himself to lead tourists over the treacherous trail from the west coast to Galway and back. Without Jamey there was no getting through; he had ridden it from childhood with Ould McElhinney to guide him, and he knew the depth and breadth of every bog and he knew how to get through them or around them. On the high mountains there was no trail. He picked his way over boulders and down wet gulleys, and any rider who thought he knew a better way to go than following in Jamey's footsteps, most likely ended up belly-deep in the quaking bog.

Oh, Charley remembered Connemara, all right; the beauty and the danger and the magic, and he remembered the sad cry of the loon over the black lake of Ussher where two children had sat in cold and fear, promising each other they would never forget.

A dull ache in his ears alerted him to the probability that they were coming down into Shannon. Outside, instead of the unreal green of the land, there was nothing but grey mist. Then, below them, the runway appeared; a bump and a jolt, and the long, groaning haul as tons of hurtling metal fought the force of inertia. "Please remain seated with your seatbelts fastened -" the soft Irish voice sounded at home.

He found a row of phones inside the terminal; the agency had thoughtfully supplied him with Irish pounds, but, damn them, no change. In the nearest shop a cheerful Irish woman gave him some pence and shillings for his pound note and tried to sell him a fisherman's sweater. He gave her a large, friendly smile and muttered something about his plane leaving in five minutes; he raced back and dialed Dublin. "Charley Gibson, here-" he said, before he realized that it was a mechanical voice advising him to call back after ten a.m. when the offices of the Embassy of the United States would be open and doing business, or else leave a message and a number where he could be reached, thank you very much and kindly wait for the tone before speaking. He stared into the face of the receiver, unbelieving. Curse and damn! Why didn't they stay up all night like they had made him do? He hung the phone up softly not to harm the ear of the mechanical voice; the gentle air of Ireland had clearly gotten to him already. Wide awake now, he headed back to the gate. An hour's flight and he would be in Dublin, hurtling through the streets with a maniac Irish cabbie.

His fat seat mate was gone and he pushed up the divider between the seats. Diagonally, his six foot two frame fitted a little better. Perhaps he could sleep. First, he'd look out the window and for old time's sake, try to identify some of the landscape. He found himself wishing they were over Connemara and he could see Ussher House in its hidden glen by the dark lake where he and Megan had huddled, waiting for the ghost of Lady Dudley through the long night of mist and chilling rain.

It was so long ago, and so much had happened; a whole lifetime, it seemed since he was that child. But, looking out the window now he thought he could feel again the wild, windy cold of that night, with the black windows of the old Mansion behind them and the dark waters of the lake at their feet. The loon's desperate, sad cry was in his ears -

No, idiot, it's only the motors, revving back to land. You've dreamt your way across Ireland and it's morning in Dublin and you have a long day of briefing ahead of you there. Then, you have to tell them how you will find and follow a half dozen men with a boat load of death in their hands, over those lovely mountains and through the quaking bogs to the north.

CHAPTER THREE
(1975)

He remembered those mountains, the bright skies and clear winds. He remembered Jamey gathering the horses together out there on the far windy shore, while a skinny, tall boy watched with eyes full of wonder, shivering in the cold, waiting to begin the great adventure, the trek over the top of Connemara, all the way to Galway. He could see the rocky coast under a heavy sky, and Bill and Paddy driving the horses and ponies to them over the piles of grey stone that were, in this unforgiving land, a field. And little Megan leaping over the boulders, dodging the bogs and whistling softly into the wind.

She was following a huge grey horse who trotted, unconcerned, away from her brothers and towards the shore. The horse stopped, ears pricked and neck arched. The wind whipped the girl's hair into her face; with one hand she brushed it away from her eyes, and with the other she reached up to the horse. Slowly, his head bent down; he condescended to be touched. Her arm slid around his neck and gently she led him across the uneven ground to where her father stood. "You're riding him today, Daddy?" she asked. "See, I've caught him for ye -"

"Sure, where would I be without my lass?" Jamey said. "Aye, I'll take him today, and maybe let this lady have him tomorrow." He smiled at Peggy. "Only my Meg can catch this lad," he said. "But sure he's the best of the lot once you're on him." He threw a rope around the horse's neck and tied him there by the wall. Megan grinned at Charley and his heart melted inside him.

"Will I get one for you, then?" she asked.

"Can I come with you?" he said. His voice squeaked unforgivably. He hoped the humiliating sound of it was drowned in the wailing of the wind through the loose stones of the wall.   "Sure ye can help," she said. "My brothers are that lazy, I have all the work to do -" She held out her hand to him and he took it in his; she pulled him along with her as she ran. When they came near a cluster of grazing ponies she slid away from him. "Cum, we'll get these," she said. "You take the grey one -"

Taking the grey one was easier said than done. It ran from him like a creature bewitched, and it hid behind a clump of gorse, where it stood, docile and quiet; then, in a clatter of stones, it wheeled away and was gone. He whirled to run after it and fell flat on his face in the mud.

Megan's laughter echoed in the wind as she ran after the pony. It stopped and waited for her; she walked right up to it. "Cum, luv," she whispered, and it put its muzzle into her hand. "Hold this one," she said, and ran off to get the others.

For an hour he followed her that day, running headlong after her, watching in awe, as one horse after another came to her and allowed itself to be caught. Then she would lead it by the forelock and, stepping lightly over the rocks and through the bog, she would deliver it to a waiting rider. Her feet never slipped. It was as if they knew by heart every inch of this stony, unyielding ground. By the time they had caught all the horses, Charley had just about made up his mind to find a way to stay here and work for Jamey and never go back home again. Deerfield Academy looked very far away.

She was the most beautiful thing he had ever seen. Dark hair blowing in the wind, her pale face washed by the swirling mists, she would race past him, laughing, and then pull up suddenly in front of him. "Charley, will we race, then?" she'd say, and before he could answer, she'd be off, yelling over her shoulder. "Beat you to yon cottage!" she'd shout. Then her voice would be lost in the wind; hair streaming behind her, she would race across the rocky fields, leaping walls or hiding behind them. He'd gallop after her and catch up to her, breathless and laughing. The pony seemed an extension of the child when she was riding, but it was when she ran free across the bogs that he most loved to watch her.

Then she was herself, only. Faded jeans covered her skinny, long legs, and a sweater, sizes too big, hung from her narrow shoulders. She could catch any pony; they came to her, laid their heads upon her shoulder and nuzzled her hand.

One day they stopped for lunch by the sea where an old musician lived. While they ate, sitting on the grass and rocks, the old man played them tunes on an ancient concertina; slow and wild, the melodies were, tossed on the wind across the water.

"Cum, give us a dance, lass," he called to Megan. Shy, she stood by the cottage wall, not smiling, just standing there alone. "Ah, lass, I'll play ye the song from the sea - cum, dance, luv." Slowly she walked into the circle where they sat. Then Mick took out a small pipe and put it to his lips. The strange, slow piping was hardly audible above the wind, and Megan stood a moment, listening. Carefully she lifted one knee and held her leg out, motionless for a moment in the air. Hesitant, she stood, until the music became more insistent and she began to move in a stately, almost formal step, eyes fixed on the misty shore, while the sound of the piping led her on. She was a young foal taking its first graceful, tentative steps. Then, with the same elegant grace, she circled the grassy plot, and her smile came from another world where things were real that have never been; for a moment Charley saw what she saw, and he felt his heart break within him for the joy he felt.

An hour later, her hoyden's yell caught up to him as they galloped along the sand. "We'll swim, then," she called, and rode her pony straight into the sea.

The long days were filled with adventure; they rode for hours each day, over rugged terrain, or galloped across miles of flat sand where the tide had left shimmering pools like mirages that shattered into fountains of gleaming spray when twenty galloping horses dashed through them. Then the nights were magic for Charley, eating dinner at 9:30 in the candlelit rooms of old lodges where they stopped, and listening, with the grown-ups around the fire, late into the night, to stories and songs filled with the melancholy longing of the Irish people dreaming dreams of freedom for their hard and lovely land. The songs were heavy with sorrow and with love, and he and Megan would sit with their eyes half-shut in sleep until at last Jamey would get up and say, "Time for bed, now. It's a long day we have tomorrow -" and, one by one, the tired riders would say their good-nights and wander off to their rooms.

One night, after dinner they sat around the fire with the grown-ups and Jamey told them the story of the sad Lady Dudley, whose manor house the inn had once been. He told them how she had drowned herself in the lake after her true love deserted her. A chill went up Charley's spine and he caught Megan's cool, blue eyes looking across the room at him. "Only the men need fear," Jamey said, "The poor lass wanders the halls looking for her luver." He paused and his mouth spread in a wide grin. "She is loony, poor thing, and will take any man she can find. She crawls into his bed and the night they have together there is one to remember, it is -"

Words failed him as he relished the thought of a night in Lady Dudley's depraved embrace. "Then," his voice was low and sad, "Then, she leads the dear lad to the lake and he follows her in - happy they say to drown in her luvly arms." The crackling of the peat fire - turf, they called it there - was the only sound in the room. Then from afar the cry of the loon

23

echoed across the lake, and a sudden wind blew down the chimney, stirring the coals into a hectic blaze. Megan moved over and sat by Charley; he felt her tough little hand resting on his. She was as cold as he, and her eyes were round with fear.

"Don't worry, Megan," he said. "You're a girl."

"Sure it's you I fear for," she whispered, and ran from the room.

She was waiting in the hall when he started up the stairs. "Shh," she whispered. "Cum out the back with me -" She held out her hand, imperious, not to be refused.

"We'll wait up for her, that's what," she said. "Daddy thinks I'm in bed already -"

So they had sat, two frightened children, huddled under the big holly tree, while the night grew cold and the subtle rain began to fall. "Where does she come from?" Charley whispered. "The lake?" He strained his eyes to see into the blackness and thought there were shapes moving in the trees. A night bird's song blew over the water to them and he felt the hair rise on the back of his neck. Megan's bony elbow dug into his side and he put his coat around her shoulders. Her hair smelt of fresh hay. "Does she really walk, or just sort of float?" Floating seemed more likely for a ghost; in fact he was sure, now, that something *was* floating, moving in the wood. Inside his coat, his arm tightened around Megan's shoulder.

"She walks," Megan said, very firm. "That's what they do. Is there nothing you know about ghosts, then? What do they teach you there in the states?" Even in the black night he could see her smile. She leaned towards him, wicked, now. "Only she can walk *through* anything, through you and me, even -" Her hand was holding his so tightly that it hurt and her face was so close he could feel her breath against his cheek.

"How long should we wait?" he asked.

"Till she cums."

He didn't know he'd been asleep and when he woke he couldn't think where he was. He knew he was shaking with the cold and everything about him was wet. Megan was asleep by his side, curled up like a puppy, with his coat wrapped around her. The rain was over; a soft, pale moon shed mysterious light through the trees and in a distance a cock announced the passing of the night. "Megan, we missed her," he whispered. "Wake up - you're freezing! We better go in -"

So that was all they ever saw of Lady Dudley - "and disappointing, she was," Megan complained. "I hope she drowns herself, next time," she said, and Charley laughed. He led her by the hand through the great French windows of the lodge.

In the dim light of the hall they said goodnight. "You're cold, Megan," he said, "And wet -"

"No more than you, lad," she said. "Just see yourself, drippin' puddles on the floor, you are -" The concern in her eyes made them go all dark, like the blue of the sea on a sunny day. He might have stood there all night, dripping and shaking, just to be near her, but she ran down the hall, blowing him a kiss, and disappeared up the stairs. "Sleep well, lad," she whispered, hanging for a moment over the rail, and then she was gone. Later, alone in his narrow bed, he thought he would die of his love for her.

The next night Charley waited in the hall for Megan, but she hurried past him with her father. He thought she wanted to say something to him; then the moment passed. He started to follow her down the hall.

"Come to bed, Charley." It was his mother, waiting at the top of the stairs. "You must be asleep on your feet -" Suddenly wide awake, he ran up the stairs and suffered himself to be kissed good-night. "See you in the morning, Mom," he said and slipped past her into his room. Fully clothed he lay on his bed by the window. Heavy vines grew outside his room, and the leaves brushed against the panes with a ghostly whisper. He was on the second floor and could see across the lawn to the wooded edge of the lake where he and Megan had waited last night, in vain, for the sight of the dreaded shade of Lady Dudley. Tonight the moon was out, an old moon, it's last half casting an eerie reflection from the black waters beyond the trees.

Maybe they hadn't waited long enough last night, or maybe she doesn't walk in the rain. Now, he lay there, wide-eyed, sleepless, remembering the chill of the night and the warmth of Megan close to him while they had waited and watched there under the dripping trees. He jumped when the cry of the loon sounded just below his window. Twice he heard it and then he leaned out to look. Instead of a bird, he could make out a white shape in the shadow of the holly tree next to the lodge. "Megan!" he whispered.

She waved once and disappeared into the darkness of the wood. The old vines held his weight easily; then he was running across the lawn and under the trees. The wood was dense, and at first he couldn't see his way, couldn't tell where she had gone. Then close beside him came the cry of the loon, a giggling sort of loon it was, and he almost bumped into Megan, standing beneath the big oak, laughing at him.

Clouds scudded across the moon, blotting out even its poor light and the wind blew cold over the water. "What are we doing, Megan?" he asked. "Why are you out here? Mom would have a fit if she knew - "

"The tinkers are camped up the road," she whispered, and they'll tell us our fortune. I've got a shilling, they'll do it for that." She opened her hand and in the darkness he could see the gleam of a coin. "Daddy won't let me - a fool's waste, he says, of good gold - but this is my own shilling I earned myself and I know the way there, along the lake, just -"

"The tinkers?" he said. "What d'you mean?"

"The gypsies, in their vans; I saw them by the road tonight. They steal sheep and sell poteen and who knows what else wicked. They even steal children, Daddy says -"

"Do they really tell fortunes?" A silly superstition, Charley thought, or had thought; something girls and other fools believed in like fortune cookies - the "Help me, I am being held captive in a Chinese cookie factory" kind of thing. Yet, here, trembling with cold under the gloomy trees, anything seemed possible, even inevitable. "Aren't you afraid?" he asked. "Your Dad may be right; maybe they do steal children."

"Well, lad, if *you're* afraid, then I'll go alone," she said.

"I didn't say I was afraid. I thought you might be -"

"And if I was afraid, would it keep me from going?" There was a little catch in her voice when she spoke; at that

27

moment Charley would have gone with her into the jaws of hell. How brave she was! It is nothing, he thought, to do what you aren't afraid to do, but to scorn your fear and do it anyway -

The trees sighed in the wind and the moon's half-light shone in flickering patches through the leaves. He could feel his heart beating wildly inside his chest. The thought of confronting alone - the lone protector of beautiful Megan - confronting alone the wicked world of the gypsy caravans, crossing their dark palms with silver and hearing the prophecy given to them from whatever evil source they knew, sent a chill down his spine, no matter her brave words or his manly courage. They *stole* children!

The path along the lake was rocky, and more than once his feet slipped and he felt the cold water soaking through his boot. Once Megan fell and when he took her hand to pull her to her feet he was surprised by its warmth and strength. He was cold in his anorak and she was only wearing the rough blue sweater she had worn all day. "Aren't you cold," he asked her. "I'm freezing -" She laughed, then, that lovely, wild laugh, and said, "Oh, you Yanks - you've not got the good, red Irish blood. Sure, a bit of a breeze won't be hurting you, now - cum, we've got to hurry. They'll not be waiting all the night."

"Do they know we're coming?"

"No," she said. "They don't -" She was close beside him on the narrow path. "When Daddy was still in the shed laying up the saddles, I ran down the road to ask them, but no-one was about. Out with the ponies, I reckon." He wanted to hold her warm hand and stop the stupid shaking of his body.

"Hssht, now," she said. "We're near to the road -" He could see lights twinkling through the trees and smell the smoke of a wood fire and of food cooking over it.

"It's after midnight," he whispered. "They're still up."

"They don't care," she said. "They're not like us, not like us at all. You'll see -"

They crept across the open ground towards the caravans that stood parked by the road. Three spotted ponies grazed, untethered nearby, showing ghostly and dim in the dark outside the vans. "Let's look in the window," Megan whispered. "See what they're doing, just, before we knock." She took him by the hand and pulled him along.

"Wait," he said. "Wait here and let me go first -" After all, he was the man, and he had to take care of her. They stepped carefully, not to break a twig or give any other sign they were there. The sky was dark now and he couldn't see where he was putting his feet unless he walked in the path of light shining from the window. What if they looked out and saw them sneaking up? They might shoot, or anything; everyone knew they had plenty to hide -

"Megan, I think we better just holler at them, tell them we're here and that it's us, not the police or something."

"Right, you," she said. "It's fools we look - shall I shout?" Before he could say yes or no the door flung open and the dog sprang into the light. He had never seen such a dog; as big as one of the ponies it seemed. And the roar from it's throat broke the stillness of the night like a roll of thunder as it lunged across the road to where they stood, rooted to the ground by fear.

"Run, Megan!" He grabbed her arm and together they plunged into the woods. He could almost feel the hot, red breath of the dog and over its wild barking he heard a man's angry voice and running footsteps after them. They ran and stumbled and ran on. Branches cut his face and once Megan cried out in pain, but terror drove them on through the dark until, close by the lake, he heard the clear, shrill baying of a second dog, coming from the path along the shore. Behind them, the man and dog crashed through the thicket, gaining space with every second. "We can't stop," he breathed. "Keep running -"

"Where?" Megan yelled. The other dog was still coming in front of them. He wanted to cry. He was helpless to save her, or himself. The dogs would be upon them in seconds - and he was helpless! They stopped to breathe at the lake's edge where the black water lapped the boulders that lined the shore. "Quick," Megan hissed. "Jump!" She grabbed his hand and together they leapt off the rocks. The water was like ice; every muscle went numb.

"We can't stay here," he whispered. "We'll freeze and drown." The water was deep and the rocky bank high above them. His clothes, weighted with water, now, pulled him down and he had to struggle to keep afloat. Megan trod water beside him. They could hear the dogs barking in confusion above them and the man swearing.

"Ye bloody damn keep away - ye hear me?" he yelled into the night. The dogs snuffled and growled, loathe to admit they had lost the track; fearing their master's wrath, they whined now, at his feet. Charley heard the sound of a boot, a good kick in the ribs to one of the animals, and it yelped in pain. Charley thought he would die of the cold. His whole body felt as if it belonged to someone else; he was numb from head to foot.

They were close under a ledge of rock and he prayed they would be able to pull themselves out when the man had given up and gone. He certainly couldn't swim far dressed like this. "Are you all right?" he whispered to Megan when it was quiet above them.

"I'm cold, lad -" her whisper was a breathe of ice and trembling. He felt the rocky wall beside him now and held on.

"Maybe we can climb up," he said. The stone was rough and he thought he could find hand-holds to pull up on. "You want to go first?" He couldn't leave her here in the water. "Get hold right here -"   He reached for her hand and she nodded. Then they heard it. The low rumble, the menace of a growl, and they knew they were not alone. Was the man still there, too?

He pressed against the wall beside her, and as he did, he felt something give way. He ran his hand over the face of the rock, and realized he was touching, not stone, but wood. Old, hardened like iron the wood was, even after ages in the water; it was boards, nailed together to make a door!   A rusty lock hung through the hasp. When Charley got it off, the doors swung open and they found they could swim in under the ledge. "Come on, Meg," he whispered. "Maybe we can get out of the water -" The dark was like black velvet; he guessed they had swum into a cave. Then he bumped into wood, a timber of some kind, down into the water. It was the pilings of a dock, and they pulled themselves out to sit, dripping wet and shaking with cold on the rotten boards of the ancient structure. "It must be a boat-house!" he'd whispered. "Have you ever seen it?"

She shook her head. "No. They just tie their fishing boats up by the mole, in the lee of it, or pull them out in a storm. Auld Ian would use it, sure, if he knew. Hidden by the trees, it must be," she said. Her teeth chattered when she spoke. He put his wet anorak around them both.

"We can't stay here," he said. "I'm going to explore. Come along; we'll freeze if we just sit here." He couldn't see anything except the square of lighter darkness where the door swung back and forth in the wind, making no sound above the lapping of the water at their feet. "There's got to be another way out. They can't just put their boat in and stay here -" He crawled along the boards of the dock, careful to feel for the edge. Megan was right behind him. Suddenly there was nothing in front of him and he almost fell headlong into the water. She held him around the waist and he pulled himself back onto the edge of the rotten boards. "It's broken," he said, "We have to find another way." He couldn't remember how long, they never knew how long, they stumbled around, blind and cold, until his hands felt stone instead of slimy wood beneath them. "It's open here," he whispered. "Stay close; I'll see where it goes -"

"I know what it is," Megan whispered. "It's his tunnel, the luver's who died! That's how he got to see her, crawling in through here with no one to know."

"Where do you suppose he died, Meg? In the tunnel?"

"Don't be daft, lad. Her husband shot him." She gave him a little shove. "Go ahead, try it." It wasn't so bad, except for the absolute and daunting darkness. And the cold. Inside the tunnel it was even colder than in the water, he thought. They might have gone ten yards when the ceiling became so low they had to bend down, at least Charley did. "It's closing off," he whispered. "I don't think we can go -" Fervently he wished for her to agree. Even the dogs would be a relief after this. "Maybe they have got tired of waiting for us."

She must have read his mind. "Let's go have a listen-" By the swinging doors they listened and the only sound they heard was the lapping of the water on the stony cliff and the sighing of the night wind in the wood.

The morning was bright, and the day was filled with laughter and beauty. It was hard to think that the night had ever been, that the great dogs had stayed slavering above their hiding place until the moon was set, and they shivering in the cave alone. And, a week later, while the plane raced over the water towards the setting sun, he sat, dry-eyed and sleepless, feeling the memory slipping backwards through his mind, until he was afraid that one day it would be nothing more to him than a remembered dream.

CHAPTER FOUR

Harry met him at the gate. Score one for the Embassy;
they WERE awake before 10 a.m.; they just didn't answer their
phone. Perhaps they didn't even know that Harry was meeting
him. "I've got a car," Harry said. "My own car. We're going to
surprise them. They can hardly wait to see you."

He hadn't changed since undergraduate days at
Georgetown. Thick glasses magnified his short-sighted eyes and
a shock of red hair still brushed across his forehead like the
forelock of a Thelwell pony. Nothing about Harry gave a clue to
the razor-sharp mind concealed behind his innocent, pale eyes.
The brain that had carried Harry through Georgetown's Foreign
Service School like a breeze from the ocean was camouflaged

nicely by a totally uninhibited outlook on life. He never opened a book that Charley knew about, and his consumption of beer was legendary. It was good to see him again; good to know he was here, a friendly face, in Dublin.

"Hey, Toad," Charley said, "Are we doing this thing together?" He found himself fervently wishing so; he remembered nights, fighting sleep, gulping coffee, despairing in lonely fear, when Harry's comforting presence and searing insights had opened his mental processes to the possibility of passing tomorrow's exam after all. The same warm confidence enveloped him now as he followed his friend through the terminal - at surprising speed for a man so short and, charitably stated, chunky.

"Not exactly together," Harry said, walking very close beside him. "In fact, I've sneaked away to meet you. Should've let you find your bloody way alone in case anyone was looking. It's just my fair bet they haven't a clue who you are - can't I meet a friend and take him to his hotel?" He paused. "No, I'm really shattered, but you're just going to have to get along with other friends, like someone who hasn't been seen greeting you off the plane like a brother." Foolish me, to think I am arriving like any other normal person, Charley thought. The sudden reality of his position startled him; he was already a marked man and he hadn't even left the terminal.

The Toad was driving an indescribably shabby Morris. He shot out onto the access road and joined the stream of Dubliners on their weary way to work. "Always a challenge driving here," he grinned, shifting lanes suddenly and with complete lack of concern for his fellow man. "I like getting away without the driver. It stimulates the mind -" He neatly cut off a huge black limo and squeaked around the corner into O'Connell Street. "You're at the Shelbourne - sort of a last meal for the condemned. Can I have dinner with you? Us peons don't live so well -"

They spun across the bridge over the River Liffey and saw Old Trinity looming, grey and dour, even in the sparkling sun. Charley saw it all just as it had been on that long ago day when he and his mother had been brought down from Belfast to arrange for the body to go home. The sun had shone that day and he had cried for his father while Mom had sat dry-eyed in the cab, listening for the hundredth time to the complete history of Dublin as revealed in endless detail by the driver. She nodded and oh, really'd now and then, not to hurt the man's feelings. He thought then, and still did, that his mother was made of a special kind of material, not available to the common man.

"Hey, are you still there, Charley?" Harry turned to look at him and smiled, narrowly escaping destruction from an oncoming bus. "Bless the man, I think he's asleep -"

"Not with you driving, you idiot. I guessed this was a hazardous duty thing, but not so soon!"

Oddly enough, they arrived at the hotel without incident. "We have time for coffee," Harry said. "I can fill you in -" A booth in a quiet corner, two cups of coffee, hot and black, and things focused a little better. "All I know is they called me in yesterday - God, was it only yesterday? - and gave me this portfolio. They said I knew the territory and good luck. Or words to that effect." Harry was absorbing diet cokes and looking smug.

"I might as well tell you," he said. "The IRA is going to get some new toys. No more of your conventional plastic, no more powder - brother Qadaffi has gone nuclear. We don't know where he got it, but we have word he's sending them something, something little and neat and very, very mean. You can put it the mail, you can drop it in a bouquet of roses, or hide it in a lady's garter belt for all I know." He tilted the almost empty diet coke bottle up and swallowed the last drops gratefully. "It'll be coming next week and they can blow up the world with it."

Charley looked up. "Where?" he asked. "Why me?"

"For your lovely blue eyes," the Toad said. "Why else?"

"Thanks - you ARE a cretin. Come on -"

"They've traced them to Galway and from there out through Connemara to the west coast. They've been using that channel for a long time, but Mossiter got word of it and we've pretty well put a stop to that. They picked up three of them and they have identities on four or five others. Maybe someone in our shop, too. A woman from Boston we've had our eye on a while." He regarded a buttered scone, briefly, before putting it on his plate. "But Connemara is where you come in. They won't try the roads again, not with this new stuff. Too easy to pick up - it radiates. They seem to think we know what it is; they have another route up their nasty sleeves." He sighed deeply put half the scone in his mouth and patted his belly, seemingly pleased with its generous contour.

He went on, "The agency remembered you taking that godawful pony ride that time. Typical; they think that means you know all about the country, a regular tour guide, that's you. All you have to do is find out how our Northern friends mean to get this stuff through - Galway into County Mayo, or what. But HOW do they get it through Connemara around us?"

Charley knew the country all right. He knew the mountains, trackless and hard, where rocks gave way to bogs and a man could sink and be forever gone, no one the wiser. They couldn't do it at night and they couldn't do it without a guide. "Have they got any locals?" It was the logical question.

"Good man -" the Toad was pleased. "Not so far as we know. The West is very quiet and very much out of it. They can't be bothered. It hasn't to do with the bloodlines of a pony, they could care less. Besides, we are pretty well set up there. I think we'd know."

Harry stood up, gave a long look around the room. "Better say ta-ta now," he said. "Back to the office for me and I won't be seeing you again, unless you want to buy me dinner tonight." He leaned close to the table. "Walk five blocks and hail a cab. Mossiter will see you at ten." He stopped a few tables away and called back, "Have you got a good sight-seeing map? Get one at the desk and have fun seeing our fair city – "

Seeing our fair city, indeed. It was a long day. Oh, God, it was a long day. He'd spent two hours being briefed by the Agency's man. He looked at about a thousand mug shots and memorized a long list of names. He could keep his identity; he'd never worked this side of the Atlantic before. "I guess I was expecting someone a little more, could I say, experienced," Mossiter had said. South Carolina was in his voice; thirty years of service on foreign soil had not succeeded in drowning it out. "Shucks, son, you boys get younger every year. Forgive a tired old man his foolishness." He looked anything but tired and old. Dark eyes darted from under shaggy brows; the angles of his face were hard. Yet there was nothing austere about him. His skin was like old leather, tanned and rough and his thick hair was steely grey. But it was his mouth you noticed. The smile was wide, and almost permanent. He looked as though life was a constant source of amusement to him.

"Oh, no, sir. I don't mind. I guess you know I haven't been with you very long -" He smiled back.

"We appreciate that," Mossiter smiled again. "And it was good of you to give up your weekend with a lovely lady just to be here with us." No sarcasm in his voice, just that quiet amusement.

"How did you -?" Charley began to ask.

"I'm afraid it will be more than a weekend. You see, we don't know when it will be, we don't know who will do it, and we don't know where they will start from or how they will get where they're going. Your job? Simple. You find them; who they are, where they get it and where they take it." He picked up the phone on his desk and spoke briefly. "I want you to be in touch with a couple of people here and you will be seeing Gene when you get to the Coast." He offered Charley a cigarette, and lit one himself. "I'll let Harrison and Bogley tell you what they know." What they knew was enough to take up another hour. Charley got it on his tape; later he would have to memorize it. Harrison had spent the last three months in Connemara, pretending to fish for salmon. "If I never see another fish -" he moaned, and confessed that in the three months he was there he'd gotten no closer to finding who their contacts were, or how they planned to get past the very effective network of observers along the way. "Good luck," he said. "You'll need it."

"Thanks," Charley said.

"Reckon you could use some sleep," Mossiter said as he showed him out. Understatement of the year, Charley thought. His head was a soccer ball and someone was kicking it down the field. He chewed two aspirins and looked at his watch. Damn! he hadn't set it yet; add five hours and it was nearly 5:30. Tea-time! Funny, not one day in Ireland and already 5:30 translated to tea-time. He lugged his bulging briefcase to the curb and hailed a cab; off to the Shelbourne and tea, he thought. "And here ye see the Abbey T'eayter, where Oscar Wilde --" The cabby woke him up ten blocks later and discharged him in front of the hotel.

It was the same grand Georgian facade he remembered, and the flowers in the windows still rioted in a hundred colors against the wet, grey stone. He fumbled with his pounds and pence - he'd forgotten how hard it was to count with the queer, big coins they had. His luggage was in his room when he got there. He lay down on the bed for a moment.

An ungodly clangor woke him. The telephone! "I thought we were having dinner at 9. Would you care to try for 10?" Harry was laughing, though probably starving, Charley thought.

Ten minutes later he was in the lobby; he identified Harry's rotund form arranged comfortably, if not elegantly, on a couch,

41

beside a half finished glass of whiskey. "I'm sorry, Toad," he said. "I guess I was asleep -"

"Forgiven," Harry said. "Just take me to the food."

The dining room at the Shelbourne was all that Charley remembered it to be and he and Harry made the most of it. By the time they had eaten their way through to dessert it seemed prudent to them to have a little exercise. Outside, the mist was thick and in the park the air hung about them cool and fragrant. They walked once around the square and Harry stopped under a light. "Charles," he said, "You are in Dublin, home of the Old Bushmill. Let not this night pass without a dram of the good stuff -"

Of course there was a pub. The whiskey came hot and straight; a lemon slice studded with cloves floated in it. "A true friend," Charley said, "Is a rare treasure. You are a true friend, Toad; any man who finds a drink like this for his friend is a true true friend -" It was lovely and warm in the pub and the whiskey was lovely and warm in his belly. The room was filled with noise and laughter and if Harry's face across the table seemed a little blurred, did it matter? The stuffed briefcase was far from his thoughts and tomorrow was another day. Looking past Harry's blurry features, he saw, in rather clear focus, a familiar looking face. Who could he know in Dublin? He was sure he'd seen him before. The man turned his head and their eyes met. For just a moment too long; he was definitely being studied. Then, as though he was embarrassed to be caught staring, the man looked back over his shoulder and motioned to a girl standing by the door. Charley decided he didn't know him, not when he had looked in his eyes. Hard eyes, now he thought of it, and cold.

Not someone he wanted to know, or meet on a dark street corner. The warm fuzziness was gone.

"Don't look, Harry, not now, but when you can, see if you know the guy behind you -"

"I just think I'll go for a pee," Harry murmured. He rose with elaborate dignity, hitched his trousers up an inch or two and began shoving his way through the clutter of bodies blocking his way to the 'Gents'. The eyes followed him. The girl was sitting on a corner of the man's chair, an arm over his shoulder. She was thin, almost emaciated, and very young. A cigarette dangled from the corner of her mouth; she meant to look tough. It was a failure, for when she looked at the man her eyes went soft; her heart was in them. The man paid her no attention; he was leaning close to the other two at his table, talking in a low voice.

Suddenly the girl spoke. Her voice was quiet and he couldn't hear her over the general din. The three men listened; did he imagine they were looking at him? The Toad pushed his way past them, back to his table. He nodded his head. "I'll tell you later," he said. "Beddy time for you, me boy. At midnight you turn into a pumpkin -"

The street lights wore glowing haloes of fog and the dark between them was a cool, grey blanket. A girl sat on the sidewalk a block from the hotel, begging. She had a baby on her lap. Charley dropped a pound note in the basket by her feet; a wide Irish smile lit her face. "God go with you," she said.

Harry took him by the arm. "Come on, Lord Bountiful - she's probably got more money than you have. You Yanks," he grinned, "Us Yanks, are the world's idiots -" They passed into

43

another circle of misty light. "You know who your friend in the pub was? One of your mug shots. I congratulate you, boy. The old photographic memory at work!" He gave a little hop and a skip. "I told 'em to bring you over; it was my idea -"

"Thanks a lot, you filthy toad -" He laughed.

He never heard the sound of footsteps and at first he couldn't figure out what he was doing in the gutter with Harry on top of him. Then he heard the sound of running feet and a police whistle. A car door slammed, a motor revved. He shoved Harry -no easy thing to do - off his back and sat up. "What the hell -?" he began, and saw a blue coated officer of the Dublin constabulary running towards them.

"You all right, sirs? Lucky for you we cum along now, just. They'd had ye for certain till they heard us. Your friend saved ye, sure enough, knocking ye out of the way like -"
Disentangled from Harry, Charley gave him a hand to get up. "How did you - did you hear them - who the hell -?" He felt entirely incoherent and reasonably stupid.

"I've been here longer than you. I look for things to happen -" Harry grinned.

"The damn-all IRA," the cop said. "They can't kill enough up north, I suppose."

They walked back to the corner under the light and he started to make out a report. "Forget it," Harry said, and showed him his badge. "It didn't happen."

"My fault," Harry muttered. "Entirely my fault. *Had* to meet your plane didn't I? A blithering idiot would have guessed, and, believe me, they aren't idiots. Plan on a short night's sleep,

Buddy; you're leaving town in a hurry."

The hotel was only a block away, but its quiet, elegant facade was far, far from the running feet in the night, and in its lobby there was the laughter and chatter of theater-goers returning and of young lovers leaving the bar, clinging to one another as they went out into the waiting night.

"See you in the morning -" Harry said, just as though he meant it.

"Sure," Charley said. "Sure you will. And, Toad - thanks. Thanks a lot -"

CHAPTER FIVE

You BLOODY fool! It was the fat one you were after getting --" Sean's eyes were black, the very blackness of hell was in them. He could kill with that look, Shiela thought, and kill he might before the night was over. They couldn't be having mistakes, not now. She felt Wolfe go tense beside her. Sean spoke again. His voice was high and hard. "It's the fat one knows who we are," he said. "You damn bleedin' should've hit him -" Jimmy's eyes met his and never wavered.

Holy Mother of God, was there no end to trouble? Jimmy was standing up to Sean; an act of sheer idiocy in Shiela's view. He didn't know Sean the way she did. She remembered him, not twelve years old, throwing the iron skillet at Mum for asking him where he had been all the night, and herself hiding behind the coal box in the kitchen for fear of his belt across her face. No, if Jim had the brains the dear Lord gave him he would go, get himself away before the rage that lay always just inside of her brother would be turned on him; Sean would kill him as soon as breathe, and sit down then to a good breakfast of sausage and eggs. She knew Sean; she willed Jimmy to run.

"Wolfe," she whispered. "Don't let him -"

"Stop your weengin', Sis! The bloody fool'll get us all killed -" The color rose in his face and he turned back to Jimmy. "They saw you, then, too, I suppose - you got the wrong one and then you damn near got yourself caught. Lucky for you if you had been!" His voice was an edge of steel. It cut across like a blade at Jimmy's throat.

"F--- you, O'Malley!" the man hissed. "It was Shiela showed him to me; Shiela, your own sister, she pointed to him -"

"Damn you, Jimmy Ahearne! Can I help you've a squint and can't see what's plain pointed out to you?" Her voice was shaking; Sean could turn on her next. "Just go, you idjit, before he kills you!"

Wolfe stood up and faced Sean. "It's dead we'll all be if we fight each other -" he said. The sound, only, of his voice stilled Shiela's fear. Mean, Sean was, and cruel, but he was no match for Wolfe. "Let him go and no harm done." Jimmy backed towards the door, careful, his eyes never leaving Sean's. He reached behind him and felt for the knob.

"Sean O'Malley," he whispered. "Sure the day I do a job

for you again the sky will go black, it will -" Wolfe's knuckles were white where he held Sean's arm. He knew how easily the hand would find the gun and the bullet would spatter Jimmy's brains, if such he had, against the dirty white of the plaster behind him. The door closed silently and the only sound was Jimmy's feet down the stairs, down and down and out into the fading grey dawn.

"Someday you'll do it, lad," Wolfe said. "Some fine day it'll be you as gets us caught. Think you the bloody cops is all asleep in Dublin? Think they'd not be up these stairs in a minute lookin' for you when they hear your gun?" He put his arm around Shiela and led her to the table. Sean stood by the window where the pale light of first day was fighting to come in; his back was to them and Shiela could see his shoulders shaking.

"Cum, lad," she said. "It's over. We'll have something to eat and we'll forget it." After a blinding rage he always fell into a silent, sorrowing despair, and she grieved for him. Then he was her little brother once more who needed to be held and comforted when the heat of his anger was over and the mindless rage that tore him in pieces was gone again. Then he was the poor wee lad, again, bloody and bruised from hitting his head against the wall; then the rage would evaporate from him like the fog over the bay and leave him quiet and sad.

"It's my fault; I should have made sure he knew -"

She went across to him and gave him a little jab in the ribs. "There's work to do, sure, and we can't be wasting our time. Be my good lad and give us a smile." He was like a baby, now, to be cajoled into humor. She looked past him to Wolfe and nodded.

He'd be all right now, he would. And Wolfe smiled back at her, that blazing smile of his, so that her heart was full of joy. "I'll cook us the eggs," she said. "And if only we had a bit of bacon for them, too -"

The flat was bleak enough, and the fridge empty enough, but it was safe. That's something of a mercy, she thought, to have a safe place in Dublin. The gas ring burned fiercely and when the coffee was done she boiled three eggs for them. The coffee was bitter in the cracked mugs, and she hated it. She needed it, though, and she drank it down, warming her hands on the thick china while she sat leaning on the table. Lord, she was tired. Not a mite of sleep since two days; they had traveled at night, and then all day yesterday the flat had been full of them, reporting to Sean and Wolfe, telling what they knew, making maps, asking questions; no wonder Jimmy had screwed it up. And, then, it had been dark in the pub when she had seen the fat pig -

"When's Kevin coming back?" Wolfe asked. "Sure, he didn't leave us much in his bloody flat to eat!" He tore a piece of bread off and chewed it thoughtfully. "Wonder how he looks, now, bloody educated and all -"

Shiela wondered, too. When Kevin had gone from Belfast and come away to Dublin to go to Trinity College they thought never to see him again. He'd tried for the scholarship and they'd laughed at him. Sure, seventeen years old they were and been fighting for years, since when they were in grammar school it was. Shiela could make a bomb when she was ten and Sean had been on the street with the men before he was in long pants. Kevin going to college! A fine kettle of fish, that was -

It had been five years, and then they had a letter from him. "I can be of help, I think," the letter said. "Think you I have forgotten the wall, the fighting; have forgotten independence, and us together? That I have not!" He said he was working in Dublin, working for the Cause. He'd a friend who had gotten on at the American Embassy, from whence all information flowed. He, himself was well connected socially; his new persona could be a valuable cover for what work they had for him. His language, Shiela thought, was very hoity-toity for a poor boy from Divis, where his Da was one of the thirty-five percent of perennially unemployed in that sorry part of Belfast that lay beneath the wall.

Sean's anger was beginning to revive with the coffee. "And who might it be that our wonderful murderer tried to kill, you think?" When he smiled it brought no warmth to his face. "Suppose they are sending out a new one just to muddle us up, now?" He turned his dark eyes to Wolfe. Yesterday's beard shadowed his chin and his teeth gleamed white in the dull light from the window. He looked to Shiela like a fierce animal; Mother of God, love my poor brother, whatever wickedness he has in him -

"Kevin will tell us," Wolfe said, "Whenever he comes." He looked a question at Shiela.

"I think not till night," she said. "Shall I get the letter, then, luv?"

"No mind, lass," he said. "You need to rest. It's a little talk Sean and I will have and then I'll come to you -"

She picked up the dishes and set them in the grubby sink. Her hands were too heavy to wash them and her feet weighed like stones when she crossed the room. The bed was unmade and the window uncurtained to let the rising sun stream in. She sank to the bed and thought, I must take my shoes off, and then try to sleep in the blazing light of this wicked day. She closed her eyes for a moment only, and then she felt Wolfe's hands unbuttoning her shirt and she twisted her hips to let him pull her skirt off. When she was naked he lay beside her and held her. He was asleep in a minute.

When next she woke she could feel his eyes moving over her body. The sun was high in the south now, and filled the room with glaring light. The window was closed; the airless room was stifling. She was wet with sweat, her body glistened with it, white under the light of the sun, and the sheets beneath her were damp and rumpled. "You mustn't look, so," she said. "It's not decent-and me naked as a babe." She tried to pull the soggy sheet over her; hadn't the nuns told her all about the sin of immodesty? Sure he was her husband now, and her body ached for him, but to be looking at each other, and in broad daylight?

"You're so luvly," he whispered. "Sure it is God's pity to hide it from me; so beautiful He made you, and no one to see?" And then she watched, too, with her eyes wide open and the hot sun on them and it was the loveliest thing in the world, and the nuns, may God be good them, didn't know the first thing about it, now did they?

"My God, it must be Kevin!" Shiela jumped up and pulled on her skirt."Give me my shirt, be quick, Wolfe - look, we've slept all the day!"

In the next room she heard him. "Sean!" he was saying, "Is that you, lad? You've grown up, haven't you?" Kevin's voice sounded like his letter. Wolfe pulled on his pants and went to the door.

"Take your time, luv," Wolfe told her. "I'll give him a pint while we wait." She scrubbed her face and tied her hair back with a bit of blue yarn. She straightened the bed and looked around the tiny room. Outside the window the sun had gone; a light mist fell on the rough paving below. Some children were playing in the alley; it looked like a scrum was in progress. She saw that the ball was a tin can, hard to pick out from the rest of the trash that bordered the playing field. The poor are the same everywhere, she thought, and the thinking seemed to her disloyal. Damn, what if we do throw them out, our long dream come true at last, and we still the same as before? Are we fighting and dying and killing for a word only; is freedom nothing but a word, no more?

Kevin stood up when she came in. He took both her hands in his and kissed her cheek. "It's no wonder you married her, Wolfe - look at our little Shiela!" He held her at arms length and smiled. "She's all grown up! And is she still so wild and fierce, Wolfe? I remember you on the wall, love, how you were there all night, once, and wouldn't go home till we all got back -" She remembered, too, but it was another Kevin she was thinking of, not this gentleman in a soft grey suit, with a silk necktie, just right, at his neck, and a white shirt, fresh-laundered. Oh, he had changed from the lad who went with Wolfe and her brother on the night raids in Belfast; she felt a shyness at his touch.

He'd brought food, and a bottle of whiskey and they sat together over the table, talking, just, until dark had long fallen and the streets were quiet and empty. Kevin told them what he knew. He had a girl, he did, this girl from Boston, and she worked at the Embassy. Bettina, she was called and she was in the secretary pool. A lot of things passed over her desk and moreover she had one of the agents sweet on her and she found out from him more than he meant her to know. She had a way with her, he said.

The thing that was wrong with him, that made him so strange, Shiela suddenly knew, was the way he spoke. Sure, by his voice he wasn't from Belfast any more at all; he wasn't even an Irishman. He could have been bloody English. "And is that what they taught you at Old Trinity?" she said. "How to be bloody English?"

"The better to hide myself with," he said. "Listen -"

Three of their people had been caught, bringing the shipment in from the coast. "It was the fat one, I told you," Sean interrupted him. "He's the one as found them out. That's what I wanted him for, Sis, when that bloody fool let him off -"

"He's off of us now," Kevin said. "They'll be getting someone else, now we know him. God knows he's done enough. Mossiter - their chief- has got every road from the West to Galway crawling with men. We couldn't move a wee mouse along those roads and them not catch us -"

"We heard it was something new," Wolfe said, "Something small -"

"Right, it is. Really new. Somewhere Qadaffi found out about nuclear. What's coming to us is radio-active like. A bit you can hide in a match box can blow a whole building."

"Can we leave it to go off by itself?" Sheila asked. "Or must we blow our own selves up with it then?"

"I said it's like nothing we've seen," Kevin said. "It can sit there, nobody the wiser, for days, and then from a quarter of a mile away, just like turning on the telly from across the room - one little punch of a button, and watch all the fires of hell break loose! We could have done it right at Brighton that year, if we'd had something like this." Kevin looked around the room at them all, with eyes that were too bright and hard by half. Sheila couldn't keep from looking at him. He's as mad as Sean, is he, then? she thought, and she leant against Wolfe, to feel the strength of him beside her. She began to wish it was all over, the killing and the hate, and the thought shamed her that she was gone so soft in the head now, and so bloody weak in the knees.

Kevin was talking again. "It would have been goodbye hotel, goodbye Maggie Thatcher - with one wee pinch of the luvly stuff." His words tumbled out so fast he almost lost his fine accent and spoke like one of them again. "Good news, bad news, lads; the bad news is, they suspect what it is and they will move hell to stop it coming in." He looked around the table; there was silence to make your flesh crawl.

"If it's such a wee thing, why can't we bring it down the roads then?" Sean's dark brows were knit together; sweat ran down his neck. "God, I can run it myself; hell, Shiela could run it, tucked in her panty-hose!" His lip rose in a sneer. "We're not bleedin' afraid to run the roads at night - of course we haven't got your fine college education neither, we don't." He swirled the golden whiskey round in his glass; suddenly swallowed it, half a

55

glass full, and slammed the glass on the table. "Tell, me where, just, and I'll go-"

Kevin waited till he was done. "Sean, lad, I'll tell you -" He spoke quietly now; authority was in his voice. "I'm doing it," he said. "That's why I came here, why I learned to be what I am." He met each of their eyes in turn. "I said the stuff is radio-active and they know it, or they think so at least. You can detect that stuff; counters by the roadside can pick it up when you pass. Click, click, click and pull over, buddy, and that's how you end up - caught with your bloody hands full. It's got to come over the mountain and stay off the roads."

Wolfe looked up. "Over the mountain, lad? Have you been there? Nothing goes over the mountain, or yet gets through the bog. Sure, your fine talk and dandy looks will not get you through, if that's what you're thinking of-"

Shiela's eyes were still heavy with sleep and the words were all running together. Kevin was talking; how he would go to the coast and join up with a bunch of American tourists who were daft enough to hire a west country horseman to guide them across from Clifden to Galway. The girl would go with him; he would be showing the countryside to his American guest. At Carna he would pick the packet up and carry it on his body, led over the mountain by the one man in all Ireland who knew the way. Safe, the precious stuff would get to Galway with never a moment on the roads, and from there it was the people from County Mayo who could get it through to the North.

When she and Wolfe lay beside each other in the darkness she said, "Doesn't he know about the Queen, then? You didn't tell him?"

Wolfe turned to her. "Sure, he'd know if he was meant to, lass. Every one of us who knows is a risk; the less the better. It's not for us to tell him-" She felt his breath on her hair; what matter who knew what - her luv was in her arms and the night was cool and clear. The silver moon showed through the window and made a pale square on the bed cover; sure, the whole world might be at peace, so beautiful the night was to her then.

CHAPTER SIX

Rain fell in soft clouds and blew across the field. Around the edge of the ring a pony trotted, led by a stout woman also trotting briskly through the mist. A shapeless tweed hat was pulled down over the woman's ears; her Wellies squished in the mud and a little spray of water shot up at each step. The pony jogged contentedly in her wake under the watchful eyes of five or six other animals who stood alert and motionless in a row down the center of the ring. The judge stood in the middle, a thin wisp of smoke rising from his pipe and curling round the edge of an umbrella held over his head by a small boy standing on tiptoe beside him. Rain dripped from the umbrella down the boy's neck and he ducked his head inside his sweater. Spectators stood all around, hatted, booted, umbrella-ed, apparently unconscious of the rain and the cold; their eyes were riveted on the ring.

Charley found shelter by the stalls along the edge of the field and watched the age-old spectacle of Connemara men at their favorite pastime - comparing ponies here in the old Clifden show ring, and trying to best each other in deals involving trades, cash, credit, any way they could exchange one pony for another. "Aye, he buys them cheap," a man was confiding to his umbrella-mate, "And he sells them dear -"

"He knows his ponies, man, don't ye forget it! Jamey Leary can tell ye the blood of every pony out there. Sure, if you're buyin' today just keep your eye on Jamey; see the animals he's for looking at -" The two moved off into the rain, doubtless trying to find where Jamey was doing his looking. Charley stayed where he was for a while, watching, not so much the activity in the ring as the constant flow of men, women, children and ponies gathering in the rain; each pony was surrounded by its own circle of admirers. Everyone in Connemara must be here, Charley thought, and every pony as well.

He had been here before, that long ago day with Mom and Jamey. "If we ride a bit more today," Jamey had told them, "Then we can go to Clifden tomorrow and see the ponies." Charley remembered the gleam in Jamey's eyes at the thought of the pony show and he remembered following him around that day in the brilliant sunshine, and listening to him talk. Of course, it had to be the same Jamey Leary, the man who buys them cheap and sells them dear; where else in all Ireland would he be today? And would Megan be with him, too, sizing up the ponies, talking down

60

the ones he wanted to buy and showing off the ones he had for sale? He looked across the glistening wet grass, almost believing he would see them.

He wondered if they were still doing the ride; if Jamey still gathered his horses out there on the far, windy shore, and if little boys with eyes full of wonder, shivering in the cold, still waited under the blowing clouds to begin the great adventure, the trek over the top of Connemara all the way into Galway. He could see a rocky coast under a heavy sky, and Bill and Paddy driving the horses to them over the piles of grey stone that were, in this unforgiving land, a field. Now the heavy, rolling clouds over Clifden reminded him of the last day when the two children had sat together by the shore at Carna, hidden from the rest, and Megan had cried and he had comforted her. Maybe it was the miserable wetness of this day that made him remember, standing here under the dripping eaves of the show barn; remember that other dismal day when he had held the child, Megan, close, and felt her small sharp bones pressed against him. He even thought he could smell the scent of her clean, wet hair in the blowing mist as he had then, so long ago.

> 'And she was a child, and I was a child,
> In our kingdom down by the sea.
> And we loved with a love that was more than love,
> I and my Annabel Lee.'

Oh, God, he thought, only one day in Ireland and I am as loony as a Connemara fisherman. You've got work to do, you fool, he told himself sternly, and he felt the beginning of a headache throbbing near the base of his skull.

"Gene will be in contact when you get to Clifden," Harry had said. "Every day around five you go to Harrigan's and have a drink for yourself. When a man sits down by you and offers you a drink, tell him, thanks you've just had one. It'll be Gene; he'll take it from there for you-" Yesterday morning in Dublin Charley had a distinctly tongue-in-cheek reaction to the cloak-and-daggerliness of Harry's plan; it had seemed like a child's game. But here, today, with the memory of last night's skirmish in the gutter still fresh in his mind, caution seemed an eminently intelligent way to go. They had scooted him out of Dublin before daybreak this morning. With the possibility of his being identified by them, Mossiter wanted him clear of the city before he was blown. The car had been brought to the hotel at four a.m. and he'd been halfway across Ireland when the black of night began to fade into the gloom that passed for morning on this dark and dismal day.

Cruising out of town onto the N1 he had turned off to go south through Kildare; he was going to use the main roads as little as possible. Before dawn he had passed the National Stud and wished he could stop; of course it wasn't open, and of course he should be thanking his lucky stars for the solid blackness that had followed him. He realized his eyes had been waiting for two points of light to appear; points of light that would grow in size until they would force him off the road and perhaps introduce him to some colleagues of his last night's friends on the street.

No, he definitely hoped to have a quiet dinner and a glass of hot whiskey in a friendly pub and then disappear into the clean white sheets of the bed-and-breakfast he had engaged on his way into town. The rented car was now discreetly lined up in the rental car park, replaced by a more local model, and with all of Connemara about the town today he felt reasonably well camouflaged from friend and foe alike.

They were calling out the ponies in the ring to pin the ribbons. The rain fell now in sheets; he could watch well enough from where he was. The child with the umbrella had left off shielding the judge and was sent running with the rosettes as the winners were announced. The PA system scratched and screeched and the spectators roared and clapped as each animal was pinned. Charley couldn't really hear the announcer; opting for relative comfort, he stayed where he was. After all, what difference did it make to him who won? They all looked good to him. Clearly, Connemara kept its best breeding here; what Irishman would send a lovely pony like these to the States, where only the Yanks would see and never be the wiser?

The first prize, a red, was being awarded. The little boy carried it through the mud across to the side of the ring. He handed it to a girl beside a grey pony and she blew him a kiss before she turned and fastened it to her pony's halter. Something in the way she moved caught Charley's attention; he stopped in the middle of mopping the cold rain off his face. Then she jogged towards the out gate. He didn't need to see her face; he'd never mistake the lovely grace, the gentle way of her going. It couldn't be anyone else. Of course, she couldn't have remained a child; the beautiful woman, running smiling through the gate was Megan.

The whole crowd seemed to move at once, then, and he couldn't make his way through them. "Sorry," he mumbled as he ran into a solid body. It was only the back end of a pony who responded with an irritable flick of its tail. A whole family blocked his way, stopping to explain to a man how their pony was clearly meant to be the winner, except for blasted Jamey Leary and his grey mare. The man knelt to feel the pony's legs and when Charley stepped over his outstretched feet a small child darted out and he fell over her, landing on his face in the mud.

"Maggie!" a woman's voice shouted. "Do be careful- look, now, ye're all muddy!" and the child was snatched away. "Oh, ye've knocked this poor gentleman down -" There was a rush of helping hands; he was on his feet being rubbed down with a horsey-smelling towel amid apologies, clearly from everyone involved. The child was pulled from behind her mother's skirt and made to offer a cold, moist hand.

"Sorry, sir," she said, "I never meant ye to fall -" She buried her face against her mother's leg and refused to be pried away.

"It's all right," he said. "Don't cry -" He smiled at the mother and patted the pony; as he hurried off he had the distinct impression that it was laughter, not tears, that shook the wretched child's shoulders.

Blast, there was no way through the crowd now. He couldn't even tell which way she had gone. Maybe she was only a vision, the kind of thing that happened in this strange and lovely land; the rain fell wetter than ever and the dark, tattered clouds raced across the sky and he felt suddenly tired and lost and very far from home.

He found the only vacant seat in the pub. It was dark in the corner where he finally sat and contemplated his hot Bushmills. A spicy steam rose from the clove-studded lemon slice; just the smell of it raised his spirits, even before he felt its burning warmth running down inside him. He had worked his way out of the fair grounds and up the crooked street, between stalls of sweaters, saddles, shoes - whatever a merchant thought he could sell in the holiday atmosphere of show-day. Never daunted by the rain, merchants stood out with their stuff by the sides of the street; with equal disdain for the weather the crowds who filled the street from curb to curb stood under umbrellas trying on bargains and arguing prices. Looking at the crowd, engulfed by the crowd, Charley thought he was in the one place in all Ireland where the natives outnumbered the tourists. It was by the sheerest luck that he had found himself outside Harrigan's.

Here, too, he saw scarcely an American face, and the noise, rapidly increasing as the whiskey worked its warming wonders, had a distinctly Irish sound to it. Even the canned rock music was recognizable as coming from an Irish group. I've come back, he thought, like I told her I would - all grown up. All grown up and waiting for my orders, orders that can lead some of us into terrible danger, or into a trap of death. He swallowed another glorious gulp of whiskey and wished he hadn't thought of the work ahead. Mossiter had said, "We can't let them get this thing through - if it's what we think it is it means they have weaponry we don't know how to combat. No one in the entire UK will be safe; last year at Brighton will look like fireworks compared to what they can do."

Why me? Charley thought, not for the first time. What makes them think I will find where it comes in, who carries it and how they expect to get it across the west and into the north? Sure, nothing to it, lad, right? Of course it was imperative to know who brought it, too. Otherwise they could try it again and again. The whiskey must be reviving him; he found that he was studying the faces around him to see if there was a flicker of recognition or a questioning look in any of their eyes. "Gene will be there - he'll find you," Harry had said. "Be your own undistinguishable self. Melt into the crowd -"

Then he saw her. Her cheeks were flushed over the whiteness of her skin and her wet, black hair hung loose on her shoulders. She pushed it back from her face and moved through the crowd to the bar. Men stood back and let her through; she smiled that wide, lovely smile and laughed when a man spoke to her. He got up, almost tripped over the boy on the chair beside him, muttered an apology and started across the room to where she stood. He saw her pick up her drink and turn to look around the room, a little hopelessly, for a place to sit. It seemed as though he would never get past all the laughing, singing, drinking faces and she would get away, vanish the way she had done at the fair grounds.

Wait," he wanted to call out, "I'm here -" Suddenly he felt like a fool - what was this girl to him at all? He'd played with her when they were children, for two weeks, long ago, and here he was in a great swivet to reach her and - and what? What in the world would she want with him? She was probably married, or engaged, just like he was. Well, no, in all fairness, he was not really engaged to Sally. Sometimes when they woke up in her Georgetown apartment they talked about it, if it wouldn't be nice to always wake up together, but somehow the subject was always dropped in the clear light of day and Sally just went on being - well, being Sally.

He felt suddenly shy, and when their eyes met, her honest, questioning stare almost made him look away. Instead, he yelled, "Megan? Is it you, Megan?" Instantly, a hundred eyes were riveted on him, and he felt his face go flaming red. Not your best example of melting, exactly; shouting across the room like an idiot. Then he heard her laugh, that lovely laugh he remembered so well. An Irish voice called out, "Who's your Yank friend, Meggo?"

She smiled in the direction of the voice and shrugged, ever so slightly. "Hisht, Paddy," she said, "It's my fatal charm, only -" and she started to turn away. Then, as though he had caught her by the arm and pulled her back, she looked full at him again and her smile was a laugh, clear and sweet, like the music by the sea. "Charley, is it?" she said. "Charley, lad, wait -" Her voice was quiet and he hardly heard her, though the room had fallen still. She pushed her way across to him and he managed to reach her midway of the room; there they stood, not one foot apart, not moving. "You've cum -" she whispered.

Then the moment was over and she threw her arms around him and kissed him. "Stand back and let me see you," she said and surveyed him with a critical eye, the same one she used judging horseflesh, he thought. "You've got bloody big -" she laughed. "What about me, lad? Have I grown up, now?"

67

"Let me look," he said, "And see if you have." What he saw was a smartly dressed young woman, country elegance in the rough tweed suit and soft silk scarf. Beneath the mud, the expensive leather of her boots gleamed darkly. "You've grown up," he said. "Oh, Megan, you HAVE grown up -" Why did he feel this dull sense of loss and loneliness? Of disappointment, almost betrayal? A beautiful woman had just kissed him and stood now, smiling up at him, and his heart was breaking for the sight of a wild little girl he had known, how long ago? for two haunted weeks on the fierce mountain slopes and in the boggy glens of this tragic land. Then he looked into her eyes and saw her plain; her soul was in them and he smiled back. "Come, sit with me and tell me what you are, now that you're grown -" He ran interference for her on the way back to his table and they were alone, then. She had a glass of Old Bush, neat, and she drank it like a man, all the while smiling like an angel and her pale eyes laughing at him.

"Can we have some cheese and sausage, then," she said. "Man, you must be starving after this day-" All business she was, now, pleased to see him, happy to be with him, but the tender moment of the kiss was over and done. The blush on her pale cheeks was the only sign it had happened and when the great, thick sandwiches came, she ate like a farm hand and asked him to get her a mug of beer. "Daddy's here," she said. "I'm to meet him after the sale. He'll be wanting to see you -"

"I wondered," he said, "Does he still do the Trail?"

"That he does, and me with him, too," she said. "He thought he'd get shed of me, sending me to college in the States. But here I am back -" she smiled, smug and pleased. "Sure, when

I was too old to show the ponies for him, he thought he'd no use for me anymore and I should go to America and cum back with a grand education and be a lady -" She sat up very straight and proper, her face severe for the moment. Then the soft smile was there again. "He needs me, though - the lads, my brothers, God help them, have gone to the city and Dad is alone but for some that hire to him. I never could leave him without one of us. It's got bigger all along, it has; every week there'll be twenty of them, most of them idjits to drive poor Daddy mad with their foolishness. Sure, he still does it, he loves it - and with Mum gone there's no one at home, neither -" She fell still and looked into the dark beer in the bottom of her mug. "Ah, it's good to see you -" she sighed and raised her eyes to look at him. "Cum with us - why not?"

"Oh, I'd love it," he said. How he would love it! to ride with her over the mountains, to gallop a big Irish horse along the shore and leap the stone walls where sheep were grazing on the sunny hillsides - his heart ached to go. Damn the IRA; damn them all and their lousy bombs! "I really want to," he said, "But I've got some business to tend to-"

"Blast," she said. "D'you have to?"

"Yep," he said. "Duty calls -" As he spoke something caught his eye across the room. There was about the man an air of not quite being Irish; American, probably, and he was staring quite openly at Charley. Suddenly the warmth of the room had lost its charm; the heat was oppressive and he felt the blood rise to his face. Damn, this had to be Gene, trying to make contact. He was bringing his drink with him and heading for their table.

The room seemed charged with danger; Megan looked a question at him.

"Is something wrong?" she asked.

"No, it's just the business I spoke of - I've got to talk to this man, you see -"

Oh, God, make her go before he sees her. I can't get her mixed up in this mess - Then, as if in answer to his prayer, Megan looked at her watch. "Oh, Lord," she said, "And here's me, leaving Dad to wait in the rain. I've got to run, myself. Take care, lad." She pulled on her slicker and hat. "Thanks for the lunch - do come if you can; it's Sunday we'll be leaving -" her words tumbled out all in a rush and she was off, gone perhaps forever from him. He drank the last drop of whiskey and it was bitter on his tongue.

"Good to see another American," a bluff voice said at his side, and the man sat beside him where she had just been. "Buy you a whiskey?"

"Thanks," he said. "I've just had one."

CHAPTER SEVEN

"And how," Marianne asked, "Do we keep the girls from telling?" She was in the kitchen of the Ussher with her husband, making very fine slices of green beans and carrots. The copper kettle was steaming on the gas flame and Pierre stood over it, sweat beading his face and forearms while he dropped tiny, well-scrubbed potatoes into the boiling water.

"Ma cherie, you know the Irish girls, they will spread the word like dandelion seeds over a windy hill." His shrug was completely Gallic, cynical and resigned; his eyebrows rose alarmingly. "Such a secret for them to keep - mon Dieu! Impossible!" He gently lowered the last of the little potatoes into the pot and dried his hands. It was clear that the Irish character was beyond his belief; the girls would talk, no matter if the instructions came from the Lord above, as soon as they knew the first thing about it.

A contingent from the royal household was scheduled to arrive that night to brief the Anhouils and their staff; security during the royal visit was going to be very tight. The letter had said, "Strictest privacy and absolute secrecy during and before the stay of the Royal Party at Ussher House will be entirely necessary. Security personnel will be in residence two days before the arrival of the party. Knowledge of the identity of the Royal Guest will be limited to the least possible number of persons." All day Marianne and Pierre had worried the problem of security back and forth between them like two cats teasing a captive mouse.

"It's no use us trying to plan," Marianne had said. "They'll tell us what they want -"

"They don't know our Bridget," Pierre countered. "Or the little Pegeen upstairs. How can they know what to tell us when we have those two to manage? Easier to keep the crickets in the scullery quiet than to keep their tongues still inside their heads."

"Don't laugh, mon cher-" Marianne shook her head. He was right, though; the two chambermaids chattered like magpies whenever they were together, and God only knew what their boyfriends heard on the way to Oughterard for the cinema on Monday night. They weren't the only ones, either. It was true that Ould Ian spent most of the time in his boat, but didn't he go for a pint in the pub each night? She knew how he liked to brag up to his mates about the great gentlemen he took out after the salmon; how they didn't know in their fine heads as much about fishing as he knew in the tip of his little toe. And the lad that did the garden and carried the luggage had eyes, as well, to see who came and went. Maybe far off in England it seemed the Ussher was a remote and secret place, but, today it looked as though they might as well publish it in the newspapers and put it on the telly for all they could do to keep the excitement from seeping out into the world.

"How did Jamey take it when you said we were full up?" Pierre said. "Every week for all these years we've had room for him - and now?" The eyebrows lifted again.

"He said he'd try the bed and breakfasts between here and Carna; he's only got eleven of them this time. I don't think he thought anything -" She was less sure than she sounded; hadn't Jamey given her a funny look when she told him?

"Sure, I feel like the Blessed Virgin at Christmastime when ye tell me there's no room at the inn for me and mine, lass," he'd said, laughing. "Ye'll leave us out in the cold, then?" He stopped and, yes, he did give her a funny look - "Must be sumbody grand to make you forget your old friends, like."

"Just a big party from London," she had said, too quickly, perhaps. At least it was partly true, and God could forgive her the other part. "Twenty of them, to fill the whole house, Jamey - I couldn't turn them away. Not after all that money for adverts in the London papers; now we know it wasn't wasted." Jamey grinned at her, then, and she thought he believed her. The last thing a French woman would want was even a sou to be wasted on a useless advertisement.

Pierre picked up the beans and carrots she had sliced and

plunged them into a kettle of ice water. The tall clock in the hall was striking the hour; its sharp, ancient chime rang out eight times. "The girls, mon Dieu, they have not laid the tables - the men will be here, and the tables not laid!" Marianne brushed past him, dropping her big kitchen apron on the stool. She stopped to pull his head to her and give him a very small kiss. "Compose yourself, mon cher. They have been doing the rooms; they arrive just now in the dining room and all will be well. When I see the car I will ring and you must put the souffle in -" Smoothing her hair, she ran through into the great hall, where, incongruous and gleaming, the reception desk tried to hide its switchboard and computer behind a bright row of potted geraniums.

Two bowler-hatted men burst through the door, shaking the wet off their sleek, black umbrellas. Marianne showed them to their rooms herself (where *was* the cursed boy?) and promised them dinner in half an hour. "Perhaps we can talk while we eat," the taller of the two men said. "Do be so good as to ask the proprietor to join us, Madame Anhouil." He made a small bow, more of a nod, dismissing her. His moustache trembled ever so slightly as he nodded; Marianne felt nervous laughter welling up inside her and she turned to go out the door.

"Of course," she murmured, "We are at your service -"

Later, sitting on the bed, brushing out her long braids, she could see the reflection of Pierre pulling his nightshirt on over his long, white body. "You are making yourself thin with worry," she said. "Just look at you -" The shirt covered him down to his

74

skinny calves.

"I can't see it," he said, "And I have worried only the last two weeks; not long enough to get thin -"

She bounced a little on the bed. "Silly man," she said. "After it's over, think how it will be. A sign in the hall, with her seal on it, gold, for everyone to see that she stayed with us - oh, Pierre, I love it!"

The two men had talked long with them, and as they talked, the whole thing became real to Marianne, not just a letter, but flesh and blood people, who talked about the Queen in everyday words; where should she sleep, what she would eat, when she would walk outdoors, when her hairdresser would come, all of it just as though she were one's auntie come to visit.

"Exactly how many on your staff, Monsieur Anhouil?" the small, ruddy one had asked.

Pierre had counted them off. "Two maids, Bridget and Pegeen, local girls; the boy, Mickey; Ian, the guide; two extra serving girls, sisters of Pegeen, myself and my wife. Eight of us. Then Annie; she does the linens, every Monday and Thursday she comes -"

The moustache quivered. "She will be known to all of them," he said. "I think it best that no-one leaves here during the visit, for any reason." He cleared his throat. "No, most definitely, everyone will stay on the premises until Her Highness has enplaned from Oughterard. The telephones will be under our supervision."

"But none of them stays here, only Ian," Marianne had begun.

"Madame, they *will* stay here now. Once they are aware of the identity there must be no communication whatever. It goes without saying that you and Monsieur Anhouil received extensive investigative scrutiny before the decision was made to come here. You are the only ones entrusted with the knowledge -"

Now she stretched, cat-like, on the bed. "Pierre, can you believe it? The Queen, here, at Ussher?" It was too delicious. Tomorrow was soon enough to worry again. At least the security men had solved the problem of keeping the news from spreading. If they couldn't go home and they couldn't phone it didn't matter what they knew. She'd need to open the old carriage house and put the extra beds up. Ian could have a room, and the boy next to him. The four girls could be upstairs, either each in her own room, or all together so they could chatter the whole night long if they wanted to. Would they make Annie stay, too? Well, they'd have to explain it to her somehow; worry about that tomorrow, she thought. She and Pierre would stay in Ian's small cottage, leaving the whole lodge for the royal party. The royal party! What a far cry from Jamey and his followers, coming in tired and sometimes wet and always starving hungry. She wondered if they even tasted Pierre's delicate pates and steamy bouillabaises; sometimes they almost fell asleep at the table before the last bottle was empty and with the chocolate mousse still in the kitchen.

Yet, she worried about Jamey. All these years he had come to them, ever since they'd bought the place ten years back. And before that, from when he'd started the ride, with just six horses and only the little boys to help. He always told her the Ussher was the best stop on the ride; he'd stay three nights when he could. Crossing over the mountains here, he could van the riders back and forth from the horses' overnight pastures along the way. She hated to put Jamey off, but one had one's own fortunes to consider. Here in the wild, deserted foothills of the mountains, Ussher House had stood alone by the dark waters of the lake and offered its ancient elegance to the few hunters, fisherman and horsemen who knew to find it. But she and Pierre had worked hard to make a good thing of it over the years, (she thought of the expensive advert) and now, the final success was theirs - a visit from the Queen! So, she decided, Jamey might cool his heels where he would; he'd be back the next week regardless, but when ever again would Ussher House be host to a Queen?

The half moon hung low in the west. It's dying light shone on the row of caravans beside the road along the shore. From the window of one, a light broke into the misty dark and a shaggy lurcher rose stiffly from the ground by its door. He stood still, the scruffy hair rose on his back and a low growl came from his throat. The spotted ponies tethered nearby shifted their feet on the stony ground; the sounds were carried off in the wind as it whipped the waves to a froth below the rockbound beach. The lurcher inclined his head to listen and then moved soundlessly into the road.

A cloud covered the moon now and the night was black. The light from the window shone like a beacon and the dog gleamed white as he cut through the beam of it. Far down the road headlights glared briefly, then winked on and off three times. The dog's frenzied barking tore through the stillness of the night. A wash of light fell on him as the door of the caravan opened and the long shadow of a man's figure stretched across the road. The man in the door turned to speak to someone inside. "It's them, it is," he hissed. "They've come -"

It had been Kevin's idea for them to come over from Galway by night. Sheila didn't much approve of it; who was Kevin to tell them what to do, after all? She leant against Wolfe as the Rover bounced and banged along the worn tarmac of the coast road and, through the heavy wool of his jumper, she felt his heart beating, steady and sure. Wolfe's heart! so true, and him so wise; fools they were to listen to Kevin. Yet even Wolfe had said, "Better do it his way - it's his bloody plan."

Sean had growled, "Not his - it bleedin' come from above him. That bird he's got, she gets it from somewhere; the States, I reckon."

Ben had been there to see them when they left Galway. "Kevin knows too bloody much, you ask me," he'd said. "Leave him do his work and we keep Her Majesty to ourselves, righto?"

Sheila hated Ben, his eyes going over her whole body as though he could see her there naked, then holding hers long enough to make her look away as though she were ashamed. She daren't tell Wolfe, so jealous he was of her; trouble amongst them was the last thing they needed. Wolfe had said, "Sure, I have no

78

love for Kevin, neither, and the girl we don't even know. Right, you, Ben - we get the stuff from the tinker and give it to him. Then he's on his way with the bloody horses and we're on our way to the Ussher -"

Sheila felt her body go hard and cold to hear Wolfe talk so. She wished they could go back to Belfast after tomorrow. Leave the bitch the Queen alone! She smelled danger in the air; it was like the smell of lightning when it strikes too near. Nothing really there, but a presence that tells you death is very close by you, and lucky you are, this time, it lets you go. I'm going soft, I am - me, Sheila, as once set off the charge that blew a hole that big in the bloody Office of the Constabulary - nothing I ever feared then! But then I hadn't the secret I have now, she thought. Then it was only me to care, only Sheila Morrison to die there in the street. Now if I die, something far more precious dies with me. Mary, mother of God, I'd be taking my luv's first child to the death with me; her hand made the sign of the cross, very small near her heart. Wolfe saw and said, "What is it, luv?" She had smiled at him, to tell him it was nothing.

So they had traveled the long road through the night. Hardly a light shined in the cottages they passed, and the streets of Ouhgterard were empty when they rolled through. Then back into the dusky night, where clouds passing fitfully over the moon made its light unsteady. The glow of their headlamps and the roar of the motor were all that disturbed the sleeping land. Once, a startled sheep jumped up, bleating, from the side of the road and plunged out in front of them. Sean hit the brake. The Rover skidded to a stop and the sheep stood there in the road, staring into the light. "F---," Sean muttered and revved the engine. "Get away from here, ye bloody fool -" The Rover shot forward; Sheila was almost thrown on the floor when it hit the animal. A scream like a woman raped came from the sheep and it fell to the side as Sean gunned the car forward.

She leaned over the back of the seat and, as hard as she could, she slammed her fist against the side of her brother's head. Wolfe pulled her back to him and held her. "Hisht, lass - leave it," he whispered. Sean never turned around; his breath went out like a long sigh, and then a wild, cruel laugh drowned the sound of the car hurtling through the night. "You know your brother, lass - be happy, now, it was but a sheep this time."

Hours later, she felt the car slowing. The road was rough here, and the sound of the sea came through the open window by her head. She had been asleep on Wolfe's shoulder; awake, now, she shook her head to clear the sleep from it. Sean had stopped the car. He flashed the lights three times and cut the motor. For a minute the only sound was the crashing of waves on the rocks below them. Then, the barking of a great dog, and she saw its white form cut through the wash of light shining from the open door of the caravan. A man stepped into the road and called the dog. It came to him and cowered, snarling, at his feet.

CHAPTER EIGHT

The crowd in the pub was thinning out. Whatever light there had been in the sky was turning to dirty black; Clifden was going home to dinner. The rain still pounded on the roof and washed down through the gutters and into the street. Charley ordered another whiskey; he needed the warmth inside to make up for the chill that was creeping in beneath the sodden sweater under his equally sodden raincoat. It gave him time to look at Gene and evaluate the man who would be his only contact with Dublin, with Harry and Mossiter.

He liked what he saw, well enough. Tall, craggy, thin enough to worry a mother sick over him, Gene nevertheless radiated a look of the outdoors and of health and of good times.

81

He could be a skier, a horseman or a hunter; his face was ruddy, and the lines in it - he was no longer young - were testimony to a lifetime of smiles and laughter. It wasn't only the drink that warmed Charley as the two of them sat in the dark corner of the pub. He felt the piercing blue eyes looking into him and he realized that he cared very much how this stranger judged and valued him.

"Enjoying your first day on the Emerald Isle?" Gene asked. "Get here yesterday?"

"I think so," Charley said. "Yep, I hit Dublin in the morning and they shipped me over here last night. Nice to get here for the pony show - I've seen it before."

"So they told me," Gene said. "You're supposed to know your way around these parts."

"Oh, sure, I was here fifteen years ago. My mother and I went on the pony trek - over the mountains, you know, with the Irish guide." He studied the ring of wet that his glass left on the table. The wood was old, and years of care had left it impervious to damage; like this land, he thought, tough from long years of use, loved by those who have struggled to wrest life from its unforgiving soil, enduring everything, beautiful for the very hardness that gives it its strength. "You know, even when I was a kid, I felt something about this place," he said. "There's this feeling you get of some kind of happiness everywere. Hell, I don't know what that has to do with knowing my way around - sorry, I just got off on that; it isn't the drink, it's just being here, I guess." He shrugged an apology.

"Damn, they've sent me a poet for an agent -" Gene's face

cracked into a smile. "You're sure going to fit right in, that's one thing. Everyone in the whole blasted country is either a poet or a killer - or both."

"Actually, I know someone who's neither one. He's here in Clifden right now." He told Gene about seeing Megan, and about Jamey. "He's meeting a bunch of Americans on Monday to do the trek."

"Tell me," Gene said. "How does it work?"

"He takes you for a week and you ride across country to Galway. It takes six days. Then he rests a day there, and starts back next Monday. My mother and I went both ways; it was kind of a blast -"

"From here to Galway, you said?" Gene's face was serious now. "How?"

"Well, over the mountains, across from south to north and back on the way east to Galway."

"What roads?" Gene asked.

"Not any. You can't imagine the country." Charley was imagining it, then. The high windy rocks and the sudden descent to flatlands where deep grass covered the dangerous bogs. "There isn't a way, really - just this guy who knows how to find one. You could get lost forever, or sink out of sight if you don't follow him; there isn't even a path. I don't know, Gene, it's just like being on the moon. You feel you're the first ones there, ever -"

"Ever go near the coast?"

"Well, they did then," Charley said. He remembered following that glowing girl into the white foam where the sea broke on the shore, and he remembered how they huddled together under the rocky ledge, watching the waves crash below them. "The second overnight is by Carna -"

"By Carna?" Gene leaned across the table. He told Charley how they had been watching the ocean traffic as it passed close to land there. Coded signals from Libyan freighters passing through the lanes there had been intercepted; it just might be something to keep their eyes on. "Could just anyone go?" he asked. "Someone sign up right now? Someone who wanted to carry something to Galway?" The blue eyes were thoughtful, they were seeing a plan, floating above them in the thick, smoky air. "Have you got your boots, boy? Because I think we're sending you on a long ride. Can we talk some more? At your place?"

They left the pub together, apparently leaning, a little tipsy, on each other; old friends out on the town. Once they were out in the street they separated in the dark and Charley found his battered Morris, holding down the town car park in solitary grandeur. The afternoon's noisy crowd might never have been; the horse boxes were gone, the merchants' stalls stood deserted, the streets were empty. He drove slowly out of town on a road almost obscured by the high hedges that lined it on either side. He was afraid he would miss his bed-and-breakfast cottage; they all looked alike, the little stone houses behind stone fences, with riotous blossoms filling their tiny gardens. 'Mrs. Leahy's B & B' suddenly appeared on his right and the beam of his headlamps showed him Mrs. L's spectacular display of roses, espaliered unforgettably around the door of her cottage and climbing over the tumbled stones of her garden wall.

He pulled into the drive and waited. Gene should be about

five minutes behind him; as soon as he saw the lights he would go round back and unlock the door to his room. Mrs. Leahy's guests had a private entrance, and, happily, a private bath. No light showed from inside the house; Mrs. Leahy had gone early to bed.

They both had to duck under the low door frame; cottagers did not grow large in Connemara. The room was tiny. Against the wall the bed lay neatly turned down; the linen was sparkling and the brick floor was scrubbed until it was smooth as velvet. Two chairs faced the fireplace where blocks of peat lay ready to light. Charley leaned over and struck a match, a little disillusioned to find a brick of 'Surefire' starter under the honest turf. "The jet age has found Mrs. Leahy," he said; the fire obediently crackled and roared into flame.

There were four bottles of dark beer, warm, of course, on the table. "All the comforts of home," Gene remarked. "Too bad you're leaving so soon."

"Am I? When? I was just beginning to feel at home - looking forward to Mrs. L's compleat Irish breakfast at nine a.m." He looked across the top of his beer at Gene. "Don't tell me I'm leaving."

"You're going take a nice long ride, my lad, beginning Monday." He smiled, self-satisfied and raised his mug in salute. "Isn't that what you had in mind?" Of course, he'd had it in mind; he'd thought of nothing else since the moment he had recognized Megan, trailing clouds of glory through the rain, leading the grey pony out of the ring.

"Not until a few hours ago," he admitted. "Though it does seem a possibility now you bring it up." He didn't want to sound like the smart-ass cat that swallowed the whatever. He continued, sounding as diffident as honesty would let him, "At least it *might* put me in the right place at the right time - and, luckily," he smiled now, "Luckily, I brought my boots and raincoat. You just never know, do you?"

"Good," Gene said. "Where do you spend the nights? Not in the saddle, I hope."

If there was a note of sadistic pleasure in this comment, Charley decided to ignore it. "Never. We stay in lovely places; I remember them. Hunting and fishing lodges, old manor houses done over - high ceilings, French cuisine, crystal chandeliers, shared bathrooms - the whole Irish nine yards." Even then, he had known it was something special. But, now, he guessed, rightly, that Gene didn't care about the menu or the decor. "I suppose you mean are they in places that are any good as far as seeing what our friends are up to? I don't know -" He thought for a minute, while the clock ticked and the wind whistled down the chimney. "Honestly, Gene, if the roads are closed for them, I don't know how they can get over the mountains without help. I remember seeing a horse sink in the mud up to its neck. Three men got it out - you just don't know where you can step."

"But suppose our friends from the north decide to take up horseback riding, now. Your Irish huntsman gets people through, doesn't he"?

"He's done it every day for fifteen years. He learned it when he was a kid from an old guy - I remember, along the way we met him. Ould McElhinney they called him; all the locals knew him because he was the only man who knew the way across.

Yeah, I guess they could just pack along with him if they wanted to and probably stay three nights at Ussher, maybe four miles from Carna -"

When he talked about it, it all came back to him as though it was just yesterday that he stood with his mother on that barren shore, and he felt the same exhilaration and thrill of expectation that he had that day. He longed to see the child, Megan, running over the rocks and across the turf, her black hair streaming in the wind.

Tomorrow he would find her and tell Jamey he was coming with them.

In the town of Clifden only a few lights still showed. The pubs hadn't closed but the few customers were quiet, seriously into their drink. On a street corner a noisy bunch of kids were singing; an old man walked by them, a terrier straining at the end of a rope in his hand. He walked past and then turned. "Shut up, ye weengin' brats!" he hissed. "Let the decent folks sleep in peace for once -"

"Go home, Dad," a girl called. "Go home - leave us be -"

A window opened above their heads. "Shut your bloody noise up -" a voice shouted, and the window banged down. Kevin turned back into the room. "God, the Irish are a bloody people!" he said. "No manners, none at all -"

Bettina was sitting on the bed very slightly clothed in a satin teddy. One strap kept sliding off her shoulder and, idly, she kept pushing it back up. "But you're Irish yourself, Kev. What about you?"

"I'm bloody, too," he said. "Bloody hungry -"

"Well, it's not my fault we didn't get here sooner," Bettina said. "And how should I know you couldn't get a goddamn bite to eat in this town after nine o'clock. It's your dumb country, not mine -"

"I don't mean hungry for food, luv," he said. "You can stop putting that thing back on; you look much better with it off -" He leaned across the bed towards her.

"Forget it," she said. It wasn't a smile; it was a sneer. "You're not coming one inch closer, not now, not ever. I only said I'd come so you wouldn't mess it up - if you had the brains of a two-year-old I'd've let you do it alone. Just keep your f---in hands to yourself-" She got up, wrapped herself in the spread and, with exaggerated dignity, swept into the bathroom. The door slammed.

Kevin sat on the bed, viewing his reflection in the mirror. What was the matter with the bitch? In Dublin she seemed as though she thought it would be wonderful; the way she'd looked at him there! The bleedin bitch! He'd like to send her packing, he would. And he would, too, only she was the one who got the money, wasn't she? She had the money, right now, the money for Thursday, for the night when the moon would be dark and the tide would be high, three hours before dawn at Carna. Damn her! Who needed a woman, anyhow? Bitches, they were, all of them!

When she came out of the bathroom he was still sitting there. "You forget it now," she said. "You fool."

She was wearing a big, heavy sweater of some fuzzy stuff

- mohair, he thought it was called - and it matched her eyes, which were violet. Her lovely legs were hidden by heavy olive drab pants, baggy, covered with pockets on the outside, rolled up at the bottom to show a pair of Bean boots with white athletic socks rolled over their tops. He still ached with desire for her, a desire turned inward, turned to rage. She musn't see it, though; he needed what she had and what she could do more than he needed to have her bleeding body.

"I'm sorry," he said, and may God strike me dead for a liar.

"Well, d'you want to know what I've done?" she said. He nodded. He had stayed in the room all afternoon - why should he be out in the rain watching the goddamn ponies? - while she had gone to find the guide, or whatever he was. Even if it had been his idea, it was a hell of a way to go. On horses, six days over this blasted countryside? God, he thought Ulster was bad land until he saw this. Connemara! A pile of rocks is what it was. No wonder the government had everyone out here on the dole; they couldn't make a living out of this land if they were God Himself, could they? The wonder was, the government caring at all if anyone stayed here. Better if they didn't, then the roads would be empty and they could go as they had used to go, straight through from the coast to Galway, and none the wiser. Then he wouldn't be sitting here wondering if he could walk after a day on the bloody horse -

Bettina was talking. "I said I was from America and I had just heard about the ride from an Irish friend and I simply *had* to go and did they have room for two more. He said he had a lot of extra horses - harses, he said, of course - and sure, we could

89

come. It was that easy - even you could've done it." She spat this at him with some satisfaction.

Damn the girl! It was his idea, he was only using her for the American money she could get, and somehow, she had taken control of it and he felt almost useless, impotent. Castrating bitch, that's what she was. Once he was through with her --- He was able to smile, then, at her. He hoped she didn't know how to ride. How he'd love to see that cute little bum rubbed raw and bleeding and hear her say, "Thanks, I'll just stand up while I eat."Serve her bloody well right, that's what it would.   "Get off the bed," she said. "We need to sleep." And she lay down with all her clothes on, turned over and cut off the light.

He pulled the chair over by the window and sat down. It was an old chair, and soft, except for one loose spring in the seat that pierced him alarmingly every now and then. Next room they took he'd make sure it had two beds.

CHAPTER NINE

He hadn't the least idea where he was when he woke; he couldn't think what day it was, either. Sun streamed in the tiny window and lay in a long rectangle of light on the smooth bricks of the floor. The chilling air in the room was remarkably damp for such a brilliant day; all he wanted to do was pull the big, downy cover over his head and stay there another twelve hours in womb-like comfort. A furtive look at his watch informed him that it was four o'clock - he still hadn't set it. It was actually nine by the time they used here. Damn. He'd have to get up.

The shower was predictably cold and, he had to admit,

invigorating. By the time he was towelled dry and shivering in front of the shaving mirror he knew it was Sunday, and he had work to do. "Get on that ride," Gene had said last night. "Tell him anything, but make him give you a horse, get your boots on and go -" He said he would arrange for contact along the way. "I'll have it all down by lunch tomorrow - be at Harrigan's by one and I'll buy you a sandwich." He looked entirely too pleased with himself, as though everything was going to work out perfectly just because he'd found a way to get Charley where he wanted him to be.

"The Ussher place is close enough to Carna," he'd said. "Mossiter feels sure that's where they make the pick up. They've identified a small Libyan freighter in the lanes off the coast there with no logical business; they've seen her more than once, and beyond those meaningless messages, there's been no good reason to stop her. She comes in at Cork and she's perfectly clean for all Ed was able to find out from the people there." He drew deeply on the pipe that he'd been trying to light while he talked. A blue wisp of smoke curled up into the still air of the room; he regarded it gravely. Then his face broke into a grin; he unfolded his thin frame and stood up. "I better let you get some sleep tonight - it may be the last you'll have for a while." He hiked his trousers up and shoved his long arms into the sleeves of a disreputable garment that showed signs of once having been a good Harris tweed. "Nitey-nite-" he said, and let himself out.

Now, Charley stepped out of the bathroom into the cold, sunlit room to get dressed. The most incredible smell filled the air; it made him forget the damp and the cold and the fact that none of his socks seemed to match. It was coffee brewing, bacon frying and oatmeal, good Irish oatmeal, cooking, and it filled his heart with gratitude and love for Mrs. Leahy, bless her fine, Celtic soul! The oatmeal came first, steaming and fragrant, with a pat of Irish butter in the middle and sprinkled with brown sugar. "Did anyone ever tell you, Mrs. Leahy," he said, "That there is nothing in the whole world as good as your oatmeal?"

"Hisht, lad," she said. "Eat it up, and you'll have your egg and bacon then-"

Filled and warm at last, he stepped outside into the new and sparkling morning. The sky was washed clean by the rain; it was breathtaking blue, streaked high above him with feathers of white, blowing in from across the water. A good day, he thought, a perfect day to go and find a wild Irish girl and tell her I will be going with her over the mountains and down to the black lake where a lady walks by night and a loon cries out in the dark, and only the men need fear.

He didn't fear, but, on this clean and lovely morning, he wished with all his heart that he was just another tourist, another silly American, looking for another adventure to fill up his snapshot album and brighten his cocktail hour conversation. "It's you I fear for, lad," she'd said. Well, this time she needn't fear; she'd never know, he could never let her guess, why he was here.

The little car choked and spluttered, complaining of the damp. On the third try it came to life and billows of smoke filled the drive. It shuddered as he let out the clutch, then lurched back and out onto the road. Once under way it rolled along nicely and Charley found that today the wrong side of the road even seemed right. It *did* look like a good day.

The town seemed deserted after the crowds of yesterday. It might have been a different place, sparkling, now, in the sun. One or two tourists wandered in the street, shopping bags in hand, discussing which of the three woolen goods shops had the best prices, and a few local women with grocery bags or babies in their arms stopped to chat on the corners. It was Sunday morning. Two old boys were sitting on a bench in front of Harrigan's. Pubs didn't open till noon on Sunday, a custom which placed considerable restraint on the drinking habits of the local gentry. They were forced, as were these two, to carry small brown bags from whose depths they were able to sustain themselves until, in conscience, the pubs could serve them their Sunday afternoon refreshment.

"Aye, Jamey Leary's in town," the more coherent of the two answered him. "Seen him down t'the pony show, I did."

"Do you know here he stays?" Charley asked.

"Aye, that I do -" He nodded, smiled and closed his eyes.

"You do? Good. Perhaps you can tell me where, then?" The eyes stayed closed. Charley looked helplessly to where the other old boy slumped forward over his bottle. "D'you know where Jamey Leary stays, then?" He spoke to the top of the man's head, with no apparent effect. He couldn't stand here and shout on a Sunday morning; he leaned down to his first informant and said, rather firmly, "Can you tell me where Jamey Leary stays?"

"Sure, that I can," a soft voice behind him said.

He whirled around and there he saw the child, Megan, laughing, teasing him, wild and beautiful, just the way he had first seen her, with her hair blowing in the wind and her mouth wide with laughter. The well-dressed woman he'd followed from the pony ring was gone; this was the girl he had known - and loved. She held her hand out to him and he took it in his and the warm reality of her there beside him shattered the moment and he smiled at her.

"Megan. How did you -?"

"Why, of course, I knew you'd be looking for Daddy," she said. "Didn't I tell you to come with us?"

"Yes, but how did you know I would?"

"Oh, you are, aren't you?" Her voice was little, now and low. "You've got to. I told Daddy - he's looking for you to come." The deep blue eyes never left his face while she spoke; her hand was still in his.

"Yes," he said, "I'm coming if you've got a horse for me -"

"Aye, we've got the big hunter - he'll do you fine." She took her hand from his and stepped back; her eyes appraised his height. "You've got so bloody tall," she said. "Lucky we brought him with us, old Padric. He's above seventeen hands, he is. The pair of you'll look a treat -" He felt as though she was judging him like a pony on the auction block. She could probably tell at a glance if a pony had gone over fourteen and a half hands; no longer considered, in Ireland, to be a Connemara at all. They threw them out of the book, then, and they were called cobs; totally useless for breeding, a disgrace to their breeders and a blemish on their sires' records.

"Will you catch him for me the way you used to catch Jamey's horse? Remember me trying to help you that day-?"

"And you fell on your face in the mud -" Her laugh was clear and loud and one of the old men on the bench stirred into brief consciousness.

"Jamey Leary is it you wanted?" he mumbled. He looked up, briefly, and his red-rimmed eyes showed a light of recognition when he saw Megan. "Ask the lass," he said. "She'll tell you, she will." He tilted the bottle to his lips and swallowed deeply; with a satisfied smile he resumed his interrupted sleep.

"Poor old, Mick," Megan said. "He used to keep Dad's horses when we were this end of the trail - his wife died and he's on the dole now." She touched the old man's shoulder. "Are you all right, Mick? Sure Daddy'd like to know if you are in need for anything -" A snuffling snore was her only answer. "Well, he's got his bottle for comfort," Megan sighed, "And to keep him warm at night. It's a shame for an old man to be alone in the night, it is."

"For any man to be alone in the night is a shame," Charley said.

"So they all tell me," Megan laughed, "But I never yet saw one I'd be ready to help out of his shame and sadness -"

"Once you wanted to show me how Lady Dudley did it; you were willing enough when you were ten years old."

"Twelve," she said, "Twelve, I was, then -" They were walking down the street, now, and, looking at Megan beside him, it was easy to imagine the child she had been; time kept sliding away from him, and the dark cloud of danger seemed, momentarily, to be drifting away. The years between were gone; they were talking as though they had seen each other every day since then. The sun was high and the wet stones gleamed in its light. The whole world seemed good.

"Come," she said, "Daddy's at the Hare and Hound, getting things together. I told him I'd find you -"

There was grey in his hair, now, but the startling green of his eyes had not changed. When he smiled, you could see how the lines around them had deepened, but when he stood up and walked across the room, the spring in his step was the same and his handshake had the same knuckle-cracking force as before. "It's good to see you, lad," he said. He clapped Charley on the shoulder as he smashed his right hand in his. "Megan said she knew you across the room - and so would I. You're cummin', she says?"

"Well, I'd like to," Charley said. He withdrew the hand as soon as feasible and put it in his pocket. "I'm here on a bit of business, but now I know you're here, I figure I can take a while off and go with you, at least to Galway if you can work it out -" As he spoke, he knew how much he wanted to do it, even with the double meaning it had for him. Even if - he wouldn't think of the ifs, now, not here, with Megan beside him and Jamey smiling his warm welcome.

Then it was all arranged; the lads would pick his bags up here at the Hare and he would meet them tomorrow at the shore. He left them, then, Megan under piles of saddles and bridles, busy with glycerin soap, and Jamey doing accounts and ordering food. It was time to go to Harrigan's. Gene would be ecstatic.

Five minutes after opening and Harrigan's was entirely filled with thirsty bodies. He bellied up to the bar to wait. A chance encounter of two old friends, it should appear. "Up bright and early, aren't you?" Gene was at his shoulder. "Get a pint for me, ok? I'll look for a place for us to sit."

Crammed, then in a corner booth, they talked quietly, the sound of their voices almost obliterated in the general uproar all around them. "It's all fixed for the ride," Charley said. "I talked to them just now -"

"Well, I can't say you seem unhappy about it," Gene said, and he knew that the joy inside him must be showing all over his face. "Do you think it's going to be a picnic out there?" Gene was serious, now, and the reality of today's business settled into Charley's consciousness like an unwelcome guest.

"We'll be three days near Carna," he said. "We stay at the Ussher those nights. Do I have a contact there?"

"Harry called," Gene said. "He's sending Bill Jordan down. Bill's been in Belfast and thinks he knows who they're sending to the coast. He's probably known to them, too, so it looks like you're it. He'll be right behind you all the way."
"Thanks," Charley said, "And who'll be behind him?"

"You know Carna," Gene said. "There's nothing there. Bill will have contact by radio, but we can't have a mob out there watching. Spook the quarry, wouldn't we?" He gazed mournfully into the mug of dark, warm beer. "God, I wish they knew what refrigeration was in this God-forsaken place." He took a reluctant gulp and set the mug firmly down. "Tell me how your days will go - what's the schedule?"

"If it's like I remember -" he said, and the memories came back to him and made him long for that other time when life was simple and the world was new and clean. "The way we do is like this," he said. "We grab the horses out of a field and we ride till afternoon. They bring us lunch and we sit around in the rain and eat - we are starved. Then we ride till dark and put the horses in another field and they take us to where we spend the night. Then we eat wonderful food and we sit around the fire and talk." And go outside and look for ghosts, he thought, and wished for the hundredth time that it was only ghosts he was looking for this trip. "We have breakfast at nine, very leisurely and then they take us back to the horses again -"

"How about your luggage? Who takes it?" Gene was all business now.

"It goes in the van, or with the girls in the horse box." He smiled to hear how Irish he was; three days in this blessed country and he was calling a trailer a horse box like any local horseman. "Why?"

"Can you carry anything yourself? While you ride, I mean?"

"A raincoat -" Charley laughed. "You never leave home without it, not here. You can take a back pack or saddle bags - sure, you can take some stuff with you."

"I'll see that you get 'some stuff', then. Communications. Things you'll need. You'll find Bill at the Shamrock B and B - about two miles from Carna. Probably the first night. I'll let you know." He approached the beer once more, thought better of it and lit a match instead. When the pipe was going again he looked up. "You *can* get out alone, after midnight, say?"

"If you say so," Charley laughed. I've done that before, he thought. History repeats itself; the darkness and wind and the bird crying over the water and the two children running along the shore and the terror following them as they ran. Only this time he would be alone in the night and she safe in her bed while he searched in the dark to find the dreadful traffick from the sea; to stop it if he could. "Sure, I can get out. Just let me know when."

Gene finished his beer and stuck the pipe in his pocket. He wasn't smiling when he spoke. "I'll be in touch," he said. "Good hunting."

Jamey Leary closed the worn ledger book on the table. "That's it, then, luv," he said to his daughter. "Fourteen of them it is, with the lad."

"I'm glad," she said, "Had you forgotten him? I hadn't."
She was doing the last few buckles back together on a pile of
bridles that surrounded her where she sat on the floor.
"Fourteen," she said, worried now. "Isn't it this time we can't stay
at Ussher? Have we got too many then, him and that idjit from
Dublin with the Yank girl friend? We hadn't counted them when
we reserved."

"I'll get around Marianne, I will. She'll let some of us
stay." His face broke into that smile of his; the one he used to
convince each lonesome spinster or dissatisfied wife who rode
with him that she was about to tempt him out of all control by her
outrageous beauty. "Marianne'll find us a bed, never fear," and
Megan knew he was right, God love him.

When she started down the hall to her room she almost ran
into the idiot from Dublin. Speak of the devil, she thought, and
brushed past him. "Just a moment, miss," he said. "Can I speak
to you?"

"It seems you are," she said. "What is it, then?"

"I thought Bettina and I were the last ones you could take.
What's this new man I heard was going? Who is he?"

"An old friend," she told him, and thought, what business
of yours is it, lad; just keep your own nose clean and tidy and
don't put it where it doesn't belong and may your life be long and
happy to you, now. But she only said, "Dad had an extra horse

and he only just got here -"

"Is he a Yank?"

"And why not? Most of them are." She was sick of this bloody man and ready for bed. "Good night, to you," she said and ducked past him. At her door she paused to look back. Bettina's door opened and, as he went in, Megan heard the hiss of her whisper, "Well, who *is* he?" What was it to them, after all? She lay in her bed thinking. Why did the words keep coming back to her from so long ago - "It's you I fear for, lad - it's you"?

CHAPTER TEN

Inside the caravan the air was thick with smoke, and the heavy smell of burning coal oil filled the tiny room. The only light came from the lamp hanging over the table; the glare from its unshaded flame hurt Sheila's eyes and for a moment blinded her. The dog still fretted and grumbled, straining at the rope that held it and flecks of foam flew from its jaws as it struggled to be free. The muscles of the man's arm rippled as he jerked the animal back. It cowered beside him then, the rope tightened about its neck and the growl, deep in its throat, was like the soughing of the wind through distant trees, low and frightening. Sheila moved behind Wolfe and took his arm.

The gypsy laughed; his teeth showed white as chalk in his

dark face and his eyes, black as bits of coal, watched her as she moved. She knew that her fear gave him pleasure and she hated his eyes upon her. She stared back at him, unblinking.

"Just watch your bloody dog," she said, with far more bravery than she felt. "We didn't come here to be killed -"

Sean was laughing at her, then. "You're silly, Sis, afraid of a wee dog," he said, and he put out his hand to pet it. She hardly saw what happened, so quick it was. The sound that came from the animal was a crash of thunder; it lunged for Sean's throat. The gypsy was pulled almost off his feet, and he swore as he struggled to keep the dog back.

"You bastard!" he yelled, not at the dog, but at Sean. "Keep your f---in' hands to yourself - next time I'll let him go, you bloody fool!"

"Can you put the dog up, then?" It was Wolfe's voice she heard, quiet and low beside her. "We've no quarrel with it, now, and we do have some business together this night." He turned to Sean. "Leave it, lad. It's you in one piece we need - have a care with yourself." He smiled, then, down at Sheila, and his arm was around her, holding her close.

"Aye, he can go," the man said. He opened the door and dragged the dog to it. "Out, then, with you," he growled, and, cringing, the animal slunk down the steps. "He's a great one for fighting, he is," and he smiled at Wolfe, dismissing the whole scene in the moment. He held out his hand. "I'm Ward," he said, "And are you him I'm to look for?"

"I'm Wolfe Morrison," Wolfe said, "From Belfast -"

"I'll need to see the what you've brought me." Ward spoke

106

low, close to Wolfe's face, so close that Sheila could smell the garlic on his breath and feel it warm on her cheek as she stood by Wolfe. "They said you'd have it with you -"

"How much?" Wolfe asked. Well he knew, Sheila thought; it was to test the man, Ward, that he asked.

"Five hundred, or it's off," Ward said. "Five hundred and in little notes, old ones, ones I can use and never anyone notice. And I see it before ever we go -" His eyes were hard, now, and there was no smile to show the gleaming teeth. But the money was to come after, Sheila knew, nothing till the job was done, Wolfe had told her that. Now she watched Sean's face where he stood behind Ward; he didn't like the man, and if there was going to be trouble over the money it could set him off again. She held Sean's eye with hers and shook her head, ever so slightly; she prayed he would heed her warning and let Wolfe handle the business of it.

"I haven't it now," Wolfe said, "You'll get half the night before and the rest when we have the cargo." He spoke quietly, watching Ward, waiting to see how he took it. Who told him we'd have it tonight? Sheila thought. Hadn't bloody Kevin said he'd only get it from Bettina when they got here? Ward was still standing by the table with the light full on his face. A long scar ran from under one eye all the way down his face. It ran through the dark stubble of beard on his cheek and ended just above his collar in a twisted red knot. Beside it, just beneath his eye, a nerve twitched under the skin. Except for his heavy breathing there was silence in the room.

Then she saw something move in the dark corner. She

shaded her eyes from the glaring light. She saw an old woman sitting hunched forward; intent she looked, hearing every word they spoke. Ward turned his head ever so slightly, enough to catch the old woman's eye. "Hear that, old lady?" he said. "They haven't got it -"   Then the old girl pulled herself out of the chair in the corner and, with surprising speed and grace, she came to the table and stood with Ward under the light. Mother of God, she was ugly. It made Sheila's flesh crawl to look at her. She could be a witch, she could; you might be sure the tinkers had witches with them, now. It could put a mark on the child just for her to see the old bitch, that she well knew. Yet she looked; it was as if her eyes were drawn of themselves to look, never mind how she tried not to see the filthy old thing.

The woman's voice was ugly as her face. She spoke close beside Ward, but the sound of her voice rasped loud in the tiny space. "You idjit," she hissed. "They'll not trust ye, no more ye'd trust them -"

Ward glared at her; the flashing smile was gone and his face was hard. God, Sheila thought, we've come all this way and for nothing? Hadn't Ward dealt with the others? and now not to trust *us*? "Shut your mouth, old woman," he snarled. "I work when I'm paid and damn who I trust -"

Wolfe sat down at the table. He was smiling, smiling up at Ward and the old bitch, and it was a smile to melt the very heart of a stone. "Cum, now," he said, soft, "Cum, it's not ours, the money isn't - we haven't got it, not with us, I tell you straight, we haven't. It's the plan we're making this night, only. Then we tell our mates and get it for you. You'll have your half before ever

108

you leave to go after it."

"Hear him," the old woman said, and Ward sat to the table, too.

"Fetch us some drink, Maudie," he said. "I'll talk, then -" They drank the burning poteen from cracked jelly glasses, and as they drank, Ward told them what they wanted to hear. The wind coming in from the south meant a good three days of bad weather, the moon hidden each night. The tide would run high after midnight Thursday; the channel would have enough depth for Ward to take his skiff out and get back before dawn. They were in luck with the weather; the moon was at the half and, if not for the clouds, the risk of discovery would be too great. Ward wanted the cover of dark until his skiff was back through the channel and safely tied up where the bushes hung over the tidal flats, and no one to see. "I'd never go with the moon on me," Ward said, "Not for your five hundred pounds nor ten times it -"

Old Maudie cackled. "Ye bloody liar," she said. "Ye'd sell your own mother for five hundred pounds -" She filled the glasses again and then tipped the bottle to her lips. Sheila watched as each gulp traveled down the scrawny neck; the old woman saw her watching and winked obscenely at her over the empty bottle. She found the beads in the pocket of her jeans and held them in her hand. Mother of God, if the old hag really was a witch -

"Then it's Thursday you go?" Wolfe said. He turned to Sean. "You'll find where Kevin'll be then, lad?

Ben had been silent since they came in, and now he barely looked up as he spoke. "Sheila's to bring them the half," he said,

"Wednesday, when dark falls. Kevin'll have the rest for them when they give him the packet." His eyes showed dark beneath the hair that fell over his forehead; a smile twisted his mouth and Sheila felt a flutter of fear, cold in her belly.

"Where do I get it, then? From that skinny bitch he's got with him, right?" Don't let him know you're fearing him, she told herself; she forced her eyes to find his and held them until his look wandered down over her body, to her throat, then lingered on her breasts and finally stopped, staring below her waist. She felt Wolfe's hand on hers and knew he was watching. He'd bloody kill the man if anything happened, that much she knew. Just pray God she wasn't alone with him, ever.

A laugh rumbled low in Ben's chest, obscene, satisfied. "I get it for you, luv, when they get to Ussher, and you come along here with it alone -'

"Not Sheila alone," Wolfe said, quiet, but not with a doubt in anyone's mind. "There's no call for her to be out by herself here - we bring it together or you do it yourself." Ward was watching them the while and she thought it well for him not to see them fighting.

So she smiled. "Oh, it's no matter, alone or with Wolfe, I'll get it here," she said to him. Easy to say; Wolfe would never leave her alone with Ben, she well knew. Ward glanced quickly at Maud. Their eyes met and her head bobbed imperceptibly; it was all right, then, with them.

"She be here by dark of Thursday or it's off," Ward said. "My boat never leaves anchor without I have it." Maud nodded again, snuffling and coughing into her filthy sleeve. It's done,

110

then, Sheila thought, and her breath came easy for a moment. It wasn't so hard after all, was it?

The night seemed colder, and the motor struggled against starting. At last they were bumping down the road along the shore, retracing their way through Carna and up the mountain to where, by the road's end they stopped in front of a darkened cottage. The door opened at their touch; the light of Sean's torch showed an empty room and a cold hearth. "Mother of God, they've left a cheery place for us, have they not," Wolfe laughed. "Not even a jug of poteen to warm us, now."

Later, they lay together on a straw pallet. Sheila rested her head on Wolfe's shoulder and his arms around her were safe. Her head fitted exactly in the hollow place between his neck and his shoulder, a place that seemed to have been made especially for Sheila Morrison's head to rest upon. "Wolfe," she said, "We're done after Thursday, is it? You're not with them for the Ussher?" Her breath stopped and she waited; it was too long before he answered her and she knew before he spoke.

"They can't do it alone, luv - you know I can't let them try." His mouth was close by her face and his breath was warm on her skin. "It means everything," he said, "If we can do it, luv, we've won, then, haven't we?" His voice was a whisper in her hair. "Then it's over, for always, and all the dying and the killing has got meaning to it -- as long as time goes on our children and their children will remember and know --" There was a catch in his throat and Sheila knew he was crying and her face was against his and wet with both their tears. She knew he would go, had always known he would go, and she with him; where else would

111

she ever be?

And the secret inside her she would keep from him till after; no need he should know, and knowing, fear to lose the very life he risked his own to save. She was so tired and the night so short; before she closed her eyes, the square of the window was grey with the dirty light of another dreary dawn.

In Clifden the skies were just as grey and the sullen mist swirled across the rocky coast and blew through the streets and alleys of the town. Charley drove the Morris, still spluttering and choking, into the town car park. He pulled into a narrow space under a tree at the back of the lot; it could stay there a week, or two, for that matter. Nothing left in it of his, no identity to it at all. Everything was either at the Hare or in the back pack that was going with him. Gene had come to the cottage after dinner last night and brought an impressive array of electronic gadgets, all of which were now neatly tucked away in rolled-up socks and tee-shirts in the back pack. "If you need me," Gene said, "Any time, press the red button - mine is on me all the time - never leave home without it, right?" The weathered face broke into a reassuring smile. "And if you need to get Bill, do the black button; he'll be as near as the closest passable road, if that's any comfort."

They were sitting with their feet on the fender in Mrs. Leahy's spotless guest room, trying to counteract the damp with a jolly turf fire while Gene filled in the details for him. "They've given you some flares, as well," he said. "I guess if you are sinking in a bog you can let one fly and produce a helicopter."

Charley grinned. "Very funny, aren't you? You're just jealous; you want to sit six hours a day on a fat pony and jog over the rocks and hills with me, I bet." You'd want to all right if you'd seen Megan, he thought briefly, before turning his attention back to the inventory of toys Gene had brought with him.

Now, he shifted the pack onto his shoulders, turned his collar up against the soaking drizzle and started up the street towards the Hare. Lights from shop windows glowed brightly through the greyness of the miserable day, and in the lobby of the Hare and Hound a blazing fire welcomed him. Jamey stood with his back to it, hands in pockets, broad-brimmed hat pushed back on his head. A girl was talking to him, while a scrawny young man nervously rearranged the three or four pieces of luggage on the floor beside them.

"Aye, they'll all be along soon," Jamey was saying. "Rob will have been on the road with them since daybreak."

The girl turned to the young man. "I suppose in Ireland time doesn't mean a thing does it? It said nine o'clock in the brochure-" She looked at her watch. "God, it's almost ten!" She might have been beautiful; Charley didn't know how such perfect features could add up to such an unlovely appearance. Then she caught his eye; he realized he had been staring. Her look was a dagger across the room.

"Hi," he said and smiled at her.

"Ah, lad, you're here!" Jamey's hearty voice filled the room and he strode over to clap Charley on the back and seize his hand in welcome. Wincing slightly, Charley retrieved his hand.

"Did my stuff get here?" he asked.

"Righto - just there by Kevin." He pointed to the pile of luggage on the floor. "Feels like enough in the pack on your back to last you the while," he said.

"Cameras and stuff," Charley told him, suddenly resentful of the deceipt he would be practicing all week on this good and honest man. And on his good and lovely daughter, as well. As though the thought of her caused her to materialize, Megan burst through the door, followed by a chattering band of men and women, dressed variously, under their dripping raingear, in jeans, breeches, boots and chaps, and carrying staggering loads of luggage. The room was suddenly a madhouse, Jamey was everywhere, greeting everyone, his ruddy face glowing with pleasure as he shook hands all around and tried to learn everyone's name at once.

Megan had come on the bus from Galway with them and she went with her father from one to another of the group, making introductions, telling him something about each rider as they went. There was no one else in the room for Charley, then. Her hair hung loose about her face and her cheeks glowed from the wind and mist. A too-big sweater hung from her shoulders and faded jeans covered her lovely legs. Then she saw him; she ran to him across the room, climbing over the piled up bags, laughing. "Oh, Charley," she said, "You look a picture, you do. Let's have a smile, lad - will we have a race to the first fence, then? And look for Lady Dudley again?" She threw her arms around him and for a moment while he held her close they were alone, children again, in that other sweet and bitter time when they had wept together by the dark waters of the lake and had thought they were parting forever.

From across the room, the fox-faced girl watched them and leant to whisper something to her pale friend. The door blew open with a sudden wind; its damp chill was not colder than the look in the man's eyes as he nodded an answer to her question.

CHAPTER ELEVEN

"Out you go!" Jamey shouted. "We'll not be letting this luvly day go to waste, now -" For a few minutes bedlam ruled the lobby; the bags piled on the floor were eventually all sorted out and loaded into the trailer. "Put yours in last," Megan advised. "Then you'll get it out first when we get there." Finally, everyone had piled into the van; once inside, Megan began introducing him to the group that had arrived from Galway. Packed in like sardines in a can, camaraderie was almost obligatory. Most of them were Americans; two middle aged couples from Massachusetts, a pair of thirtyish librarians from Philadelphia, a fat young man with a voice as thick as Mississippi mud and an assortment of single females that Charley hoped to have sorted out in his mind before the week was over.

"Who are those two?" he asked Megan. "Are you ignoring them, or what?" He nodded toward the two who had waited with him at the Hare.

"I'd bloody like to ignore them," Megan whispered. "He's a right pig, he is; no manners to him at all, and she no better, if you ask me." Her nose twitched like a rabbit smelling the morning air and she shrugged. "But, they're Daddy's business for better or worse - Kevin and Bettina, they're called. He's from Dublin and she's his friend from America, Boston, I think. They signed on late, just here in Clifden -"

The van jolted to a start; in fifteen minutes they were at the coast. The rain had stopped and ragged clouds raced in from across the water. Jamey stood by the wall with the wind in his face and Megan beside him while the rest climbed out of the van, stretching their legs, looking around in wonder at the wild sea and the rough, rocky land.

"Where the hosses?' Mississippi asked. His fat legs were stuffed into impeccable breeches and shiny brown field boots, probably for the first time in their chubby lives.

"Just there," Megan said, at pointed toward the sea. There the horses stood grazing, their tails to the wind and their heads buried in the tall grass. She handed the fat man a bridle. "Go with Dad," she said, "He'll show you which one is yours - I'll fetch it for you then."

"Can I come with you," Charley asked. "I promise I'll do a better job than I did back then-"

He followed her over the fence and across the stony field.

It was the same field and the same wind and the same clouds, and the girl running ahead of him ran with the same wild grace and abandon he remembered from that long ago day when their great adventure had begun, and he felt the years fall away and the memory was more real than the turf under his feet this day. For an hour they worked, catching horses, giving novices a hand readying them for the ride, and all the while his mind was living again those two weeks of love and terror, the two haunted weeks when he had left his childhood behind him forever on the shores of a black lake set there in the middle of a wild and brooding wood.

"Penny for your thoughts." He jumped at the sound of her voice, close by his side. "Sure you look in another world -"

"Ah, Megan," he said, "I was remembering the night of the tinkers - how close we came to not getting back and how we lied about it when we did." He could laugh about it now, but the memory was still a cold terror inside him.

"Did you ever tell?" she asked.

"Never," he said. "Did you?"

She shook her head and her hair flew across her face. Impatient, she brushed it aside and smiled. "Tell my Dad his wee lass was out in the night with a lad, and visiting the tinkers as well? You don't know my Daddy, then."

"Remember how we cried?"

"Maybe you cried," Megan said. "I never would've."

"- how we cried when we came to the end?"

"And how long it took us to go back? And how long we stayed in the boathouse? Oh, Charley, it's brave you were, then -"

She smiled again, looking down. "I thought I loved you, then," she said.

"Are you two cummin with us, or lollygagging all day there?" Jamey's shout across the wind shattered the moment. Megan grabbed Charley's hand and dragging their startled horses, they ran over the rough ground to the van. "Don't wait, Daddy," Megan called. "We'll catch you right enough!"

Jamey mounted his little grey stallion, spoke a word or two of encouragement to each rider and began to lead them off, up the narrow path that would lead them over the mountains and through the bogs, all the way across Connemara.

Kevin and Bettina were at the end of the ragged line, holding back from the rest. Leaning down to pick up his girth, Charley could see, under the horse's belly, Kevin's face turned toward him. Their eyes met and Charley held the stare until Kevin looked away. When he stood and pulled the girth tight, he saw the two riding off together; Bettina's head was close to Kevin's and they seemed to be arguing about something.

"You don't know them do you, those two?" Megan looked puzzled.

"Not that I know of," he said. And even as he spoke, the moment shattered in a glare of light; he was in Mossiter's office with pile of photographs in front of him. "These are some of the people you might come across," the old man had said.

Then danger seemed to fill the air as thick as the Irish mist that blew in from the sea and it was all around them and he could feel it cold in his heart, as cold as the dark that had sheltered two frightened children on that long ago night by the black water of the lake of Ussher.

CHAPTER TWELVE

He watched morning come, at first only a pale light in the east, then a steadily growing brightness above the ragged edge of the mountain behind the lodge. He was standing at his window, had been standing there since before dawn. Yesterday, the first day, had been a hard ride, hard for the horses and ponies, and hard for the riders, climbing the steep, cliffy side of the mountain in the morning and galloping the length of its ridge, past the trenches where peat had been cut, and through - incredible, here on the mountain-top - bogs to sink a horse to its belly in. A girl from New York had panicked when her horse almost lost its footing; her hysteria was catching.

Bettina was riding right behind the girl and when the horse

began to sink in the treacherous turf, she snatched her horse's head up angrily, so that it wheeled to the side, lunging up the rocky cliff. "Oh, Jesus!" she yelled. "We're going to be killed up here!" She jumped off her horse and grabbed Megan's horse by the bridle. "Does your Dad know what the hell he's doing?" she demanded. "We've paid good money to come out here for him to sink us in a goddamn mud-hole -" The girl from New York sat frozen on her horse, a thin scream coming from her throat.

Megan got down and walked past Bettina without a glance. She took the reins from the terrified girl and stood beside her. "Come on, luv," she said. "Sure, this old mare has been deeper than this a thousand times - just hsssht yourself, now, and we'll be right before you know it."

The girl looked at her with eyes round as silver dollars, shining with tears. "I'm scared," she whispered. "What happened?"

"You got off the path, you didn't follow Daddy," Megan said. "And then you should've never stopped in the middle. But, not to worry - just you sit still and I'll have old Maggie free before you know it." She handed the reins back to the girl and got behind the mare. "Git up, there, old lady!" she said, and gave the animal a good smack on its rump. As the mare lunged forward she shouted to the girl, "Just let her have her head, now - she knows what to do," and in three or four plunges the mare stood on solid ground again; the girl managed a feeble smile and walked gingerly on.

Kevin stopped by Bettina. "Get back on, you idiot," he hissed. "You've got everyone looking - just what we need!" She

124

fixed him with a piercing stare; sullen she looked, enough to kill. Was she part of it, then? or did Kevin share with him alone the burden of keeping their dark business a secret? Were the two of them, riding to their ultimate meeting, living the same lie? He ached to tell Megan what he was doing; each passing moment he longed to stop the charade he was living and tell her, if only to protect her, to see that she wasn't there when --

Standing, now, at the open window, with the morning fresh before him, it was hard to get his mind in gear for the next part of his job. The day was innocent, and new as Eden, waiting, in all its loveliness, for the sordid reality he would bring it. Only he and Kevin, only the two of them, caught together here in this beautiful place, held violence and death in their hands.

Last night, long after the rest were asleep, he had raised Jordan on the radio. "One of them's with us," he'd said. "And a girl with him - I think they're the only ones."

"Have they a clue? You, I mean. Any recognition?"

"He's looked at me, maybe too hard, a couple times. The girl is American -- she could be our Boston bankroll. Everyone else is American, though, but she certainly came with him. Bitchy girl. They fight a lot for a loving couple -"

"Stay with him," Jordan had said. "You can sleep next week -" Did the sadistic bastard actually chuckle?

Tomorrow they would leave the horses by the shore near Carna. He remembered the place, another rocky field, fenced by ragged stone walls, an abandoned cottage to one side of the field and the sea pounding the shore just over the wall. It was reached over a stretch of dirt road that followed a long, narrow inlet where water rushed in at high tide, and slithered back out, six hours later, leaving a dry bed of sand and sea weed. Because the inlet was narrow, the tide rushed in and out with the force of a mountain stream; a boat caught in it would be whirled about like a chip of wood. In a few places, little stands of willow and unlikely palm trees sheltered the channel. It was off this shore the Libyan freighter had been sighted.

They would spend the night, then, at Ussher, and he would make his secret journey alone, while Megan slept and dreamt, he hoped, of that other time when fear had held them all night long in its frozen hand, and they had loved each other with a love that

'was stronger by far than the love
of those who were older than we --
of many far wiser than we --'

By the time he went down for breakfast, the pale pink of dawn had been smothered in grey, scudding clouds, and sheets of rain dashed against the windows. He looked for Megan; he needed to have breakfast with her, needed to look deep into the blue of her eyes and lose himself there, for a moment at least, in their cool shadows. Or laugh with her over a silly joke, or feel the light touch of her hand on his - or, impossibly, what he really wanted, take her in his arms and hold her forever. Control, Gibson, he told himself, you need control. You don't even know how she feels about you, now do you? Moreover, she wasn't in the dining room, at all, waiting to be ravished or not. The day looked even greyer. In the end, the only place left for him to sit was at the table with Kevin and Bettina, where he made a fair attempt at normalcy. "How are you two getting on with the ride?"

126

he asked, his deceitful voice oozing a bluff sort of friendship.

Kevin tried a smile. It was not a success. "Jolly good fun," he said. "And you?" Bettina was busy with the toast and marmalade; she did *not* reflect the jolly good fun at all.

"It's a bit harder than it was when I was thirteen," he said. "I came here with my mother then."

Kevin's interest picked up. "Then you know the territory?" he asked.

"Well, it was a long time ago -"

"I mean, you know what to expect then? The different stops along the road? Things like that -"

Bettina was watching closely now, the toast and marmalade abandoned on her plate. Then she was guessing, too. He felt her eyes on him and had to force himself to keep looking at Kevin. "Yes," he said, "I do, at least if it's like it was then -"

"Maybe you know, then," Kevin said, "How far it is from where we leave the horses the night we get to that old lodge - what's it called? the Asher?"

"Ussher," Charley said. "Well, it really doesn't matter how far, does it?" He was watching Kevin's eyes. "They bring us back and forth in the van anyway. Once we're there, stuffing ourselves with dinner, there wouldn't be any reason to want to go back out there, would there be?"

"Just wondering, he was," Bettina said. "I made him come on the trail, to show me Ireland, you know, and he's done nothing but complain -"

Kevin's eyes, under the pale brows, glowered at Bettina. "You needn't pretend you find it so grand, either, girl." He

127

sniffled and wiped his sleeve across his nose. "I've got this bloody cold, now -" he turned to Charley and his mouth twisted in a kind of grin. "You should see her bum after yesterday - it looks like a side of bacon!"

"Shut up," Bettina snapped. "At least I'm not making a damn scene over it. I came to see Ireland close up, and I *will*! If you want to chicken out, just go right ahead - I'm finishing the ride, with you or without you."

Charley was paying very close attention to his bowl of porridge. At least he had found out one thing. He and Kevin both had the same idea as to where it would happen; the question was when, and who - and how?

"Mon Dieu!" Marianne's voice was a small shriek as she swept across the narrow courtyard by the main entrance. "My primroses! He's pulled them out, they're gone! Pierre, come see - vite! vite! That boy, that idiot -- with my own hands -" she held her hands up, trembling, in front of her, then wiped them on her apron front in despair. "With my own hands, just yesterday, on my knees, I planted them -"

Pierre came and stood beside her, his arm over her shaking shoulders. "Cherie," he whispered. "Do not weep. Instead, find the child, and find a good oak switch, and when he can no longer sit down, he will plant again your flowers."

"There aren't any more," she sniffed. "It was the cuttings Lady Grosvenor brought me. I saved them for - you know - for this week. To have the garden not be a disgrace to us when -"

The intensity of her sorrow was too great; she hid her face in her hands and leaned against Pierre's bony, though reassuring chest.

"Boy! Get out here! Do not hide yourself --" His voice echoed from the stone walls and rang out to the lake's edge. "There is work --"

"Do not alarm yourself so, mon cher. Myself, I will find him - at least, he can clean up the mess and perhaps plant some of the geraniums from the terrace." She patted Pierre's arm and turned from her ruined garden to seek the unfortunate Timmy and lecture him on the astounding variety and beauty of the ill-fated primroses; a painful conscience would last far longer than a hurting backside, and teach the lad something in the bargain. Pierre stopped her.

"Listen," he said. "Would that be Jamey?"

The Land Rover announced itself before it came in sight. Detached from the horse box it could travel at alarming speed in Jamey's hands, and now it came rattling and roaring up the drive, complaining and grumbling as it bounced over the uneven cobbles. "Luvly!" Jamey cried. "You're a treat to see, lass - " He turned to Pierre. "She's prettier each day than the last, God luv her! D'you know how bloody lucky you are, man?" He clapped Pierre heartily on his skinny shoulder and siezed Marianne in a bearish hug. She laughed and pulled away from him.

"For shame, Jamey Leary!" she said, "With my man standing right here to see you -" She reached up to push back her hair, thought better of it when she saw the mud on her hands and wiped them again on her apron instead. Then, remembering, she looked back towards the house. "Jamey, you're not to be here!

I told you, we're full this week."

"Aye, you did," he said. "Not too full to give us a drink and a little chat, are you, now?"

Marianne looked helplessly at Pierre. His brows and his shoulders shot up simultaneously; he looked past Jamey as if some invisible help were to be found in the air behind him. Jamey looked from one to the other of them, waiting. "Well, what is it, then?" he said.

Pierre shrugged. "Only it is a special party -" He hesitated, his eyes on Marianne.

"You must never tell; *never* a word - I have promised them!" Marianne took Jamey's hand in hers and pulled him close to her. Her heart fluttered in her chest and beads of sweat stood out on her lip. She would tell him part, but never all; she was far too clever for that. Oh, she was up to the deceit, the lies, even, of the intrigue with which she was trusted. "It's the Duke of Edinburgh," she whispered, "And ten of his friends, all royal persons - they have trusted to us to keep their privacy intact, Pierre and me, so, you see, you must see, we can't have anyone enter the place, have anyone know -" She smiled her most beguiling smile at him and squeezed his hand. Pierre's head bobbed in a series of encouraging little nods.

"But, luv, now I do know; you've just told me," Jamey laughed. "As well hang for a sheep as a lamb and give us few rooms for the while."

"C'est impossible!" she whispered. "I am forbidden! Even the girls are forbidden to leave, and Ian also. We stay in the carriage house each night." She paused. "And *you* are forbidden

130

to say a word - I have told you nothing! *Nothing*, you understand!" Her dark brows almost met in a fierce scowl. Jamey was laughing!

Pierre put his arm around Marianne's shoulders. "Cherie," he whispered. "You know Jamey. He can be trusted, no? Do not disturb yourself so -"

"Marianne, lass!" Jamey said. "You've done just right, then. The carriage house is opened up; you'll have a bed there for me and my Megan and no trouble to you at all - and one or two more, maybe?" His smile was that of an angel and his clear green eyes full of trust to melt the heart of a stone.

"Already, before, I told you about this week; you found other places, no?"

"Ah, Marianne, you know how they are; three new ones signed on to us at Clifden and I've no place to put them. You'd not let them sleep on the ground, now, would you?"

What was she to do? If she sent him away unhappy, who knew what news he might spread; who knew if he'd come back again each week, in season and out? Her nerves could take little more after the strain of the past three days. She looked up at Pierre; speaking more to him than to Jamey, she said, "It could be done. There are the rooms in the loft - none of my good feather beds, there, you see, but rooms where one could sleep, no?" Again Pierre nodded. Encouraged, she went on. "It must be understood, the lodge is not open, it is only the carriage house. And you will eat with us there, no?"

The carriage house should be safe enough, she thought. It stood beside the lodge, but a high stone wall was between the

131

two buildings; the carriage house could be approached directly from the road without entering the garden (the poor destroyed garden!) in front of the lodge. And Jamey and his crowd came in late, always - quite often late enough to spoil Pierre's dinner as well as his temper - and they were off again as soon as they finished their breakfast. Not a lot of time to be snooping around, looking. They were tired and slept well without much care to where they laid their heads.

Besides, what was there to see? The Duke and his friends went off each morning at daybreak and *she* kept to her rooms till late. Then she walked by the lake with her Corgis - imagine dogs sleeping in the same room with a QUEEN! - and he came back for a long, late lunch with her and her ladies. Ian would take him out again late in the afternoon, returning often after dark. *She* would walk out on the mole and watch for them across the lake. The silly little dogs went with her everywhere, and she with that scarf over her head, looking - Marianne giggled inside as she thought it - like a French housewife going to the fish market.

So it was settled. Jamey and Megan would stay three nights; Wednesday, Thursday and Friday. They would bring with them two young men; an American, a Dubliner and his American girlfriend. It should be no trouble at all, Jamey said.

Megan was tired when she climbed into the Land Rover after dinner. It had been a long day and that fool Bettina screaming like a Banshee over a bit of a bog - wanted to see Ireland, she did; well, why not shut her mouth and look around her then instead of yelling filthy words at everyone. Even the poor little girl on Maggie, who after all was the one in trouble, hadn't made as much a blather as Bettina. She was just turning the motor over when she saw Charley standing at the door, outlined by the yellow light from the hall. She let the old Rover splutter and die. Her foot lingered over the gas pedal a moment and then she pulled the key out and stuck it in her pocket.

Fool, she was, right enough, to be mooning over Charley. It was so long ago, a wee girl she had been then, and he just a lad. It was daft to think he remembered, remembered the way she did, or to think he'd ever felt the way she had, just the look of him making her go all soft inside. And how she had cried when he was gone away! And how, when Daddy sent her to the States to show ponies and, later, the four long years there in college, how she had watched every tall, thin man she saw, waiting for him to turn around and be Charley. How often she'd wondered what she'd do if it ever *was* him, and now here he was, and here she was, sitting in the Rover like a bloody idjit, staring at him across the dark courtyard, and the same feeling of her heart doing rabbity leaps inside her and her tongue struck dumb.

She started the Rover again and put on the headlamps. Over the roar of the motor she heard him call. "Wait, Megan! Where're you going?" He ran across the yard in the dark. "Can I come with you?"

He couldn't know how she felt. She spoke, quiet. "Sure, if you've a mind to carry feed bags to the field with me -"

He jumped in over the door on the other side. "After that dinner I need the exercise." She could see the gleam of his smile

133

by the dim light from the dash; he looked still like the lad who followed her into the dark on the trail of a ghost that long ago, rainy night and she longed for his arm around her keeping her warm and safe. She was daft all right. Here she was, 25 years old, meant to wed Jimmy Regan next year, and longing for the arms of a man who surely had no use for her, who probably was laughing at her every minute for the silly fool that she was.

She pulled out into the road, the van complaining aloud at every bump, its gears grinding ominously. She had to shout to be heard. "Daddy had to pick up some extra feed and I told him I'd take it out to them -" She pointed to the back where three or four one hundred pound bags of feed bounced along with them.

"You shouldn't do it alone," he shouted. "I'm glad I saw you!"

How could they be sitting here shouting at each other about feeding the bloody horses when her heart had gone wild inside her. She'd forgotten how it had felt; she'd told herself it was a child's fancy only, and long dead. "Aye," she said, "I'm glad, too -" and she kept her eyes on the road as it unrolled before them in the jiggling light of the headlamps. In the field the horses were grazing; it was so still when they stopped that they could hear the sound of horses munching the heavy grass long before their eyes could see them there in the shadowy dark. Megan filled some empty sacks halfway up with grain and together they carried them, stumbling and laughing, to put them down in front of the nearest few horses. In the still night, then, they could hear hoofs beating on the spongy turf, as from over the field, the distant horses heard them, and came trotting up to get their share of the dinner before it was gone.

When they were finished, Megan did up the wires that served as a gate in the rough stone wall. The sky was heavy with clouds and the only light came from a cottage far down the road. The only sound was the wind in the brush and the distant cry of a night bird, calling its mate. Charley stood beside her, listening, too. She willed him to speak, but when he did, his voice beside her made her jump. "Remember," he said, "Remember the night before I went home?"

"Aye," she said. "You said you'd come back -"

"Well, I have," he said.

"I said you'd never look at me, after all the rich and beautiful girls you'd know in the States -"

"I didn't know I was coming back to you," he said. "If I'd known, I'd have come sooner." She was very close beside him and the happiness she felt was half pain, for behind it stood good, honest Jimmy, whose devotion to her was so great that it made her weak with pity for him - *pity*! Pity wasn't love and never could it be. Never mind how hard she tried to love him, it was pity that had made her say she'd marry him. Next year, only, she had said, for she thought next year would never come. Something would stop it, for how could she lie with her whole life, her heart and soul and body, and live this lie for a lifetime with a man whose love she could never return, not in the searing, rending passion that Jimmy had for her? Yet she had promised. And now that promise seemed to wither up like a cinder and blow away, clean far away in the yearning she had now for this man by her side.

Then his arms were around her and holding her so close

135

she could feel his heart beating against her. She leaned her head on his chest and felt warm tears running down her cheeks. She was home and safe here in his arms, where she had no business at all to be. She felt him lean down and kiss the top of her head. She looked up and saw the moon break through the clouds; its light was dim and cold. She saw the tears shining in his eyes and put her hand up to touch his face.

His kiss was warm on her lips, then, and their tears of joy turned into laughter that broke the still of the night like a song.

CHAPTER THIRTEEN

Sheila pushed the ragged curtain back and looked out into the pale mist that hung over the mountain. "I can't see a bloody thing," she said. "How are they finding us, then, in this fog?" It was chilly by the open window away from the fire that sputtered on the hearth and the wind blew through the mist, damp and cold as a dead hand reaching out for her. She pulled the shawl close around her shoulders.

"And won't Kevin be having a treat out in this?" She smiled, thinking how fine he thought himself in his American jeans and boots; thinking, too, how loony the rich were, to be paying good Irish pounds to spend six days flogging along on a pony, and over these dreadful mountains, when they could be home in

137

America, sitting warm and dry in their grand houses. She couldn't credit it; life was so hard here for them as couldn't help themselves, and then all them who didn't have to suffer went right out and found a way to live as miserable as the poor Connemara sheep men, fighting their way over the rocks and down the steep glens, no matter the weather. She knew how much Kevin was enjoying it, and that bird he had with him! Mother of God, what a bitch she was!

Wolfe was at the table having a pint, waiting while the potatoes boiled in a pot over the fire. She came and stood behind him and put her hands on his shoulders. He reached up and took them both in his. "Ah, luv, it's a funny world, it is," he said, as though he read her thoughts. "And only us born to put it right -" She stood, happy for the moment, there beside her man, and longed for it to be over, for Kevin to be on his way, and his bitchy girl with him, and for the whole awful week to end and she and Wolfe be back in Belfast again. She couldn't be easy in her mind about the kidnapping. Why not leave it to Sean and Ben? Happy enough they were to do it, and her and Wolfe back home, safe and free? And the baby - "Wolfe," she whispered. "I worry so, all the time - "

She sank to the floor beside him and laid her head in his lap. If only Ben hadn't started this dreadful plan; if only Wolfe hadn't agreed. He must know it was daft - what would they be doing with the Queen, hiding her away, while they thought how to make their demands? "We haven't thought enough, Wolfe; Ben doesn't know what to do once we have her." Her voice choked up at the words. "Wolfe - I hate him; don't let him have his way with you -"

"Is it my own Sheila saying to me to have a care, now? Telling me not to do what I must? Luv, you know me more than that." He held her head against him and stroked her hair. "Only I wish I'd thought of it myself, I do."

"Ben can do it, with Sean. We can go home as soon as we finish at Carna." As she spoke she knew it was no good. Wolfe held the dream too dear; useless it was to fight it.

He took her face in his two hands and turned it up to look at him. "I promise, lass, when it's over, we'll be back home, and you'll not be fearing in the night again -" He kissed her gently on the lips. "Be brave for me this one more time and I promise - sure, we'll not need to fight, never again, we won't, not after what we'll do this week, luv -" His voice was a whisper now and his breath warm on her cheek.

So sure he was; so sure of himself and so filled with his dream of freedom there wasn't a thing else in the world for him until it was done. He wouldn't be her Wolfe if he were different, nor would she love him so. She got to her feet and he held her to him, his face buried in her breast. How could she fight with this man? She knew she would go to hell and back with him, no matter the danger - no matter what.

The door to the little back room opened and Sean burst through it; sleep still clouded his face. "You'd ought to have waked me, Sis - suppose they'd got here and me asleep in there -" Now it was anger that shadowed his eyes and Wolfe got up to stand between him and Sheila.

"Leave it, Sean; he's not due another half hour yet. Have

a pint with me while we wait." Sheila bent over the bubbling pot, testing the potatoes with the bent fork she had found on the hearth. Stay out of his way when he's like this, she thought. Just keep still and out of his way. Sean sat down on the bench with Wolfe and opened the bottle.

Then she heard the footsteps on the stones outside the door, hurrying, knocking loose stones away to roll down the hill. Before the steps reached the door she started across the room. Wolfe jumped up and brushed past her. "I'll get it, luv - wait you here," he whispered.

"Kevin?" he called through the door.

"Ben. Let me in -" the voice was rough, short of breath. He'd had a time of it, climbing the mountain, he had. She wished him dead, with his filthy leering looks and she was glad his breath was short; may he have a leaky heart, as well, she thought. Wolfe eased the door open, just enough to let the man in. Uglier than she remembered, he was, and her flesh crawled when he looked at her.

"Sit down," Wolfe said. "Be quick, now. Kevin's on his way and we won't be wanting questions from him."

Ben sat by the fire and rubbed his dirty hands to warm them. He was smiling to himself, pleased, he looked, with something.

He *was* pleased. He had talked with his cousin, Annie, before daylight, in the wood behind the carriage house, and a good thing it was they'd planned it before - there was no way of getting a message in or out now *they* were there. "How can I tell you a thing, then?" she'd said. Poor Annie, not so bright she was,

140

after all.

"You'll meet me when they're asleep," he'd told her. "They've got to sleep, just like you and me, do they not?". So there she was, all fifteen stone of her, hiding in the wood, waiting for him at four o'clock this morning. "And what she told me!" he grinned. "Man, you'll not believe how easy!" He reached over and held Wolfe by the arm, excitement bringing drops of sweat out on his face, that shone in the firelight, ugly and greasy, Sheila thought. "The Duke, he's out fishing till dark. Everyone is inside drinking before dinner. Except *her*. She's out, with her two doggies, walking along the lake, out on the mole, watching for the boat to come back. *Alone*." A drop of saliva ran down his chin. Sheila looked away, fighting the gall that rose in her throat. "Understand me? She's alone. Every night she walks there-"

Sean's eyes were red and hot. He leant forward over the table. "We need a skiff, and three of us there, right?" He loved this. How swiftly evil ran through his head, she thought; how easy he is with death in his hands. But she was watching Wolfe; his plan would be the one they would follow. His mouth was a hard line and his eyes were cool, but there wasn't the hate in them that passed between Sean and Ben. Two of a kind those two were, and might the Blessed Virgin save her man when he dealt with them. Then Wolfe spoke.

"Right, you, Sean, we need a skiff." He looked to Ben. "Can you get one? Do you know the lake, the shore there by the lodge?"

While they talked, Sheila put the potatoes on the plate, with a little bacon for each man and sat with them, listening while

141

she ate. Ben could get a boat, he would bring it along the shore and stay hidden under the rocky ledge until *she* came along to the mole. There was a dense growth of rhododendron and other shrubs along the path where it came to the shore. Two men hidden there could throw a bag or a tarp over her head as she passed, overpowering her and silencing her at one blow. They could tie her up and gag her, drop her over the ledge into the skiff, jump in themselves and then let the boat glide away into the dark waters of the lake. If they missed one night, there was a whole week more to watch and wait. Wolfe nodded.

"It could work," Wolfe said. "We can do it." He rested his head in his hands for a moment, then looked up at Ben. "Where do we keep her?" he asked.

"I'll find a place, not to worry." He growled, more than spoke, his words. "My other cousin, as lives up the mountain, he's got a shepherd's hut - I know the way there. Or some say there's a cave, like, by the lake. One or the other we can take her to -"

"Who else knows?" Wolfe asked, careful.

"Only the office in Belfast. We've to let them know whenever it's done." He was still rubbing his hands together, an obscene gesture it looked to Sheila; he couldn't still be cold. "I've got a man in Clifden with the code to send -" So smug he was, she could vomit just to look at him.

When Kevin and the girl came they wanted to know who was the little man fumbling his way down the mountain road. "He was in a some kind of hurry," Bettina said. "He saw us all right

- who in hell -?" Kevin cut her off.

"Are you straight with us, Wolfe? We never heard about anyone else in it." His eyes were black in the unsteady light from the lamp on the table; though he spoke to Wolfe, his eyes were on Bettina.

She had the money, right enough; was she running the game, as well? Sheila's blood ran cold in her. What had they come to now? Ourselves alone, it always was, us against the world, sworn together with blood and tears, and now the air filled with suspicion, and that girl casting judgement on us all - Mother of God, she wished it over! A skinny bitch, she was, that girl, and looking scorn down her nose at them, at them who'd lived their lives fighting, while she knew nothing of what it was to watch while your men risked their lives and died, and you left to carry on alone.

"Ah, lad, listen now -" Wolfe's voice was quiet, but it filled the room. Outside, the wind screamed against the walls of the cottage, wrapping cold fingers of rain around it and a broken shingle whined in bitter disharmony to the song of the wind. Bettina pulled her coat closer around her; she was shaking with the damp and the cold. Kevin stood, staring, like a stubborn sheep, waiting, just, to make trouble it seemed to her. Water dripped from the peak of his cap and he brushed it from his eyes. "Listen, then," Wolfe said. "He's one of us, from here, he is, and knows the land." His look passed over Sean with a warning, and by a mercy, Sean nodded and was quiet. "Telling us, he was, things we need to know. It's us as has to get it for you, lad; all you do is give us what we need and we come back with the bloody packet for you. The less each of us knows, the better for us all -"

Sheila filled two more plates and set them on the table. "You can eat," she said, trying to ease it over. Wolfe smiled then, his blazing white smile, and he laughed.

"Come, now," he said. "It's as good as done - let's drink to it!"

He handed two more pints around, and clapped Kevin on the back. "Now there's a good lad -" he said, and only Sheila saw behind the laugh, and knew the truth of what it cost him. He was fearful of the days ahead, fearful of Kevin so close to their plan, fearful of the crime turning in on them, who once were brothers together against the world - now their eyes were shadowed with distrust and they stood apart, silent and cold.

Bettina did the talking, and Kevin sat sullen by her side. The light from the fire flickered over her cat's face as she spoke. Sean's eyes never left her and Sheila could see the knuckles of his hands white, his fists tight, resting on his thighs. His fingers worked back and forth and the sinews stood out on his wrists. Now and again, Bettina caught his look; she seemed speaking to him more than the rest of them. "Sheila's to take it alone," she said. "They don't want a whole mob around when they go." Wolfe's eyes narrowed and his hand on Sheila's arm tightened. "She's got to go with them to the boat; how else be sure the money gets there and not into Ward's pocket? Ward can get his half then and no sooner -"

"They'll not like it," Wolfe said. "The money first, they said -"

144

"They'll damn well do it, like it or not," Bettina snapped.

"Sheila'll not go alone." When Wolfe said this Bettina's head swivelled to look at him.

"Man, it's *my* money and it goes how I say it goes." The threat was under the quiet words. Sean stood up.

"We're sick of you, Wolfe Morrison!" he hissed. "Think you can run the whole bleedin' world, you do!" His fist came down on the table to shake the plates and splash beer out of the mugs. Quicker, Wolfe's hand flashed across and smashed into his face. Blood spurted from his nose and his yelp was the cry of a wounded animal. Kevin's mouth was open; soundless he watched while Sean glared back at Wolfe and Sheila pressed a rag where the blood flowed from her brother's face. She spoke to him, quiet, and he listened, the fight gone from him now.

In the end, it was agreed that Wolfe should go with Sheila to the caravan and wait on shore while she went with the tinker to the boat. He nodded his agreement without taking his eyes from Sheila's, and she knew he never meant to leave her alone with them, not ever would he leave her alone again.

Kevin was fidgeting over a cigarette that wouldn't light. He looked at his watch. "Christ, we've got to go; they'll have that girl out after us -" Bettina gave him a look of sheer disgust.

"Stop mewling, you fool," she said. "They'll damn well wait - we told them after lunch. Megan's got plenty to do just feeding them and getting them back on. I told her we'd be a while in Clifden" She got up and looked around the dusky room. "Sean," she said, "Be a love and get my backpack for me -" A thick wallet was handed over to Wolfe and he put it into a pocket inside his anorak.

The day outside looked brighter when Kevin opened the door; the fog had lifted, blown off by the winds that still whistled over the mountain. The light glistened like the mother-of-pearl inside a shell from the sea. Kevin paused by the door. He whispered something to Wolfe and Wolfe took Sheila by the hand to walk down the hill to where the Rover waited by the road.

"A right bitch, that Bettina," Kevin said, as if he would settle that slight to his manhood before anyone took notice. Sheila nodded and Wolfe smiled.

"You didn't bring us down here to tell us what we know, lad. What"s up?"

"I think someone's on to us," Kevin said. "One of the bloody Americans. He signed on when we did in Clifden-"

"Could your imagination have a hold of you, boy?"

"Damn, you," Kevin snapped. "I don't bloody like being followed around, I don't. I guess I can tell if I'm being watched, can't I? He butters up to me and Bett - spying on us, he is, sure I know it."

Sheila was looking back, waiting for Bettina to come out of the house. Through the blowing door she saw the two figures merge for a long moment in the shadows; then the smaller one pulled away and Bettina came running down the path. When she turned, she saw the look on Kevin's face. Black it was, and filled with loathing; he had seen it, too, then, poor Kevin. The brightness seemed only cold, now, and the wind cut through her like a knife.

146

CHAPTER FOURTEEN

He couldn't think for a minute where he was. Light was just beginning to seep in through the shutters and a bird made tentative sounds outside the window. Charlcy moved, gingerly, feeling the effects on his bones and muscles of spending two days in the saddle. Could 27 be the beginning of middle age? He pulled the cover over his head to cut out the light. It couldn't be time to get up.

The bird's early chirping became a raucous song now and even the pillow over his head couldn't dull the shrill, insistent sound. Where was he? Peering out of hiding he caught sight of a rough plastered wall, with shutters set into a deep window high over his head. Heavy timbers formed the rafters that slanted up to the roof tree, and bright sunlight lay in patterns on the scrubbed, pale wood of the bare floor. The Ussher? That's where they were supposed to be. Then he remembered. He had been riding along beside Megan in the late afternoon drizzle yesterday, when Jamey came trotting up beside them. "What'd you find out?" Megan asked him. "Can we stay?"

"What do you think, girl? Think I couldn't get old Marianne to find us a place?" His face wrinkled with laughter. "Sure, you think I've lost me fatal charm, then?" He turned to Charley. "She thinks her Dad has got so old he can't have his way with a good French girl like Marianne, now -"

"Oh, Daddy," Megan said. "You know I never doubted once you'd do it-" She put her hand on Charley's thigh. "That's my Dad for you," she laughed. "Sure it worries me, the poor opinion he has of himself -"

So the van had dumped the five of them out in the yard of the carriage house and Jamey explained the high honor of staying there; it was far older than the lodge, historic-like, he said. Just anyone might stay at the lodge, but only very special guests could lay their heads to rest here, free from the ghost of Lady Dudley, to be sure, but doubtless inhabited by far older and more satisfying shades. Charley threw a look at Megan; her eyes caught it and returned the answer - they should indeed try a bit of ghost-hunting tonight. "For old time's sake," she whispered.

A girl showed them to the rooms in the loft. He noticed Kevin hanging back to see where the boy took Bettina's bags. "Bring mine down here," he said, and stalked along to the far end of the hall.

"True love," Charley said to Megan, and she laughed.

"I told you she's a right bitch," Megan said. "Will you dare have the room next to me, lad?"

The rooms were tiny, whitewashed plaster and snowy white linens, as bare as a monk's cell. They had dinner downstairs in a long room like a refectory, off the kitchen. "Business must be good," Charley remarked. "The whole lodge full?" Jamey heard him from across the table.

"Aye, they've a big party from London, she says -" He swallowed a spoonful of steaming boulliabaise; pausing, he looked around the room. "You three signed on late, so what was I to do with you, then, and the others all around in bed and breakfasts wherever I could? You'll sleep like the dead here, you will -"

No ghost had come, though they sat long around the dying fire, long after everyone else was asleep. Not unless you counted the ghosts of the two children who had run through the dark and the rain and the cold on that haunted night, with fear behind them and terror cold in their hearts, and had sat, next day, beneath the dripping trees and wept to part forever.

His breeches lay folded on the chair and his boots on the floor beside them. He'd hung his sweater and shirt and raincoat all on the one hook high up the white wall. When he moved his arm he felt the tug of the strap fastened to the backpack under his bed. He pulled it out and checked its contents. Everything in place, just as it should be. Oh, God, it was time to get up, to come out from under the warm downy cover, to shiver in the wretched

149

damp and cold, and try to warm himself in the clammy garments left out from yesterday. The sun was actually coming up; it might be a fair day. The thought of the day made him think of Megan, and he was humming a small happy tune to himself, trotting down the hall to the primitive chamber where it was possible, he hoped, to shave with warm water, and luxury of luxuries, to shower as well. He ran right into Megan, wrapped in what had to be her father's robe, engulfed in it, she was, and laughing at him.

"A treat to see, you are," she said. "Running people down on your way to the loo, now, is it?"

She was soft in his arms and he found it possible to laugh and kiss at the same time and the day was bright and the world was good. He wanted to run into his room, grab the backpack full of toys and dump it in the deepest part of the black waters behind the lodge. He wanted to hold her forever in this sunny hallway, while the bird sang outside the window and lovely Megan -

"Are ye standing there all day, then, lass?" It was Jamey, towel around his waist, emerging dripping from the shower, ducking into his room, where his laugh echoed against the thick walls like, Megan said, "a great jackass braying there."

Then there was the struggle to get everyone's bags loaded in the van, everyone fed on Marianne's wonderful omelet and kippers and then the bouncing ride to the field where the horses grazed, rested and content. The sun shone with amazing consistency, for hours at a time that morning, and they climbed the mountain over trackless outcroppings of rock and past awesome

fields of cut peat, where water gleamed, dark and still, in the deep
channels left by the turf-cutters. He rode at the back with Megan,
to help her goad the stragglers on. Mississippi suffered
constantly. He claimed to be raw and bleeding in unmentionable
sites on his person. It was all he could do to keep up. Megan
chivvied him on from time to time; his patient beast went forward
bravely.

They were near the top and the trail was getting hard to
follow. In places they went along rocky ledges or walked
carefully over smooth outcroppings of rock. Looking ahead,
Charley could see the long line of riders going single file behind
Jamey. Now and again, the wind brought the sound of Jamey's
voice to them, chatting up a tired rider or pointing out some
natural wonder to those nearest him. The line snaked upwards,
the last ones almost meeting the head of the line sometimes where
the trail took a sudden switchback to scale a particularly steep
face of the mountain. "What's that idiot trying for?" Megan
pointed to where Kevin had turned his horse back and was starting
down towards them. "There's no room to pass," she shouted. But
he continued down, inching past other riders, sometimes perilously
close to the edge. Bettina had stopped, too, but stood where she
was, holding up those behind her. Jamey, never looking back -
why should he? Megan was to bring up the rear - had almost
reached the top.

"Stop there," Megan yelled to Kevin. "What is it you
want?"

He kept right on until their horses met on the narrow
ledge. "Bettina's in trouble," he said. Urgency roughened his

151

voice. "Something broke on her bridle and she can't go on. You'll have to go up and help her."

It sounded too much like a command and Megan didn't like it. Charley could see her back stiffen and her mouth made a little straight line in her face. The pale eyes were cool and clear as spring water. "Of course, I'll go. You needn't order me about." She looked at Charley. "Can you watch the back, then, while I go? Daddy'll want someone to -"

Slowly, carefully she rode her pony up past the line of horses. Charley waited for Kevin to turn around and start to follow. "Can you make it?" he asked. "It's not a lot of room -"

The rest of the ride was almost over the crest now, out of sight. Kevin didn't answer. He didn't try to turn around. He drove his spurs into the horse's sides and as the startled animal charged forward he brought his whip up and slashed it across the face of Charley's horse. "What the hell-?" Charley yelled as the horse stumbled back. The man was bonkers. The drop from the ledge where they stood must be over a hundred feet. Straight down.

Kevin's horse charged forward again, forcing his way between Charley and the side of the hill. Charley heard, more than felt, the solid crash as the animal's shoulder rammed his horse. He heard the scrape and clatter of loose rocks as the horse lost its footing. For a moment they hung at the edge. Then he saw the sky above him and felt the rush of air as, together, he and the horse plunged over the cliff.

Megan looked back and saw Kevin galloping along the ridge, catching up. His voice blew across the mountain-top.

"Stop!" he was yelling. "Accident! Help!" Some of the last riders were looking back over the ridge they had just climbed.

"My God!" someone yelled. "He fell -"

She didn't know how she got there. Her hands were bleeding from the rocks where she fell, scrambling down the side of the cliff. Her jeans were torn and her knee didn't feel right. She couldn't stop running; she had to get to him, to where he lay face down in the bog, and the horse thrashing about on its back, half on top of him. She couldn't get across the struggling animal to reach Charley. Then Jamey was beside her.

"Get his head, lass," he said. "We'll get him right out - " She saw the horse's white eyes, rolling in terror; blood ran from its mouth and its breathing was shallow and bubbling. Poor creature, it was dying and in fear. She got the reins in her hands somehow, and prayed it would live till they could get it up, let them get to Charley - Mother of God, how could he breathe, his face in the muck like it was? She pulled with all her strength while Jamey got ropes on the horse's legs and together they rolled it over. She had a picture for a moment of a dozen faces, far above them, white, staring, while she and Jamey fought to keep the dying horse from rolling over to crush the man who lay half sunk there in the mud. They were in the bog half to their waists as they worked; each step they took was a battle in itself. They worked their way through the muck until Jamey could get his arms under Charley's shoulders.

"Hisht, lass, we'll have him now - don't cry, luv." Jamey's voice was soft; she felt a little girl again to hear him. She was crying, the salt of tears was in her mouth. Slowly they pulled the still figure from the bog and onto the quaking turf. Jamey turned him over and Megan cleaned the mud from his face.

"He's dead, isn't he?" she whispered, low, so only she could hear. If no one heard, then it wasn't true, was it? His eyes didn't open and she spoke his name; still he didn't move. Frozen, she seemed, too, where she knelt by his side. Her eyes moved to look at his chest, to watch for the rise and fall of his breathing. Nothing. Nothing at all.

"Daddy?" she said.

Jamey knelt beside her. He leant his face close over Charley's. Then he looked up, and a smile broke across his face. "He's breathing; I felt it against my face," he said. Her hand moved in the sign of the cross and she laid her head on Charley's muddy chest.

"I can feel it, Da," she whispered. "And hear his heart -"

"I'll have to get lads with a stretcher and block and tackle to get him up from here," he said. "We're no doctor to know what to do. Best you stay with him, lass." He put an arm around her shaking shoulders. "You'll be all right, will you, now?" He knew, didn't he, he knew all about her, nothing you could hide from Jamey Leary, then could you? How she loved him now, this flamboyant, loud, outrageous man, her quiet, tender father. He kissed her and she nodded her head against his grimy shoulder.

"Sure, and why wouldn't Jamey Leary's daughter be all right?" Her voice was steady and her eyes were dry now. "Hurry, only -" she paused. "I love him, Daddy -"

"Lass, I know that," he smiled and was gone, climbing, scrambling, running up the cliffy hillside.

She sat on the wet ground, holding his head in her lap. The shallow breathing made no sound; she could hear her own heart beating. Under the mud his face was white as chalk, vulnerable it looked, and so at peace. Her tears dropped on his cheek; pale lines ran through the dirt. She could see Jamey, far down the hill, pushing his pony dangerously fast over the rough ground. The rest of the ride straggled behind him and he paid them no mind. How long till he could get back? How many hours to get Charley safe to hospital where they could know -?

Then he began to tremble, long shudders going through his body. Holy God, don't let him go into shock! She pulled off her sweater and tried to wrap it around him. The pack on his back was in the way; he'd been lying on it, heavy thing that it was. Hurting him, it must have been and she so dull not to get it off. He was a dead weight and she had hard work to get the straps undone and pull the pack from under him. Still he didn't move, just the cold tremors shaking him; wet and cold he was, and helpless lying there in the muck.

Finally the back pack was from under him and he lay stretched flat on the turf. Mother of God, she was tired! She lay beside him, rubbing his hands for warmth. She was afraid to move him; she should lower his head and get some blood to that pale, white face - what did they tell you in Girl Guides? Face pale, raise the tail? It didn't sound a bit funny now, looking at the still, chalky features lying there calm as death and as cold, indeed, as the grave. She rested her head on the backpack. She wouldn't rest on his shoulder, for all she longed to feel him close, lest she hurt him more.

Bloody uncomfortable it was! Was it rocks he carried there, or bricks? She undid the buckles and dumped it on the ground. A long, black box with a dial and buttons and a coiled antenna, a sleek black notebook, zippered shut - what did the lad want with stuff like that, here on the high mountain? She laid them carefully on a dry, flat rock and closed the case. For long she sat on it, imagining Jamey firing up the Rover, racing to Ussher, calling the ambulance - how many minutes? How long she sat there she had no idea. A lifetime, it seemed, and still he lay there, no more, no less alive. Cruel, it was, to have found him again, only to lose him like this.

She jumped at the noise. It was a choking sort of sound in the middle of the quiet breathing. Another cough and the breathing became a rasping, gasping struggle. Still the white face without expression. She ripped his anorak open and his shirt. Then her hand felt the hard leather strap going under his arm. The gun lay there, dark and menacing, close to his body. Charley carrying a gun? Here? His breath was quieter again, the choking left off; except for the stone-white of his skin he might have been asleep, only.

She laid the nasty thing out beside the radio (?) and the notebook, trying to put together in her mind what she was looking at. She picked up the zippered notebook; her fingers held the tab of the zipper for a moment. Holy Mother, forgive me for a snoop and a cheat, she murmured, and opened the book. Pages covered with close-written words, lists of names there were, and numbers she didn't understand. What jumped from the pages and stopped her reading further were the words, "Central Intelligence

Agency" at the heading of a letter. No business she had, looking at people's private papers, or their private guns, for that matter.

Slowly she closed the book, put it and the radio and the gun back into the pack; if they were not meant for her to see, surely much less they were for others. Her mind flew to the night at the Hare. "Who's the new man signed on?" he'd asked her. "I thought we were the last?" What was it to bloody Kevin? The wind blew cold again; through the clear blue of the open sky it penetrated to the marrow of her bones and it seemed to cut through her like a knife in her heart. Far off the scream of a siren broke the stillness. "Charley, luv," she whispered. "Don't leave me now -"

There wasn't anything but a grey fog, everywhere, and he couldn't breath in it. It was cold, and a brightness shone through the fog. His chest hurt and the effort of breathing was too much for him. Just as well give it up; it was too hard. But if he gave it up, Megan would die, because only he could save her. He saw her, far above him, and he saw a blazing ball in the sky coming after her. It was so bright he couldn't look at it and she didn't even see it. "Don't leave me now -" she begged and he reached out for her. The bright light was screeching now, it hurt his ears.

He couldn't see anything but the light, though he realized now that his eyes were closed. If only he could open them - but it was too hard. "I love you so -" she said, and he opened his eyes. The sun made a halo around her head and she was leaning over him and her bright tears fell on his face like a blessing.

157

CHAPTER FIFTEEN

They didn't need the ambulance after all. The medics checked him out, put ice on the ugly bruise by the side of his head and congratulated him on having the luck of the Irish. "Just a bit of the wind knocked out, and the brains addled for a moment is all," the chief medic said. "Take it easy a while and you're right as rain, then."

Charley didn't share the man's optimism about his condition, but one look at Megan's radiant smile gave him at least a reason to hope. Perhaps his head would quit roaring by tonight - good God, he had to contact Jordan before dinner. His hand went automatically to reach for his backpack. Was it all right? Where in hell was it?

"I've got it, Charley," Megan said. "Lying on it in the muck you were when we got you out -"

He took it from her, winced as he hunched his arms through the straps. God, he hurt! Adjusting the shoulder straps, his hand touched where the gun should be and found only the empty holster. Megan was watching him, her eyes growing large as they followed the movement of his hand feeling one more time for the hard steel that wasn't there where it belonged. "I took it off you," she whispered. "It's in your pack." Her eyes met his, unblinking. "I know, Charley; I saw --"

"You f---ing incompetent!" Bettina hissed. "Can't kill a man dropping him over a hundred foot cliff!"

"You can hardly blame me he landed in a bog -" She was hell to fight with, Bettina was. Hadn't he risked his ass going back down there and hadn't he actually forced the man over the side. He never believed he could have done it; now the little bitch was laughing at him, ridiculing him, and him barely escaped with his own life!

"In any event, we'll not be needing you again. You're leaving the ride tomorrow. I've told Jamey you've got a bad case of dysentery -"

"You lying little cunt! I'm taking the packet; you know that -" His voice betrayed his fear, and his hatred for himself rose with the decibels in his voice. They were walking before dinner along by the lake where the wood was deep and they were unseen from the lodge. The clear skies of the day had vanished under scudding clouds and a white mist floated in layers over the water.

"Oh, shut up!" she said, her voice quiet and low, disdaining him, speaking as she would to a dog or a child. "If you were a real man it would be different -" His head was filled with a shrill whining noise and a red light glowed all around him. Did she think he hadn't seen her and Sean the minute his back was turned there at the cottage? Did she think he would stand her scorn when she was nothing but a whore? Her voice was far away when she spoke again. "Sean will give it to ME tomorrow; he'll be at the lunch stop -" she said. The red around her head filled his vision -

"WHORE!" he screamed. "Filthy whore!"

Her eyes showed white in the burning red; she was afraid. Her mouth opened wide, but no sound came out. His hands were too strong, closed around her throat. He forced her down onto the wet stones; his hands moved of themselves, pounding her head against the rock. His own body felt light as air and the desire in him was a throbbing heat, at once an anguish and a joy so intense he wanted it never to end. One more time he smashed the lolling head into the stones and he heard the sound of it shattering like clay; then he felt release and a warm wetness against his belly, and he held her to him, sobbing, his tears mingling with the blood that matted her hair.

Filthy Sean could keep his filthy prick to himself, now, and serve him right, it would. Bitch! he sobbed, you f---ing bitch! and he lay on top of her until his sobbing ceased. It was dark and, through the trees, lights winked from the windows of the lodge. It took a long time to scrape out a shallow grave, and he covered it over with leaves and sticks. They'd be days away before anyone would find it. Crossing the darkened courtyard he could see them all at dinner in the great room of the carriage house. He went in the narrow back door and up the stairs to the loft. He hadn't thought blood would be so hard to clean up; he was at least fifteen minutes getting presentable.

"Sorry I'm late," he said, entering the room, casual, not to attract notice. They were at the second course already. "I've had a hell of a row with Bettina - she said she'd not stay another day. We were arguing in the road and she just left, got a lift with a guy in a lorry and left." He shrugged and smiled a helpless smile, as to say "Women! Who can understand them? least of all me." He pulled out one of the two vacant chairs and sat down. God he was hungry!

Charley lay awake in bed thinking. The only reason for Kevin's attack could be that he was the runner, and that he knew, or suspected, what Charley was there for. Charley had accepted the apologies and feigned belief in Kevin's whiny excuse. "I simply couldn't control the bloody horse," he had said, "Jolly good you're all right." If he let Kevin think he believed him now, he'd have him running on a long tether, leading to the point of transfer. There was some advantage in knowing, now, who Kevin was, but not much comfort in Kevin fearing that he had blown his hand and his cover. He wondered how soon he would try again.

"He meant to kill you," Megan had said. "Turn him in to the constabulary-"

"I can't, Megan," he whispered. "It's not what you think." Then he had told her, and she listened with eyes wide, like a child, while he explained. "I've got to follow him until we find what he's up to. It's no good my getting rid of him now."

"But he'll try again -" she said. "Even more. Now he's done it, he knows you know. He gave himself right away doing it -" She smiled, almost, then. "And bloody fool he is, he couldn't even do it right," she said, and the smile faded from her face.

He hadn't bothered to undress; if he heard Kevin go out there'd be no time to fumble around for his clothes in the dark. He felt sorry for Bill Jordan, sitting in the car, hidden from the road, waiting to hear. He'd made contact before dinner, thankful that the radio had survived the crash as well as he had. Maybe better; it didn't ache in every bone.

"I've heard from Harry," Jordan had said. "They've spotted the freighter. It altered course at 3:30, veering towards our coast. Better get your beauty sleep early. Our friend may be on the road to Carna sometime before morning -"

"I hear you," Charley said, "Loud and clear." He paused. "Guess what happened to me today - our man tried to get me." He told Jordan, briefly, about his slide down the mountain. It didn't seem necessary to mention how pleasant it had been to return from the dead in the arms of the girl he intended to marry; it was hardly part of the drill.

Jordan was properly sympathetic, also briefly. "I'll have

wheels for you," he said, and explained the hidden entrance a quarter of a mile from the lodge where he could wait in his aging BMW in case Charley needed a ride to the coast.

Now he looked at his watch. It was almost two and no sound from Kevin. He couldn't have got down the creaking stairs without Charley hearing him. A pin dropping could have been heard, so still it was in the lodge. The possibility of another contact entered his mind; Kevin might well sleep soundly here all night while the stuff was being picked up along the coast to be passed on to him somewhere tomorrow. At last he thought he'd better chance going with Jordan and watch along the shore. Hang Kevin; it was just possible he was missing something waiting here.

The stairs DID creak, and the door as well. No lights showed in the courtyard and he kept to the shadow along the wall as he made his way out to the road. The air was still; for once the wind wasn't stirring the trees and even the night birds were asleep. The ragged clouds raced across the sky, driven by a silent wind far above the sleeping earth, sometimes covering the moon, sometimes letting its eerie light scurry over the silent land below. He moved soundlessly, careful of the loose stones in the roadway, until he was well away from the buildings. Trees leaned over the road on his left, and an impenetrable hedge closed off the moon's unsteady light from the other side. He walked close to the hedge and as fast as he could without running.

Then he heard, felt more than heard, running footsteps behind him. He plastered himself against the hedge, pressing his back into its stiff branches. Clouds covered the moon and the night was black. The steps were very close, just around the turn.

His hand went to the holster under his arm. Then he saw the small, pale figure outlined against the blackness, illuminated by the light of the moon that showed itself briefly among the racing clouds.

"Megan," he whispered. "I'm here -"

She stopped and ran to him. "Charley, I know -" her breath came in quick little gasps. She must have run all the way. "I'm coming with you."

"You can't," he whispered. "You've got to go back -"

"I'll not be in the way," she said. The face he looked down into was a little girl's face, eyes big with excitement, lower lip caught under her teeth, begging to go with him on a grown-up treat.

"You don't now what it is," he said. "I can't take you."

"Charley, you TOLD me what it is; and I read your papers, too." Her eyes held his for a moment; then she looked down. "I know I shouldn't have - but when I found that thing on you, that gun, you know, sure I couldn't help myself till I found out why, could I?"

"Then you must know why I can't take you." She was very close to him there in the shadows; he could smell the fresh scent of her hair. He leaned down; very gently he kissed her lips. "Go back now, love, please go back-"

"You can't find your way here alone," she said. "I know the land - I'll not have you getting lost in the night. Nor getting shoved over any more cliffs." Her mouth was set, very firm she looked. He loved her too much and there was no way he could help himself. Afterwards he would tell her -

"Besides," she said, "I can't. The door locked after me - you don't want a great row getting me in do you?"

Jordan would be waiting in the car, wondering. She shouldn't go back alone; Kevin was there. "I'm meeting someone," he said, "In a car down the road. If you come with me you must stay in the car, no matter what. If anything goes wrong, you must bring the car back yourself. It belongs to my friend -" Safe enough, he thought; safe as he could make it under the circumstances. Fine circumstances! When Mossiter found out he hadn't even been able to keep his identity covered he could be in very deep shit. Yet some irresponsible part of his being, deep inside, was filled with an unaccountably smug sense of happiness, of the rightness of being together in whatever the night would bring them.

Jordan might not like it, but there they were and not much he could do about it. "Keep close to me," he whispered. "It's just down the road."

"Where are we to go?" she asked.

"Towards the coast," he said. "We're looking for someone there -"

"Can you tell me who?"

"No. No, I really can't," he said.

"I thought not." She sighed.

The car was hidden well off the road. Jordan was a little touchy. "She knows the area," Charley told him; he tried to sound as though it was all a super plan he'd thought of long ago, making use of the locals when appropriate is what they called it. "She's been doing this trek with her father since she was, what? five years old, Megan?"

She nodded. "Just about," she said.

Jordan pulled the car out onto the road. "Not a lot of traffic this time of night," he said.   "Just get me close to the shore by Carna," Charley said. "Scuttle the car there and we'll have a look."

"Charley," Megan whispered. "Not it's any of my business what you two are up to, but if it's what I think it is and I was you, I'd look where the tinkers have their camp along by the channel -"

"Tinkers?" Jordan said. "What -"

"Sure they camp there half the time, down by Carna - people come and go from them in the night. Mrs. Loughran sees them from her B and B down there. Doesn't sleep well, she told my Dad, and lots of times in the night she sees a car go by without lights and it stops close by the caravans -"

"Luv," Sheila whispered, "Wake up. We've got to go -" She was sitting on the side of the cot where Wolfe lay asleep, his long frame cramped on the narrow straw pallet, his lovely dark hair mussed like a little boy's and his face as innocent in sleep as a child's. It was midnight; they had an hour's walk to the shore, to where the tinker, Ward, waited in the channel and another hour on the sea to meet the Libyan where she lay off the coast in deep water. That made it two o'clock to start back, before the change of tide, Ward had said, or the devil's own time bucking it they'd have, when it started rushing out to sea again.

"You needn't come," she whispered. "They want me to go

167

alone; suppose there's trouble when they see you with me?"

He was awake and sitting up before she finished speaking. "You know I'll not let you," he said. He held her to him; his arms were hard around her and she could feel his breath on her cheek. "They know I'll go to the caravan; there'll be no trouble there, I promise."

"I don't mind, Wolfe," she said. "I'll go alone with them; it's Ben I fear, only-"

"You'll need fear no one," Wolfe said, "Not while I live, you won't -"

Not while I live, he'd said, not WHILE I LIVE. The words were cold in her heart and rang inside her head and she wanted to scream; she bit her tongue and felt the blood hot in her mouth and her face wet with tears while the words rang back and forth in the night air like the clanging of an anvil. Not while I live - while I live - while I live -

CHAPTER SIXTEEN

The BMW suffered audibly over the disastrous condition of the road. Bill Jordan winced at each shock and slewed from side to side not to hit the worst holes. "It's been through a lot with me," he said. "I hate to treat it like this." Charley nodded, unseen in the dark. Just making a conversation to keep our minds occupied, he thought. A thoroughly nice guy, Jordan was, and with this thankless job - ferrying nervous young agents, agents who had blown their identity, ferrying them around in the dark and living in this wild, far place, for what months on end he could only imagine. He felt a warmth of affection for the man.

"God, I'm glad you're here," he said. "Out in left field

without a glove, is what I thought when Gene turned me loose -"
He hadn't even properly seen Jordan until now; he'd just been a
voice in a little black box before tonight. He still couldn't see too
much of him, bouncing along in the dark, but the voice, released
from its box, was very reassuring. "How long have you been
here?"

"Six months," he said. "It only seems like ten years -"
There was a sound that might have been a laugh, or a sigh.
"Spend six months in B and B's out here and you know why the
pubs are full at two in the afternoon."

"Right, you," Megan said. "Unless it's sheep or ponies a
man could feel himself right out of it in Connemara. Or drink,"
she added.

"You could build walls," Charley said.

"Thanks." Jordan grinned and swerved to escape an
unusually large pot-hole; Megan and Charley slid laughing across
the (fine old leather) seat as the car lurched almost into the ditch.

"Are we nearly there?" Megan sounded hopeful. "Sure,
I'd be happy to walk -"

"No insults from the passengers, please," Jordan laughed.
"We're about there; my home sweet home away from home, Mrs.
Kennedy's finest hostelry -" He turned to Charley. "Actually,
you've got about a quarter mile from here to the caravans, and
good cover from the hedge most of the way."

They left the BMW behind the house. Mrs. K. had
apparently turned in for the night. No bit of light showed from her
cottage. The moon was high overhead and when the clouds blew
off it cast an eerie, cold light on the silent countryside. The walls

lay like exposed ribs across the land; old walls they were here, some of them tumbled down and trampled over by generations of wandering sheep. Mrs. Kennedy's small house was surrounded by a rather more cared for version of the local wall, quite high enough to hide a person who wished not to be seen from the road. The fitful light of the moon seemed to race across the land, rippling over the walls and spilling in and out of the tiny fields.

"Is this the only road?" Charley asked. They were standing in the small garden, behind the wall. He strained his eyes to make out the road in the velvet dark. "I mean, if anyone comes, he has got to come the way we did?" he asked Jordan, but before he could answer, Megan spoke.

"Aye, if he came from the west" she said. "It follows the channel to the sea, where we leave the horses tomorrow night, just. It turns there and goes east along the coast. You can go up to the forest there, or all the way to Galway -"

"It's the only way," Jordan said. "Not exactly a network of super-highways out here. That's why it was so easy to catch them when that was the route-"

"But didn't you find how they got it in?"

"Never. It was Gene and Harry down near Galway that got them. They suspected the freighter, but since traffic along the road has dried up, this is the first time we've looked at this end." A match flared in Jordan's hand and he lit a cigarette. "Actually, we'd been pulled off it till that chick from Boston surfaced. The Brits were handling it for a while by themselves."

The light from his match shone in the sleeping countryside and briefly illuminated Jordan's face. He was younger than

Charley had thought; crew-cut hair and the face of a varsity quarterback, except for the expression. He had the eyes of a man who had seen more of life than most of us, Charley thought, the kind of a man it was good to have with you playing the sort of game they were playing tonight.

The damp air penetrated Charley's coat and the thick fisherman's sweater he wore underneath it. The air was, for once, still, but the light from the moon seemed to spread a silvery coldness on all it touched. When it disappeared behind the scudding clouds the air was warmer, friendly, it felt to him, then. Megan stood beside him, her face glowing white in the cold light; against the pale skin her blue eyes were dark, and her hair blacker than velvet, hanging loose on her shoulders. *She* wasn't cold, and only wearing a sweater against the night air.

He looked at his watch. "Twelve forty five," he said. "Let's go."

Through a gap in the garden wall Jordan and Megan followed him. It was one of the goddamn rock piles they called pastures here and he hadn't gone ten feet before his foot slithered off a rock and landed him on his knees in the muck. With some loss of dignity, he scrambled to his feet. "Let me go first," Megan whispered. "Do I not know these fields like my own face in the glass?" She took Charley's hand in hers. "Careful, lad," she said, "You'll be no treat with a twisted ankle to hobble along on now -"

They picked their way over the rough ground in silence. It was very dark behind the hedge; even the intermittent light of the moon didn't reach into the shadows there. At last they came into the clear and his eyes adjusted to the dark. He could see the lights of the caravan now (they never sleep, she'd told him that night) and the craggy top of the stone wall picked up enough light from the sky that he could at least see where he was going.

"Get down!" Jordan's whisper was a rasp, cutting the air.

They crouched behind the wall; the sound of their breathing seemed to echo across the silent spaces. And in the quiet air of night he heard the clatter of a stone, rolling down the hill across the road. It was a small, dry sound, an ordinary sound, but the hair rose on his neck. Then another, scraping little sound, and another. Across the road someone was coming down the mountain.

"Stay behind the wall," Wolfe whispered. "We'll not need to be in the open till we get there -"

Sheila stopped, kneeling by the wall, looking over it into the road. The shadow of a cloud covered the ground and for a moment all she could see were the pin-pricks of light that showed them where the caravans lay by the roadside. Pray it stays dark, she thought, let it hide us from the world for it's a dark and dirty job we do tonight. Mother of God, she was going sappy! Times back she'd have loved the danger and laughed at the fear; now she feared for herself - no, not herself, after all, but the child she carried, the son she would give to Wolfe when it was over at last. Carefully they moved along, hiding behind the wall, bent almost double. Her back ached and her knees hurt where she had fallen on a boulder and she wished to God for the night to end, and them back in the hut on the mountain and her safe in his arms. If this night is ever done, she told herself, if ever we see the morning break, then I'll get a hold of myself, and I can talk to Wolfe and make him see the madness of going on, of believing Ben that it could be done. Tomorrow he'd listen to her; in her arms and warm with their love, then he'd listen -

The still of the night was rent by the dreadful baying of the lurcher, the heart-stopping, thundering sound of the animal's terrible anger as he strained at the rope that held him tied to the wheel of the caravan. "Sure, they've got the welcome mat out for us, luv," Wolfe said, and in the dark she could feel the warmth of his smile. How she loved him, then, in that moment - laughing in the face of danger, banishing fear with a smile; she leant against him, stopping by the wall to watch across the road.

The man, Ward, opened the door and light spilled out into the yard. It seemed they were on a stage, crossing that light, on a stage for all to see. She ran close beside Wolfe; the man stood back and held the door for them. He closed it quickly behind him. The dog's dreadful howling ceased. Sheila stood, blinking in the light, looking around the tiny room, hoping not to find Maudie's baleful stare upon her. Her hand, in the pocket of her jeans, wrapped itself around the beads - Holy Mary, Mother of God, pray for us sinners now and in ---

Maudie wasn't there. Five men stood around the room; the glare from the single lantern etched sharp lines on their faces and reflected pinpoints of light from their dark eyes. An empty bottle lay on the table. The quiet in the room was like a presence of its own, heavy it was, and pressing on her chest until she could feel her heart beating, the pulses in her temples pounding as though her head would burst.

Wolfe spoke first. "Let's get on with it," he said. "We've not the time to spare -"

One of the men spoke from the shadows. "She was to be alone," he said. His voice was high pitched, complaining.

"You bloody were told," Wolfe snapped, "She'd not come here without me." He glanced at Ward. "It was your word," he said.

Ward leant towards the man and whispered something. His eyes never left Wolfe's face as he spoke. The man grunted. "As far as the dock, then, is all - only her to the ship or they'll blow us off." He looked back to Ward. "I told them only the woman -"

Ward's ruined face came close to Sheila. "You'll do what we damn well tell you and you'll come back safe, ye hear me?" He turned to Wolfe. "You want your woman back? Then don't trouble us -" The hoarse whisper ran through Sheila like ice water in her veins.

"Leave it, luv," she whispered. "It's right enough -"

Ward banged his mug down on the table. The sound was like a shot in the stillness of the night; his voice held danger when he spoke. "Are we bloody staying here the night? Miss the tide, you'll not get your f---ing bomb, now, will you?" His eyes were on Wolfe's face. "But we'll have your woman and your bloody pounds. Ye hear me?"

"I said, let's get on with it," Wolfe said, his voice quiet; he wasn't afraid, then. He looked into her eyes and she knew. He'd a plan, he had, a way to keep her safe. She'd never fear to go, now. His hand was on her arm and the strength of it hurt, so hard he held her.

Ward turned the lantern down and snuffed out the light. The blackness was like a solid thing around them; when he opened the door, the fitful light of the moon looked bright as day to them. He pushed them out ahead of him into the night. The air was clear and the wind rising from the sea. In the channel she could hear the rush of the water as the tide rose to cover the muddy flat that lay there. There was no need for words, now. In single file they followed Ward and his men across the field to the scrubby grove where she knew the boat lay.

Hidden, now, by the trees, Ward struck a match. "Let's see it, then," he said. "We never leave here till we see you've got it."

Sheila turned from them and reached under her sweater. She pulled the thick wad of bills out and gave it to Wolfe. "Count it," Ward growled, "Where I can see -" Hundreds of pounds, it was, more than she'd ever seen in her life. All the times they'd brought things in before, it was never this much. Sure, the bloody Americans could afford it, living there across the sea, with all their money and their - their freedom! Here we fight so hard, have fought our lives and our father's lives, for a bit of our own freedom, and they just *have* it, have it, they bloody have it, without a fight, without the dying and the tears, only for being born there they are bloody born free!

Wolfe stood on the bank, then, watching as two of the men fiddled with the engine. The skiff was big, a whaling boat, it looked, with an inboard motor set amidships. Sheila sat alone on the seat directly in front of the oil-smelling engine; two men were hunched together in the stern while Ward was in the bow casting off. The channel was wide here, he could see where it stretched for hundreds of yards of mud flats when the tide was out. Now it was almost filled to the rocky bank where he stood. It was quiet here, not like the terrifying torrent that poured and tumbled through the narrows a hundred yards away, yet its murky surface rose with astonishing speed, covering the mud and rocks beneath where he stood. The moon was almost directly overhead; high tide was less than an hour away.

This was Wolfe's second visit to the hidden docking place. In the afternoon he'd come, working his way across the fields, hidden by stone walls from the caravan. He'd waited, scarcely breathing, in the thicket not ten yards from where Ward and his men were readying the boat, bringing petrol, checking the spark and straightening the lines. It lay in the mud, then, for at low tide only a few flat pools remained of the sea water that had flooded it six hours before; they glinted in the sun, reflecting the sky like mirrors. He lay there, hidden, till their voices died away along the road. When he heard nothing more, nothing but the cries of seagulls circling above the channel, he pushed his way through the bushes and went along to the dock. A white gull swooped low over his head and dived after a poor wee herring left aground by the tide. Aloft, it was attacked by a larger gull who snatched the fish from its beak and flew off, screaming its triumph in the wind. Wolfe smiled at it and waved. No better the bird's life than theirs in Belfast, he thought. Try and hold to what you have; time and again you lose it, no matter you've fought and bled and died for it.

Then he saw what he was looking for. The other boat lay in the mud, tied under the pilings of the dock. A wee skiff it was, but oars lay in the locks; sturdy oars they were, oars that could face the open sea, could carry him out to the ship tonight, unseen, unheard. His hand went to his side, where the heavy steel piece lay, ready if he should need it.

Now, he touched it again, feeling it as his hand would once have touched the beads; a prayer was on his lips. He'd need to be quick, to get through the narrows and out to sea before the sound of the whaler was lost to him in the crash and roar of the waves. A thick cloud covered the moon and threw the earth into darkness; it was hours until day would break. The dark was a blanket, or a shroud.

The current was nothing here, and he rowed easily against it. Then he heard the thundering water crashing through the narrows. The channel turned to the west, towards the sea, and for the length of some three hundred yards, steep rocky banks confined the rushing waters of the incoming tide, turning them to a boiling white cauldron. He could hear, now, the motor of the whaler struggling, coughing and starting again, driving the big skiff through. His own tiny boat began to bucket about; he had reached the mouth of the narrows where millions of gallons of water released themselves into the wide mud flats.

Wolfe knew the water, and boats. As a lad he'd lived by the sea near Belfast. Two summers he'd worked as a fisherman, taking up the nets, working till his back ached and his hands were raw, bleeding, sometimes, from the oars. He knew the tides, too, the strength of them; he'd have a job getting through this night.

The throb of the engine was still in his ears and it seemed a talisman to him; Sheila was safe so long as he could hear its steady drone. The sound of it held him somehow close to her, and she was safe.

He must be more than half-way through now. His arms were burning, the muscles screaming against the strain of pulling the oars, forcing the boat against the current. He daren't rest for even a moment; the frantic motion of the water would engulf the wee boat. It wasn't his life he thought of then, but hers, alone out there, hostage to the cause she loved, and the pain in his shoulders became nothing, only the need to hear the sound of the motor, whining above the crashing waves, a tenuous thread holding her to him through the weary night.

There was water in the boat now; it sloshed over his feet. Waves broke over the bow and it was like riding a wild horse when the current twisted and pitched the tiny boat about like a matchbox. He couldn't stop to bail; an oar almost slipped through his hand and pulled out of the lock when he was thrown against the rocky wall of the channel. Then there was a sickening crash, the sound of breaking wood. For a moment the skiff hung, motionless, plastered against the rocks, battered by tons of surging water. Then it broke loose and whirled wildly out into the current again. He saw that one of his hands was empty, still gripping the handle of an invisible oar. He seized the remaining oar in both hands and tried to fend off from the rocks as the boat careened from bank to bank. He saw that he had lost a good hundred yards; he was almost back to the tidal pool. There was no more sound of the whaler, nothing but the rushing water, and she was alone out there, then. Helpless against the current, he was, with one oar and a leaking boat and he swore to heaven, his voice an anguished howl above the dirty waters.

He saw, for a moment, the black shape of a boulder, surging towards him; he leant forward with the oar to deflect his course from it. The oar smashed as though it were a twig in his hands, and he didn't feel his blood as it stained the water around him. The boat shot forward again, driven by the maddened rush of the tide. He didn't even see the rock; only the smashing noise he heard, as the frail shell of the boat exploded. A merciful coolness closed all around him, then, and felt himself transported smoothly along a shining, white way, where Sheila waited for him, smiling. A little boy stood by her side; his sister's lad, Willy, he thought. What was he doing here with Sheila? Then Sheila put her arms around the child and held him and began to cry. He was closer to them, now, and he could see the lad smile. "Don't cry, Mum," the boy said. "Look, it's Daddy cum for us -"

Then Sheila was in his arms and his own little lad, and all the pain was over and his body was gone from him. Everything was gone, everything; only the love was still there and it was all around him and through him and the light was so bright he couldn't see anymore --

CHAPTER SEVENTEEN

The air was so still Charley could hear his own breathing; whoever was there beyond the wall on the other side must hear it. *They* were very quiet for the moment, waiting, he thought, there in the shadow of the cloud, waiting and listening. The line between hunter and hunted was almost non-existent; they lay there like two predators, each preying on the other. Jordan shifted his weight from one knee to the other, a minute scraping of leg and boot on the rock, and Charley wanted to shout at him to be still. Then the cold moon broke through again and the shadow slithered off, leaving the roadway bathed in silver. The protecting wall felt transparent, leaving them vulnerable behind it. He wondered who it was that waited there, listening, across the way.

181

His ears strained for a sound from them. Every bone in him ached; he longed to move and prayed for them to go along, to go where they wouldn't hear him. Then it came, the slight rustling noise of a bush brushed aside, and, very faintly, the almost inaudible sound of feet moving cautiously, with great care not to disturb a single stone along the way, feet moving slowly towards the single light that now shone by the caravans. The sounds faded; whoever it was that crept along beyond the wall must have decided they were alone, and gone their way.

He looked at Megan's white face, close beside him. She had been holding his hand with a firmness almost to equal her father's iron grip; he thought she was afraid. "We've got to follow them," she whispered, "And get them." The moonlight reflected from her eyes and it was not fear he saw in them, but a fierce joy; the lioness tracking her prey through the night.

"Not yet," he said. "See where they go, first." In Dublin they had been very clear about it; they mustn't flush the quarry too soon, not until they had the stuff in their hands and could be nailed with it. He needed to know who was meeting the ship tonight and he needed to know if this was the courier himself, or only a go-between. Then it would be up to Gene, perhaps to Mossiter, how to handle them. "You'll have to wait," he said. "They'll send someone to help us. We just keep our eyes open -"

"Oh, Charley," she whispered. "You mean we've to let them walk right out of here with their bloody pockets full of bombs -?"

They hadn't long to wait. The baying of the lurcher broke the stillness of the night like an explosion; it raised the hair on the back of his neck to hear it. He was the child again, running by the lake, with terror close behind him, and Megan's hand cold in his. He put his arms around her and a tiny breath of a scream was muffled against his shoulder. "Mother of God," she whispered. "Sure I thought it was just here beside us -" She pushed away from him then and smiled, a sheepish sort of smile. "It's not I'm afraid, you know -" she stopped in mid-sentence and they watched in silence as the caravan door opened, and in the light from it they saw two figures run across the road and up the steps. Then darkness again; they heard the slamming of the door, a tiny sound in the distant dark.

"I told you," she said. "The tinkers -" She turned to Jordan. "They're a bad lot always, you've got to watch them. Haven't you seen these down here the last months? Never moving on, just waiting there, they are." He could feel the shaking of her body, with fear or cold? he wondered. Sharing the memory somehow doubled its power; he wished the damn dog in hell. Its voice echoed through the darkness and his blood went cold in his veins.

"Look," Jordan said. "The light's out."

The blackness was thick enough to cut. Not even an edge of silver showed to tell them where the moon was hidden; the racing clouds covered most of the sky, now. Only along the horizon one or two stars winked at them, little diamonds of light in the glooming dark that covered them.

"There's the door again," Megan whispered. They're coming out." He felt his eyes straining to see; it was a physical effort, looking into the dark distance, trying to make out the

183

shape, or shapes, he knew were moving there in cover of darkness. Blast the moon! Where was it? How many of the bastards were there? As in answer to his curse, the moon suddenly showed through a hole in the clouds. For the moment it seemed light as midday and the seven men - no, the small one might be a woman - hurried away from the van; walking quickly, they headed for the trees along the channel.

As fast as it came, the moonlight vanished and they were alone in the dark again. The dog was silent at last, and Megan had stopped shaking. "Now, let's go," she said. "See where they're off to."

"Stay close by the wall," Charley said. "Follow me." In front of them a wall went off at right angles to the road, heading toward the channel. "If we think they have it with them when they come back," he said to Jordan, "then we let Gene know. I'm sure Kevin's our man -"

"Bloody clever they are to think they can use my Dad for their rotten business," Megan sniffed. "How will you get it from him?"

"We've got to see if they come back," Charley said. "And then see where they go. We're not jumping the seven of them tonight, if that's what you want, love -"

They were even with the caravans, now, and perhaps two hundred yards from the dock on the channel. The wall lay between them and the dock; in any event, the moon had gone as abruptly as it had come out, and the darkness was a shield and a hiding place for them. And for *them*, Charley thought. They could be just on the other side of the wall. He put his hand on

Jordan's arm. "Better hold it here," he whispered. "Don't move, love -" Megan stopped close by him; it seemed they held their breaths, trying to hear, and when they did hear something it was the soft, dry sound of earth being disturbed by the tred of careful feet upon it. It wasn't a hundred yards away.

He raised his head above the top of the wall. There wasn't anything to see as long as the damn cloud was over the moon. Then a flare of light among the trees and he could see the outline of several heads leaning close over something, and the light went out. Now there were voices. Voices careless of being heard, though they were too far away for him to hear the words, only the murmuring sound, now low and deep, then an angry excited shout. He breathed out softly. "They're sure they're alone," he whispered.

God, it was getting cold, crouching there behind the wall. "Get on with it, you fools," he muttered, and Megan giggled beside him.

"Listen," she said. "They are." He could hear the creak of wood, of weight coming down on it; an old boat and people getting in. The motor choked and coughed, then the spark caught and it growled and roared into action. Whoever it was, was in a hurry. The sound quickly faded, and at last they were left with only the wind sighing in the trees above them, and the far-off cry of a sleepless loon came to them over the water.

For an hour they sat, the three of them huddled together. Megan's head fell against his shoulder once; she was sound asleep. And his want for her then was a dull ache that wouldn't go away, and he cursed the IRA, the Central Intelligence Agency, the

British government, Mossiter, anything and anyone he could think of that was keeping him out here, sitting on a rock, freezing, when he might have been in a nice warm bed, with nice warm Megan -

The scream was like the sound of death. It came across the water, cold, clear as shattered crystal and it ran through him like the screech of a piece of chalk on a blackboard. It woke Megan and she stopped her own scream with a hand over her mouth; her eyes were wide, shining white in the pale light of the moon.

Sheila huddled in the bottom of the boat where only the spray from the lashing waves could find her. Soaked to the skin, she was; the sea was rough and the boat slammed into each wave with a sickening crash - her head ached from it, and her body screamed for it to stop. She wanted to vomit; nausea was a white, whirling nothing behind her eyes and she could taste the bitter green bile in her throat. She held the dreadful, precious packet close to her, under the mackintosh, and she thought she could feel its menace right through her clothes - death clutched to her side, close to the life that she carried there, the secret she carried there, the secret she was keeping for Wolfe.

Oh, Wolfe! When I have lived through this, I'll tell you. This morning, when we lie together, alone, then I'll tell you. She could feel his arms around her and it helped to stop her shaking so, and she could hear his voice, clear as if he were there beside her now. "I luv you more than my life," he had said, and she knew it was true, she knew he would die for her. And now she would give him this new life, this life they had made together; of their own love they had made the child and one day Wolfe would hold the tiny baby in his hands, and on that day all the danger would be long forgot and they would live in a proper house and Wolfe come home each night and they -

Her head slammed against the edge of the seat behind her and she was sprawled in the bottom of the boat. Suddenly, they were carried forward in a great rush; the motor stopped struggling and the old whaler sighed with relief and raced ahead on the incoming tide. She struggled to sit up, not so much to see as to get out of the dirty bilge that sloshed around her where she lay. The package she clutched in both arms; one of them had offered to carry it for her, but after the price she'd paid she was letting no one take it from her. Not till she gave it to Wolfe would it leave her hands. And happy she would be when Kevin was on his way with it - who knew what might set the bloody thing off? Reckless, the skiff shot through the narrows and, as it came out into the calmer water near the dock, the motor started its chuff-chuff-chugging again - Mother of God, you'd not hear yourself think with the noise it made. She could sense the nearness of land; the chugging changed key as it echoed and reverberated against the rocks. She pulled herself up to look over the gunwale and, as she did, the moon broke out from the clouds, turning the surface of the water into shiny grey metal that the bow of the boat cut through effortlessly. They were almost to the dock.

"What the hell?" the man in the bow yelled. "What's this hanging about here?"

She saw pieces of wood floating past them, like parts of a boat, she thought, a boat all broken to bits and drifting off, like, with no one to guide it at all.

Two of the men were leaning over the side, poking at something in the water, something bobbing about beside the boat. It was a man, floating face down in the steely grey water; how odd, she thought, to be in the water this time of night, and so cold, too. Poor devil, may God help him -

One of the men reached out and grasped the man's arm. He pulled him over to the boat and, together, the two of them turned him over. Blood ran, black, into the grey water and sightless eyes stared up at the pale, cold moon. Water washed over his white face, running in and out of his mouth and when she screamed the world fell in two pieces around her and there was nothing but her scream and the rough hands holding her, keeping her from him there in the water and they covered her mouth with their hands so the scream was all inside her, burning and cold and red.

A man swore, and she tasted his blood in her mouth. "Bitch!" someone yelled, and she spat the blood and spit and tears in his face. Why was Wolfe still there in the water? Why wouldn't they let her go? The moon was so bright, now, and it was floating, too, and she was sinking and falling and her body was as light as thistle-down drifting through a summer's day.

She was waking up from a bad dream; she thought she was lying on a cold, hard bed and she didn't want to open her eyes.

The dream was still with her, the way dreams will be, staying after you wake, seeming real as life. She couldn't breath, so bad the dream had been. She'd seen Wolfe dead, white and cold in the water and she knew that couldn't be. Wolfe was alive and there was something she had to give him. In a minute she'd open her eyes and the dream would be gone. Jesus! it was good to be awake and know it was only a dream. Wolfe dead?

She felt beside her where he'd be, still asleep, God love him. Funny bed, she thought. Am I asleep in a bed of rocks and turf, then? Wolfe, where are you? Don't frighten me so, luv - Her eyes were open, then, and she saw only the sky and the clouds that scudded in from the water, and she heard the small frogs chirping in the water by the willows. Christ, she was cold! And there she lay, her clothes soaking wet, and Wolfe nowhere and this big, ugly package under her, cutting into her side. She saw the package and seeing it she knew, knew why she was here, why she was lying out here alone under the sky and she knew that the nightmare was her life, her whole life, for now and forevermore.

She stumbled towards the water; a thin, high sound came from her lips and she thought she would fall. He'd be there, her own Wolfe, and she would get his body and wash it and clean his wounds. She'd get a priest and - at the edge she stopped and fell to the ground. Below the rocky shore there was only mud, wet, dark mud and scattered through it a few pools gleamed, left by the tide as it raced out to sea, and she knelt alone by the empty shore with nothing for comfort but the cry of the gulls as they hunted the leaden sea.

CHAPTER EIGHTEEN

The scream lingered in the air, blowing on the wind, stretching across the black sky, echoing against the stony mountain side and reaching into his guts. Charley thought he had never heard anything as full of pain and despair and terror as the thin wisp of sound hanging over them there; hearing it seemed to make him a part of some burden of grief too great to be borne. Jordan and Megan knelt beside him, frozen by the sound.

Men's voices, then, rough and angry. Christ! he wished he could see what was going on. An occasional word came to them clearly; now and then a whole sentence. "We'll not be found with him - bastard tried to - damn, she's fainted - out with the bloody tide -" Then the wind turned or they lowered their voices. He

191

couldn't make out anything they were saying, now, but for maybe twenty minutes they stayed by the dock. Crouched there behind the wall, his knees felt rooted to the ground; he fervently wished them all in hell, or at least home in bed.

"What are they doing?" Megan whispered. "Can't we go closer?"

For a moment, then, they showed a light; they were starting back to the road. Then the light flickered out and they moved in a huddled group, sometimes dimly outlined against the sky but mostly hidden from him by rocks and walls. They passed within fifty yards, in silence. Were all of them even there now? He couldn't tell. Still hidden in the shadow of the clouds, they opened the caravan door and went in. He could hear it close behind them. It was two thirty.

"How long do we wait?" Jordan asked. "Till they come out?"

"Well, I need to see the transfer," Charley said. "Get Kevin with it on him."

"Or Bettina," Megan said. "I don't believe a minute she really ran out on him. She's too cool, that one -"

"You're turning into a real pro, kid," he said; he felt himself smiling there in the dark and he wanted to hug her and laugh and make love and forget Kevin and Bettina and spend the rest of his life waking up to look into her lovely pale eyes.

Instead they watched there until the grey clouds began to lighten in the east and a dull red glow showed along the horizon. Once he almost slept and woke with a start. He thought a stone had been dislodged and rolled into the road, but when he looked there was nothing to see except the outline of the wall, and nothing to hear but a complaining sheep, bleating it loneliness into the night. Megan stirred, too, at the sound. "Bill," Charley whispered. "You awake?"

"Yep, and I heard it, too."

"Are they sending it by a sheep, then?" Megan said.

"You never know -" Jordan answered.

Then he was wide awake, watching, trying to see up against the mountain side, see if anyone went there. He cursed the cloud cover that lingered through the night and when the dawn came, all rosy and pink, pushing the clouds back to show them a clear, pale sky, he shrugged and looked at his watch. "I think we just wasted the night," he said. "They'll not come out now -"

"How d'you know?" Megan asked. "They're Irish, you know - I'd not put it past them so quick. Wait you - " She had been leaning against him with her back to the wall. "God," she said. "I can't move. Can you?" She stretched her legs out in front of her and rubbed her knees. "I'll never walk again."

Charley straightened his back and wondered, as he did, if it was possible to fuse vertebrae by sitting for three hours against a hard, wet Irish stone wall. His arms ached and where he had sat on the spot of turf under the wall, his butt was numb and cold. He raised his ruined body to peer over the wall. "We've got to get out of here," he said. "They'll be out and about soon -"

"Bloody fools, we'd look," Megan said and knelt beside him.

"Oh, damn - there's someone on the road," he whispered.

Megan followed his look.   "A local lass, only," she

whispered. "Mother of God, she looks a sight! Out in the bushes all night, she was. Just wait till her Da sees her!"

The poor girl walked along the road, her head down, her feet dragging. Her eyes stared at the road in front of her; stared sightlessly, it seemed, for she stumbled often and once fell to her knees. She was quite close to them now, and they kept low behind the wall. Charley had one good look at her face as she passed them. Tears streamed down her cheeks and her eyes were blank; she looked as though she had seen the face of death and, having seen it, longed to have it for herself.

She turned from the road and started up the mountain on a narrow footpath. The packet she clutched to her side, and it was heavier with every step she took. Her throat ached and burned; her breath was hot and dry and the tears ran unnoticed down her face. The sun had risen full before she was in sight of the hut but it gave no heat to warm her shaking, shivering, trembling, crying body. Its white, wicked eye glared over the top of the mountain, its rays shattered into shining crystal in the tears that filled her eyes. She moved her feet over the rough pathway; cut and bleeding they were and she didn't know it, didn't know where her shoes were at all.

She saw again and again, in the hard light of day, his white face and staring eyes and then only the filthy stretch of mud where the tide had run out, where she had searched till her head ached, looking, hoping the careless sea might have left him there for her to bring home at the last and then giving up and her soul empty and her heart a stone.

When she came to the door of the hut, she could hear them inside, Sean growling and Ben whining his reply. They couldn't hurt her now, could they? There was nothing left to hurt. She stopped there in the slanting sunlight; leaning against the door she thought she would fall. The sudden wave of nausea bent her double and she fell to her knees retching and gasping while the bitter bile choked her and filled her head with its sour sickness. She lay on the ground, then, and tried to stop the spasms that were tearing at her as though to break all the bones in her body. Holy Mary, she'd lose the child if it didn't stop! And the child was Wolfe's, would *be* Wolfe, not dead, but living, and she to love him and see him a man one day. Wrong she was to think they couldn't hurt her; if anything happened to the child she would tear their eyeballs from their heads, her own brother, even, and that bleeding bastard with his ugly, leering -

The door screeched as it flew open and she pulled her legs under her in a ball, rolled up like a hedge-hog, to protect herself. The nasty packet she held against her breast. "What the bloody hell?" It was Sean, standing over her, the sun behind him outlining his head and shoulders against the cloud-washed sky. "Shut up, Sis, you'll have the bleedin' RUC here from Galway -" She thought he would kick her and she rolled away from him. Against the wall she pulled herself up and stood, looking square across at him. Her breath came in quick sobs that caught in her throat and she could taste the vomit, green and foul on her tongue. Damn if you see me crying, Sean O'Malley, damn if you do, ever again.

She stood there, then, by the wall, and he took a step

towards her across the unkept yard of the hut. "Stay you there," she hissed. "I've got what you bloody sent me for." She held it out to him and almost fell from the weight of it in both her hands. She bent and laid it on the ground. "Pick it up," she said, "And do with it as you like. I'll not touch it again, never mind what you do -" Ben was with him then and she moved away along the wall.

"What the f---?" he said. "A pretty sight you look this day, Missy!" But his eyes were all over her body, dirty they were and that crooked smile, too, when he looked. Her hand went to her throat and then she knew her blouse was torn and open and she saw that she was barefoot and her wet clothes clung to her body and she felt naked in his eyes.

A chilling wind came, now, from under the clouds that were blowing in, blotting out the sun, and she was shaking again with the cold of it. Sean leaned over and picked up the packet. "Where's Wolfe?" he said, and she turned from him to walk down the hill. "Where's Wolfe?" he yelled. "Come back, you little bitch!" She didn't hear him, wouldn't hear him, would never answer him, no matter how he screamed. His hand was on her arm, then, and he pulled her to him. His face was an inch from hers and his hand on her arm was like iron; she asked God's forgiveness that she hated her brother and she sunk her teeth in his arm. He threw her to the ground, yelling in pain and she got up and ran. How far she ran, or if he followed her, she never knew; only that she was away from them, and, at last, alone on the high mountain, she found shelter where a ledge of rock hung over a little field of turf and the gentle sheep grazed beside her when she fell asleep there.

"Was it my lass that kept you out so late?" Jamey was finishing off a plate of kippers, looking disgustingly fit and ready for another day of bog-trotting and mountain climbing. "You'll need to watch yourself with this girl," he grinned. "She's a right one for a good time - she take you off dancing in Oughterard, then?"

Not exactly, Charley, thought; not exactly a good time, though certainly a late one. It had been broad day when they climbed the back stairs of the carriage house, cold and aching, clinging to each other for warmth, and it was clear to him, now, that even a hot shower and fresh clothes were insufficient to conceal on his person the ravages of the sleepless night. Megan was already at breakfast, sitting next to her father, and her face was as bright and guileless as a babe's, as though none of last night had ever happened, or if it had, she had been sleeping the sleep of the innocent in her own warm bed. He marveled briefly at her undiminished beauty and sank slowly into a chair, careful not to jar the ache behind his eyeballs, or affront too rudely the parts of him that still bore the marks of long hours pressed against the rough stone of this God-forgotten piece of land. Megan's smile was brilliant. "What's been keeping you, Charley? Breakfast's got cold waiting for you, now -" An empty porridge bowl was on her plate and she was attacking a thick rasher of bacon like a starving animal. His own stomach was cleaved to his backbone, and the hollowness echoed inside him; a piece of cold toast was manna from heaven.

"Here, lad, have some bacon," Megan offered and pushed her plate over to him. "I'll get us some more -"

Kevin sat alone at the next table, picking at his food. Nervous, aren't you, Charley thought - today's the day, isn't it? He caught Kevin's eye for a moment; hastily Kevin turned, looking out the window as though the sight of a wren in the holly tree was of all-consuming interest to him. Then, of a sudden, he got up and came over to Jamey. "I'm not riding this morning," he said. "Can I pick you up at noon break?"

"Aye," Jamey said. "We'll be at Carna for the swimming. Will you be going with Anna, then, when she brings lunch?"

"Someone's hired a car - a friend, you know, someone who couldn't come with us." He kept catching his lower lip in his teeth as he spoke and his eyes were looking just past Jamey, shifting back and forth, uneasy. "Thought I'd spend a while with him; he just might know where Bettina has gone off to -" An effort produced a smile; not much of a smile, but it was a try.

"Not to worry," Jamey said. "You'll find us all right, then?"

"Anna told me," Kevin said. He was staring now at Charley and there was a question in his eye. Charley gave him the satisfaction of a politely raised eyebrow and a small smile. "Well, I'll see you all later," Kevin said; then he turned on his heel and started out of the room. He stopped by the door and came back. "I say," he said to Charley, "I *am* sorry about yesterday - the damn horse just went on out of control, you know. Delighted you didn't get bashed up too much -"

"Forget it," Charley murmured. "It could happen to anyone."

As he left, then, Kevin nodded, an odd sort of ackowledgement. "A queer one, that," Jamey said.

"He can stay as long as he likes for all I care," Megan said. "Looking for the bitchy girl friend, I reckon -"

So there were two ponies running with them that had no riders that morning. The thin sunlight soon gave way to low clouds and the wind came off the water, sudden and cold. Jamey led them through fields where the turf was deep and for a while they larked over the low walls, sometimes surprising a small flock of sheep napping in the deep grass. The silly sheep would leap up from the ground, bleating piteously in high, complaining voices; from a safe distance they would stop and stare, accusing, baleful, their eyes following the horses until they were out of sight. Nearing the sea, they came to long stretches of sandy earth covered in bright green grass, smooth and firm to the foot, and they galloped till they were breathless, pulling up by the narrow road that followed the channel to the sea.

Trotting down the road, Charley could hear from far off, long before they saw the camp, the baying of the lurcher; his spine stiffened. Megan was close beside him and she leaned over to whisper. "There's the music for our dancing last night -" She smiled, a wicked, scheming smile.

"You *told* Jamey we went dancing," he said.

"And was I to tell him I lay all the night in the bushes with you, then? You don't know my father -" She laughed at him and booted her pony off down the road.

The dog roared his hatred at them as they passed; three filthy children played in the dirt beside one of the vans and smoke came from the tin stove pipe. There was no other sign of life. The largest child, a boy, shouted at the dog to shut up; it paid him no attention, and its cries were still in Charley's ears when they came in sight of the sea itself, a quarter mile past the camp.

Megan and Charley sat behind the abandoned cottage sharing a plate of salmon and cheese and heavy Irish bread. "D'you think he'll show up?" she asked.

"Yes," Charley said. "I do." He couldn't afford to be wrong. Last night he'd been so sure he would find out who was getting it from the boat, and he hadn't even found out if that's what they did, let alone who had it. Sure, he'd seen them go out in the skiff, and come back, but his eyes still ached from watching for one of them to leave in the night and he was actually no wiser than before. It *had* to be Kevin carrying it across; he must be right about that. Gene had been disappointed, he could tell he was, when he'd talked with him before breakfast; he hadn't actually blamed Charley for not getting a better fix on the loot, it had been dark, and if there were seven of them, of course he and Jordan couldn't jump them. At least that's what he'd said. "We can pick the courier up in Oughterard if you're right about him." He hadn't sounded too sure that he thought Charley right about anything. Self doubt crept into him like the cool mist off the water. Blast Kevin! Where was he?

They stayed close by the cottage on the shore after lunch.

The beach was long and smooth and they galloped the length of it and back. Then they rode the ponies into the surf - Megan raced him to the shore and her tomboy yell came back to him across the sand and for a moment the worry fell from him and the years, and he galloped through the crashing waves and laughed like a boy out of school. "Look, you," Megan said, close beside him. She pointed to the road, where a ruinous Land Rover rattled past the gypsy camp and stopped by the gate.

One figure detached itself quickly and the Rover wheeled around in the road and was gone. He could tell it was Kevin, even from this far away. Anna was still picking up from the lunch and Kevin stood by her a minute, chatting her up, it looked.

At last, Jamey brought them all back from the sea, the wind drying them as they rode. Kevin was sitting, uneasily, it seemed to Charley, on the grey hunter he'd been riding the day before, the same one who'd knocked him over the cliff. He had his raincoat neatly rolled and tied to his saddle, as they all did. The same pack he'd worn the day before was on his back. Charley could see how the straps cut into his shoulders, pulled down by the weight of the pack.

"It's a load you've got there," Megan said to Kevin. "Is it bottles of poteen you've brought for us then?" She was close beside him and she gave him a comradely nudge on the shoulder.

He pulled away from her; she might have been a venomous snake, for the look he gave her. "What I carry can't be of any interest to you," he said. "It happens my friends have brought my photographic equipment along, so please be good enough not to shove it around. It's quite expensive and, as you may know,

201

fragile -"

Megan's smile was evil. "Perhaps you'd better let Anna carry it in the truck, then, and keep it safe, as you seem to have trouble managing your horse-" Charley breathed a sigh of unmitigated relief. So he did have it with him, after all. Let him worry it for three more days and they'd pick him up before Galway. "You were right, luv," Megan whispered, when he had gone. "Too clever by half, you are -" As they started up the mountainside into the forest the sun broke through the clouds; it cast slanting rays across the fields. The long twilight was beginning and peace settled over the mountainside like a blessing. Sheep were grazing here; their woolly shapes cast long shadows between the rocks. The tired ponies walked more slowly as they neared the tree line.

Megan caught his arm. "By that rock," she said, "Look". Under the shadow of an overhanging ledge he could see a pale shape huddled. "It's the poor lass we saw this morning," she said. "Her cottage must be near and she's feared to go home lest her old man beat her."

"Are you all right?" Charley called out to the girl.

"We'll help you, luv," Megan said, but the girl never looked up at them at all.

"Leave me be," she said. Her voice was harsh from crying, the words thick with tears. "Get away! I'll be going on soon - just leave me!" Huddled, later, in the van on the way to the Ussher, her voice was still in his ears and in bed that night he couldn't forget the sound of it, and he wondered again at the strangeness of this wild land, and he wished to God Megan was here beside

him. Sleep, when it finally came was full of dreams and he woke
often with the lonesome cry of the loon in his ears and it seemed
to be the cry of the girl up there alone on the mountainside, and he
thought that day would never come; this night would be forever.

He pulled his mackintosh on and crept down the stairs and
out into the yard. He could hear the waves lapping the shore of
the lake, now, but the cry of the loon was gone; there was nothing
more than the lapping water and the soft wind in the trees.

Her voice was soft, close by him. "Are you daft out here,
lad? Sure, you need some sleep -" She was soft in his arms, then,
and he held her to him against the damp of the night.

CHAPTER NINETEEN

The two corgis, Millicent and Roger, raced across the lawn. Their mistress was taking them for their walk early today. They chased a squirrel up the pine tree by the corner of the wood and then came running back for her approval before they shot off towards the path to the lake. It was sunny this afternoon, and she wasn't wearing her mackintosh or the scarf over her head. She brought them out, no matter the weather, of course; they didn't mind and neither did she if it was rainy or foggy or wet, and she came every day, just before dark to watch for the boat to bring her husband back from the fishing.

They ran down the path towards the lake. It was a good path for running, narrow and twisty, and often they could surprise a sleepy dove into terrified flight, or pounce on a water rat, sunning himself on the rocks. It must have been too early, for nothing was in the path and they hurried along to the shore in hopes of finding the mother duck waddling along there with her babies. If she was in the water their fun would be spoiled; their mistress was quite firm in not allowing them to go into the lake after anything. For some reason she was against taking wet corgis into her room.

She stood a long time on the shore, looking out over the water, but it was too early for the boat to come back. There wasn't a sign of it to be seen. Roger raced to the end of the mole and back; he brought a stick for her to throw, and she did. Millicent got it, and then there was a chase over the rocks. They surprised the duck, but she was in the water and swam off, giving them a haughty look. Millicent began to amuse herself by reaching into the water after a shell she saw close to the edge. Suddenly she slipped and fell in. Their mistress was not pleased even though Millicent carefully shook the water off her coat when she came out. "Bad dog," their mistress said, and snapped their leads on them.

She had started for the lodge when something caught her eye on the lake. She turned and walked to the end of the pier. "Wait," she said to them. "I think they're coming in early," and she stopped to look out over the water. The dogs watched, too, and Roger wondered why she thought it was *his* boat. Clearly, as any dog could tell, it was quite different.

At last she shrugged and said, "No, it must be someone else." The fog was getting quite thick and had covered the sun completely. It was delicious and white and soft. They could hardly find the gap in the wood where the path took them back to to the lodge.

Kevin was in the front seat with Jamey, his backpack stored between his knees. The Rover cruised along with Jamey's usual reckless abandon; Kevin was ashen-faced, clutching the dashboard with both hands. They had a very close encounter with a big lorry, and almost lost the road wheeling around a blind turn. On Charley's shoulder, Megan slept in blissful ignorance of the danger she was in. On the other hand, she had driven with her father all her life and there was no reason to believe he was any worse now than he'd ever been. Maybe she thought she was safe.

At any rate, she needed the sleep, as Charley well knew; she'd spent no more time sleeping than he had in the last two days, and that clearly wasn't enough to sustain rational life. They had stood there in the dark hour before dawn, clinging together, leaning on each other as though if they didn't, they would fall. "I'm so tired," she whispered, "And I can't sleep -"

"I can't either," he said. "I can't stay in that room another minute - I feel like a monk in a cell."

"P'raps you'd better pray for us then," she said, and smiled.

"Well, I feel less like a monk, now," he said. She leant her head on his shoulder, standing there in the night, and her breath was warm on his neck; her hair smelled like new hay - no, he definitely was not ready to take holy orders. She was laughing softly.

"Well, lad, I have to tell you, Megan Leary never in her life felt like a nun, so you've not to worry there -"

Her lips were soft when he kissed her and her body fitted against his as though they were the two halves of one person. He held her there for a long time, while the loon laughed at them from the lake, and the night birds made the beginnings of a song for the break of day. The mist was very thick, and where the light shined across from the stable yard he could see her hair frosted with little jewels of water.

"You must be freezing," he said. "God, I shouldn't keep you out here-"

"Aye, that you shouldn't, and me in my night-dress only." She laughed and pulled away from him, and he saw that she was barefoot, standing there in a shift of white cotton that clung to her body in the damp, cool breeze but her hand in his was warm and comforting there in the dark sadness of the night.

"We'll go in then," he said. "We can't stay here -"

"It'll soon be day," she said. "Night's almost gone. You can come to my room if your cell's too cold -"

No, definitely, neither of them had enough sleep, not enough sleep for a day of watching Kevin carrying his pack like a baby all the day long. Careful of his 'camera', he never laid it down; it was on his back at lunch time and it bumped along on his back while he rode. Pretty heavy, Charley judged, whatever it held. He'd radioed Gene with the news in the morning. "He's got it with him," he said, and Gene's strong voice came over the air, congratulating him.

"Good man," he said. "I'll pass it on to Harry. Don't

wonder he'll be out to meet us in Oughterard. Stick with him, son, night and day -"

Not exactly good news, not when his muscles screamed for rest and his eyes tracked at about half speed. It was good to see the pack still with Kevin, now. Maybe he was tired, too, and would go up to bed right after dinner like a good boy. Dinner! He woke Megan up when they were screeching around the last turn before Ussher came in view. "Time to eat," he said. "Wake up -"

She smiled in her sleep and muttered a little nothing to him. "Come on", he said, "Dinner time." Marianne would have food on the table for them as soon as they could wash up. She'd not mind their being late; he understood there was a large party staying in the Ussher, a very demanding party, who must be fed and cossetted first, in any event. Charley had seen two quite discreet gentlemen, unobtrusively armed, he had noted, attending to the entrance, through which, clearly, no-one entered.

Jamey swooped into the yard with considerable loss of rubber on the cobbles, and lurched to a stop beside the door. Megan sat up straight, looking around her; sleep still clouded her lovely eyes. "Not dark yet," she observed. "But one hell of a fog, isn't it?" The lights were on already in the carriage house, making fuzzy squares of yellow that floated in the soft whiteness of the still air.

"Out with you, then," Jamey said. "Be down by half after or Marianne will have it out of my hide; a right witch she can be if we keep her dinner waiting -"

"I'll put the truck away for you, then, Dad," Megan said.

"You can go and tell her we're here -"

"I'll come with you," Charley said, "So you don't fall asleep at the wheel."

"Not bloody likely, from here to the back," she laughed, and he climbed in beside her. They watched Kevin go through the door, holding the pack, now, in his arms, careful he was, not to bump it against anyone in the narrow passageway. "Look you, Charley," she said. "Watch the lad - what's he got there, so precious, will you tell me?"

"Some games for his friends in Belfast, something they won't ever get-"

"Why don't we take it from him now?" she asked; the lioness out on a dangerous foray, homing in on her kill.

"Harry is coming to Oughterard with someone," he said. "Someone who understands what it is. We could blow ourselves to hell-and-gone and take a good piece of Ussher with us if we get too eager -"

"Sure I hope he knows how to take care of it, then," she said.

Charley thought a moment. "Or they may want me to see who he gives it to; kill two birds with one stone. Gene will know when I talk to him tonight -"

She pulled the Rover into a spot under the bushes by the back door and jumped down. They started for the door, hand in hand. "You can have the shower first," she said, "At least if you beat Dad to it. I want a bit of air before I come in -"

"You're sure you're ok out here alone?"

"Aye, the many times I've stayed here, why should I not

be?"

"Just remembering the night of the tinkers and their dogs," he said. "About the same kind of night -"

"Go along, you" she said. "I'm grown old, now, and can take care of myself. Just hurry along with the shower, or I'll come in and shove you out myself, then -"

So he went and she was alone in the white mist. She pulled her mack out of the truck and tied a scarf over her head. The pale blanket of the fog covered everything and its chill went through to her bones, and she turned the collar of the mackintosh up to her ears. Well she knew these nights and the cold that seeped through to make your spine tingle and make you forget the day had ever been, with its warmth and sun. She'd just go down by the lake for a bit and think.

So much there was to think about. Last night there was, the thought of it to warm her heart until it beat inside her that she could feel each thump of it pounding against her chest, and the knowing that she'd need to tell Jimmy, and she could see the hurt in his eyes, now. Not that she need tell him of last night, never mind that, only he must know she was Charley's now, forever, and her heart was sore with pity for the lad and the shadow of guilt was heavy over her, for had she not let him hope these years along that one day she might love him with the same love he had for her? God forgive her, she never meant to hurt him.

Then, supposing Charley'd never come back and they'd married, as well they might have? How long could she pretend a love she never felt? and then how cruel the hurt would be when at last he knew. When they got back to Galway she'd need to see him and tell him straight what had happened -

She hardly noticed that she'd walked all the way to the lake along the path under the dripping trees; didn't notice till she heard the water lapping against the rocks of the ancient mole. The white mist was darkening and a chill wind blew across the water, ruffling the waves and throwing them against the rocks with a new sound. The fog was so thick, now, she could hardly see the edge of the lake, not four feet on either side of her. The waves were a steady roar, and she didn't hear the creak of oarlocks behind her, so she was startled to hear a voice, harsh and rasping, close at her back.

"It's her!" the voice said. "Alone -"

She whirled around and saw two men jumping from low a skiff onto the mole. "What would you want?" she asked. "Who -?" The younger of the two moved like a cat; neither man spoke, and before she could run, an arm was locked around her throat. The sound she made was only a muffled croak; her breath was cut off. She couldn't see them clearly, it was that dark already and the fog so heavy; only the other one reached from behind and stuffed something in her mouth and tied a rag around her head to hold it in. Then she couldn't see at all; something was pulled over her head and tied around her neck. So tight it was she thought she'd never breathe till it was off.

She fought to get her arms free. She felt one elbow connect with the soft part of a man's belly, and was cheered to hear him gasp a moment for breath. "Old bitch!" a voice hissed beside her, and she staggered when a fist slammed into the side of her head. She lost her balance and the next blow knocked her to the ground. She struggled against the weight that was on her back

212

and fought to keep her arms free, but strong hands held them crossed behind her back while other hands wrapped wire tightly around them.

A cruel laugh broke the silence. "Is Your bleedin' Majesty comfortable, eh?" a voice said, close by her feet. She twisted around and kicked as hard as she could in the direction of the voice, and felt the satisfaction of hearing the laugh turn to a yelp of pain as her foot connected with solid flesh. "Damn, you bloody bitch -" she heard him yelling, just before the stars burst in her head and the pain ran searing through her brain. She tried to roll over, but one of them was still on top of her. The other was trying again to tie her feet. He was bending her legs up to tie them to her hands behind her back. A right mess she'd be in then.

She used all her strength to kick her legs free, keep him from tying them. Her head was a balloon, filled with fire instead of air and she could see bright flashes of light in the red behind her eyes. Damn them, bloody bastards, what did they want with her? She gave a last heave with her body and almost dislodged the man on her back. Then a blaze of light shot through her skull and there was nothing, nothing but black and cold and hollow nothing, nothing at all was there.

CHAPTER TWENTY

The water was actually warm in the shower, and Charley lingered, luxuriating in the soothing warmth, whistling under his breath a tentative reconstruction of the song the old piper blew for the child, Megan, when she danced that day by the sea, and he could see her there, slowly and shyly circling the green of the lawn while the wind blew in her hair and whispered through the grass where she moved among them with another world shining from her pale, lovely eyes. The water began to get cold and he was reminded that Irish plumbing, most notably rural Irish plumbing, while charming in its way, did not provide limitless quantities of hot water, and he was not the last one to need it. He smiled, thinking that his subconscious mind had probably kept him there waiting for Megan to make good her threat to come in and throw him out. Well, Megan or not, he wasn't staying in an icy shower any longer.

Passing her room he beat a little tattoo on the door. "Megan?" he called. "Hey, I'm sorry - the hot water gave out -"

Not a sound from inside the room. "Hey, you in there?" he called. "Megan?" No answer. Maybe she went in to eat without a shower; probably knew he wouldn't leave her any hot water. She understood the Ussher and its vagaries that well, after all; she probably knew he'd forget how quick the geyser was to give out of heat.

He hummed while he dressed, happy little songs; happiness seemed to bubble up in him uncontrolled. He was stricken with guilt to think how he had cursed this job, the agency, Mossiter, the IRA, anything to do with tracking the smuggling operation; now, he realized that if not for them he'd be back in Washington, regretting the weekend with Sally in Middleburg, instead of being here, here with Megan, who loved him. She did; she loved him, she really did. He looked in the mirror and saw the silly, smug smile on his face and broke into a laugh. He loved her and she loved him; life was so simple that way, and so good! She'd be downstairs now, waiting for him; waiting for dinner more likely. He'd never seen a girl with an appetite like hers.

Jamey and Kevin were standing by the table, drinks in hand, while Kathleen carried the first course and laid it on the table. He looked for Megan, but she wasn't there. Jamey saw him come in. "What have you done with my girl?" he said. "Just parking the truck, I thought you were-"

"She went for a walk," Charley said. "I came in and showered. I thought she'd be here." A little black shadow walked across behind his eyes and hung there a moment, just a little shadow, not quite a fear, but more than a doubt, and his eyes turned to look at the doorway, hoping to see her come in and send the shadow away.

"A right bad night for a walk," Jamey said. "The lass has the sense of a paycock sometimes." He shrugged. "Never saw her late for dinner, that one," he added, and laughed. "Well, no matter at all; she'll be along -" And that seemed to end it for Jamey. He was probably right; there was nothing here to worry about. No one had seen them at the shore last night, and Kevin wouldn't know she'd been there. Anyway, Kevin was here, standing behind Jamey, looking with intense interest into the bottom of his half-full glass, without the pack on his back for once, Charley noticed. Pretty sure of yourself, aren't you, boy, he thought - where have you left it? Suppose it was in his room and Megan knew about it? She wouldn't be snooping around up there right now, would she? Yes, she would; she might well be in his room this very minute, examining the device itself, her eyes bright with curiosity, checking on the loot, as it were, for her own satisfaction. The black shadow moved in again and this time it was a real fear, fear that she had the thing in her hands, and not knowing what it was she might-

Kevin was watching him, now; the glass was empty and he had set it down. Marianne came in from the kitchen and told them to sit down. "Before it's cold," she said, "Only a small boullia-baise, but a good one, the clams fresh from the water today -"

217

Jamey moved towards the table, but Kevin remained staring at Charley, who felt himself immobilized by indecision. He thought Kevin knew what was in his mind, and he didn't see how he could get away to check the upstairs. Surely, if he was right, and it was still in Kevin's room, then Kevin must have thought of Megan, as well, must wonder if she was up there now, in his room, searching and finding it. Before he could move, Kevin turned to Jamey. "Sorry, I've left my allergy medicine in the room - don't wait the soup for me." Much too quickly, he brushed past Charley and hurried up the narrow stairs.

"Shall I go give a shout for Megan?" Charley asked Jamey, moving through the door as he spoke. Briefly he saw Marianne's stricken face as her guests, one by one, abandoned her good boulliabaise to run, no doubt, foolish errands while the soup lay cooling on their plates.

"Aye," Jamey said. "If you want, lad." Charley was in the hall before Jamey finished speaking, and started up the stairs. Kevin's door was closed and there was no sound from his room. The whole loft was quiet as night. He stood in the hall, listening. Was Kevin *in* his room? Or had he gone somewhere else? Or was Megan in there alone, quietly getting ready to blow herself up? He tried the knob, ever so gently; it turned, but the door wouldn't move. Someone was inside, then, to have thrown the bolt. Megan's door was across the hall. He stood between the two doors and called her name. "Megan," he called, "You're missing the soup," It was loud enough to be heard through either door. Then he tried the door to her room; it was unbolted and pushed open easily. The room was empty; the neatly made bed looked innocent, virginal, the soft down covered with a white cotton spread. Good job, he thought, that she never wanted to be a nun - she was right when she said she had no talent for it at all, none at all. The happiness kept coming on to bother him; it shoved its way into his mind, sharing space uncomfortably with the panic that was building in him. She hadn't been here, not since they came back. Her clean clothes lay waiting for dinner, and they looked sad to him, abandoned and lifeless.

Then he heard water running and he raced out into the hall. She was taking a shower! But it was only the loo flushing, and then Kevin came out, adjusting his fly; concentrating on what he was doing, he almost ran into Charley. "What's happened to the girl?" he asked. "D'you find her?" He stood with his back to the door of his room, blocking it from Charley.

"No," Charley said. "She's not up here." Unless she's in your room, Kevin, and God help you if you find her there.

"You'd best get down for dinner," Kevin said, motionless in front of his door.

"I'm not that hungry," Charley said. "Maybe something we ate for lunch- not feeling so good, either?" He nodded in the direction of the bath.

"I told you, I've got this allergy. There's nothing wrong." Still he stood by the door. "You go on; I'll be down in a minute."

For a man who tried to kill me forty eight hours ago, you are one cool cookie, Charley thought, and be damned if I leave you alone up here until I know who's in that room of yours. If Kevin knew who was in it then he knew it was locked and he wouldn't try the door, not while Charley was there. All the doors

219

fastened with the dead-bolt only; there were no keys.

How long they might have stood at this impasse, Charley never found out. Jamey came bounding up the stairs. "Marianne's having a right fit," he said. "Come, get your soup, lads, before she has my head on a platter -"

"Right," Charley said. "We're coming." He looked Kevin straight in the eye. "We were on our way, weren't we, Kevin? Or did you want something from your room?"

Let him try the door now, with Jamey here. If he's surprised to find it locked, then we know where Megan is. Or, if he knew who was there and wanted it to remain a secret, he wouldn't try it. Kevin forced a weak smile. "Just coming, we were," he said. "I've taken my pill." He didn't even glance at the door; they went down together, herded along by Jamey.

"The soup's a treat -" Jamey was saying. "Sure my lass will be sorry to miss it."

He spoke with maddening calm, as though Megan disappeared on a regular basis, as though no danger possibly lurked there in the dark beyond the old carriage doors. Kevin sat down and attacked the soup with enthusiasm; innocent as a lamb he relished each steaming spoonful. Charley looked at his plate and felt his throat go dry. The ticking of the old clock above the fireplace sounded in his ears like distant shots echoing from far off. When its harsh bell chimed eight o'clock, a cold finger of fear touched him; it was over an hour since she had left him, drifting off alone into the cool, soft, dusky night.

Her remembered smile, the wicked grin flashed over her shoulder, laughing at his fear for her - the memory of that smile cut through him, now, and he cursed himself for a fool to have let her go. "You're not eating, lad," Jamey said. "Are ye still hurting so from your trip down the mountainside?" Wasn't he even wondering where she was? Didn't he know? Of course he didn't; this was just another trip over the mountain for him. The darkness and the fear didn't touch him, and Charley briefly gave thanks that Jamey didn't even suspect what he feared.

"No," he said. "I'm fine. Just not too hungry, I guess. Anna really filled us up at lunch." He tried a confident smile. "Guess I'll just take a look outside for Megan - we know she'll be hungry." Jamey laughed, then and returned to his boulliabaise; Kevin seemed preoccupied buttering a slab of soft white bread.

"Right, you," Jamey said. "Go have a look-about. Down by the lake you'll find her; whistling for the loon, she'll be, or watching for the night owl in the trees - some foolishness or other, you'll see." *He* wasn't worried, not in the least. Charley nodded and got up, too quickly, perhaps, dropping his crumpled napkin on the floor.

"I'll find her," he said. His voice held far more conviction than he felt; a kind of emptiness filled him and something buzzed inside his head, something that said, "You have lost her - you let her go, you let her go and you'll never find her, ever again." He stumbled out the door into the night. The damp air was swirling through the courtyard, carried by a small wind that blew in from the shore. It was cold on his face after the glow of the turf fire and its chill went through his jacket, through him, and he felt his heart grow cold standing there in the lonely, silent dark with only the wind for company. He remembered another night, remembered himself standing just as he was now, in the dark and the cold, knowing, as he knew now, that something he loved was lost forever because he had been careless and had let it go.

It had been a night in early spring and the slow, white fog had drifted down over the mountain, blown in by a soft breeze from across the ridge. He had been eight years old; he knew that because the puppy had been a birthday present. Ever since he could remember he'd dreamed of having a dog, a wonderful dog all his own; he'd prayed for a dog, begged for one, even smuggled a small, mangy creature into the residence in Teheran one time, only to be told there was no way they could keep it there - diseases were rife and dangerous - and it was given to the cook to take home to her children. But now they were at home in Virginia; Dad had a Pentagon assignment and they lived on their own place, in an old stone house, nestled among great oak trees, under the shadow of the Blue Ridge.

So it happened that on the morning of his eighth birthday he heard the door to his room open, heard Mom's voice, with laughter in it, saying, "Wake up, Charley! Happy birthday!" Then something soft and warm landed on his face, nuzzled under his blankets and covered him with wet little kisses. It pushed against him and wriggled with joy and he held his puppy in his arms, laughing, unbelieving - it was his Dog! It was very small, a Jack Russell terrier ("Terror, more likely," his mother said) six weeks old, and it was his, his very own!

He named the puppy Bear, and together they learned the countryside, its long valleys and rough hillsides. The fat puppy body followed him tirelessly, short little legs working like pistons and tail whipping back and forth in ecstacy as they searched under rotten logs and in hollow trees and waded in the freezing water of the pond behind the barn. They had secret hiding places in the loft and under the house; Bear was his best friend and he loved him totally. Days at school were endless, waiting to be home, where Bear would greet him like a tiny black and white tornado, leaping and whirling in the air.

But that night he had stood silent, tears running down his face. Two hours before he and Bear had been playing at the pond. A sudden wind swirled dust and leaves around them; big drops of rain splatted on the dry ground. Thunder suddenly split the sky and bolts of jagged lightning crackled around them. The storm came over the mountain with terrifying speed. "Come on, Bear," he yelled. "Run!" Bear was across the pond from him; the rain was like a white cloud between them. Then he saw the little body shooting like a bullet towards him and he turned and ran.

The thunder rolled over him and lightning struck beside him, splitting a tree. "Hurry, boy!" he yelled again and then he covered his head with his jacket and ran. Bear must be just behind him. He was a smart puppy; he'd find his way all right.

But he hadn't. When Charley got to the house he waited, dripping, on the porch, calling, "Bear, Bear! Come, boy, hurry up!" While he stood there, the big oaks in the yard thrashed wildly in the wind, the new spring leaves heavy with rain. He started back to look for Bear, running, crying across the grass. He heard the sound before he saw the giant tree by the gate crash to the ground; the whole yard was filled with its great, wounded branches and he couldn't get through.

Later, standing there, as he stood now, he was filled with the sick knowledge that he had abandoned Bear, in danger, poor little Bear, out there alone in the storm, afraid and cold. Now he remembered how he found him, the small wet body washed against the side of the creek where the flashing flood waters had carried it.

God, his head ached and throbbed, and through his brain the picture of the little dead dog alternated with one of a lovely girl, lying battered and still where the black waters lapped the shore beside the ghost-haunted lake of Ussher. "Megan!" he shouted into the night. "Megan, where are you?" and his voice came back to him, empty and cold. The loon gave answer, its crazy laugh echoing wildly through the trees, telling him nothing.

He walked into the deeper black of the woods, remembering the path, feeling his way through the bushes that grew on either side of the path. By the lake, once out from the trees, his eyes could make out the dark bulk of the mole, stretching into the lake, and he could see, on the other side of the wall, the lights from Ussher itself, but he knew he was alone. She wasn't here, nor would she answer him, however he should call. "Megan!" His voice sounded hollow and useless. He scrambled around the end of the wall and up the slippery rocks onto the mole. Auld Ian's skiff was tied up there, bobbing quietly, bumping against the stones.

He ran the length of the mole then, panic catching hold. He lit a match - stupid, what can a match show you in all this night? - and saw that his hands were shaking. The loon's wavering call sounded again; he shouted at it to shut up. It only made him remember and he wanted to cry. She couldn't be gone! She could be back at the carriage house; it was just his aching head that imagined things that never were. He began to run, ran until he was breathless at the kitchen door. She must be there; God wouldn't let it happen, not if there was a God, a good, just Episcopalian God, the One he always thought you could count on. He stood catching his breath on the smooth stone doorstep. Through the window he saw the kitchen girls washing up, chattering to each other as they worked.

He pushed the door open. "Mind if I come in this way?" he asked.

"Sure, you're welcome, sir," the little red-headed one smiled. "And welcome to help us, if you like -" Her smile faded and she became very busy in the pantry as Marianne came in, bustling, sweeping Pierre and Pegeen ahead of her. Marianne ignored her; her attention was on Pegeen.

"And why were you taking a so pleasant stroll before dinner, with the table not laid yet? And plates to be prepared. Mon Dieux! am I to do everything myself?" In anger, Marianne was formidable, and Pegeen was, in fact, close to tears.

"Perhaps, Cherie, she can explain -" Pierre's long face was composed in a resigned smile.

"Oh, ma'am, I'd never done it, but *she* asked me herself. The wee dogs had got out, running to the lake they were, and she said, she said it herself, she said, 'Will you be a dear and go fetch them in?' so what was I to do, ma'am? I was that frightened." Pegeen dabbed at her reddened eyes with the corner of her apron. "Almost dark it was and them so wilfull as they might be lost. *She* said I must go -"

Not easily mollified, Marianne attacked from a new base. "Look at your apron! Would you serve *them* looking like a miner straight from the pits?" She turned to Pierre, tears starting in her eyes. "Look, only, how the abominable child has ruined her good clean uniform -"

"But, ma'am, I caught them, down by the lake they were, and I had to carry them in, the naughty wee things!" Pegeen clearly felt on stronger ground now. "That happy she was to have them safe, she took them from me her own self -" A small giggle interrupted the story. "And, ma'am, she's dirty as me, she is now!" The smile was pure triumph.

"Very well, mon petite, so it is done! No need to stay the whole night chattering - get a clean apron, wash up and make yourself helpful." Marianne strode from the room, nodding, "Bon soir, m'sieur," as she passed Charley in the doorway. Then she turned back. "All is well, no? M'sieur? The dinner was satisfactory?"

"It was great," Charley heard his strange hollow voice reply. "Thanks, everything's fine."

He started to follow her from the kitchen and almost ran into Pegeen, struggling into a fresh, white apron as she came through the door. She was still giggling a little. He caught her arm and stopped her beside him. "Sir?" she said, pulling away, looking up from under heavy, pale lashes.

"Oh," he said. "Sorry -" He dropped her arm. "Could I just ask you something - something about what happened before dinner?"

"If I can help you, it's that glad I am," she said.

"When you were catching the dogs," he said, "When you were out by the lake, did you see anyone there, you know, someone just walking?"

"Only the boat is all I saw," Pegeen said. "A right queer thing it was, how it was there one minute, and then, before me own eyes it was gone!"

CHAPTER TWENTY-ONE

The loft was deserted. Just as he thought, they weren't back from the day yet. Sean could feel the silence heavy around him. Every step he took seemed to echo that loud it could be heard in Dublin. The ancient boards creaked under him and he clung to the wall as he went up, trying to step where the wood was less worn, less likely to scream out as he put his weight on it. Passing the window, Sean stopped to look out over the lake. From here he could see the mole extending out into the dark water and he could almost see over the high wall dividing the carriage house from the main lodge. The sun slanted low over the lake, but already a heavy fog was blowing in from the sea; it would hide everything from his view before the coming of the night.

A bloody good thing it was, too, the fog. If her royal majesty chose to walk in this bright day, Ben and Liam would be hard put to surprise her, they would. He stood there a moment in the still emptiness. From the kitchen next door he could hear voices, excited, Gallic; Marianne marshaling her troops, chivvying them into perfection for the Queen's pleasure. He looked at his watch. There was a good hour before they'd be starting on their drinks; she'd plenty of time for her bloody walk. He wished he could see the back of Ussher House, watch for her to come out.

The sound of wheels on the gravel of the courtyard echoed through the empty building and he turned from the window, furtive, feeling eyes upon him from behind. No one was there; the doors of the Rover slammed and pieces of conversation floated through the white, solid air. He heard the heavy front door swing open; they were in the hall downstairs. Get to Kevin's room, he'd better, and bloody quick, too.

They'd met with Kevin the morning before. He'd come to the hut by himself; Bettina'd run out, he said, and left him to do it alone. Ben wanted to know where she'd gone. "We'd never should of let her in," he said. "Trust a woman and they screw you every time -"

"She had the cash," Kevin reminded him. He took a long swallow from the bottle on the table, "From the States. I didn't see you bloody having the thousand -" He looked around the room. "Where's Sheila?" he asked.

"She run -" Ben began.

Sean shoved Ben aside; he leaned close over Kevin. He

took hold of his collar and twisted the cloth tight in his fist. "It's nothing to you where my sister is," he hissed. "And if you want to be long in this lovely world you'll be minding your own business, then." It was wonderful to watch fear crawl up around the man and to see him, craven, shrink back in his chair. The hand that held the bottle was shaking to rattle the glass on the table.

"Bettina'll not be giving us trouble," Kevin whispered. "I promise you that." His eyes held Sean's, but the fear was cold to be seen in them.

They had emptied his pack and Ben carefully stuffed the three boxes into it. "Bloody heavy," he said, weighing it in his hand. "Think you, can you manage it?" Scorn was in his voice; he stood behind Kevin and buckled the straps, snugging the pack in place.

Kevin straightened his shoulders. "It's all right," he said. "I'll get it there -"

"I'll be at Ussher tonight," Sean had told him. "Keep an eye on it for you while you eat. We don't need it laying there by itself at all; no more we want little Miss Leary and her Yank friend wondering why you bloody never put your cameras down and rest your aching back -"

Kevin started to speak, then his mouth closed in a narrow line and he was very busy with the adjustment of his pack. It crossed Sean's mind that Kevin knew something he wasn't telling. Briefly, he wondered if it was worth making him tell. Probably not; it was vital to the mission that Kevin attract as little attention to himself as possible, and Sean felt sure he would have to alter Kevin's elegant facade to some degree trying to get it out of him.

231

Better leave it then, whatever it was; something about the Yank, maybe?

Sure, he'd found nothing more last night, for all he'd stayed in Kevin's room till the middle of the night, waiting on the blasted fool from dinner downstairs. Nervous, the man was, as a dog with a snake by the tail, afraid to hold it and afraid to put it down. Sean had a good look-see at it while Kevin was downstairs eating his fancy dinner and, after, he'd made Kevin show him; so simple it was, you'd never believe it could send this whole building and everyone in it to meet their Maker, and only at the touch of a wee button. The three boxes must hold enough to blow London to hell and back. Christ! the power he had with this in his hands!

This afternoon, he and Ben had met with Liam and Padric. The skiff was Liam's; he would meet them at five o'clock a half mile up the shore from Ussher. They would kill the motor several hundred yards off and row up to the far side of the mole where they could anchor out of sight until she came. Alone, she would be easily overpowered; tie her up, dump her in the boat and it was only a hundred yards to the hidden door under the rocks. Once she was in there, locked safe as in church, they'd wire Dugan in Belfast. Wait till it hit the bloody papers!

It had been just past six on Thursday when she came and she had walked all the way to the end with her two dogs running all about her. A long time she had stood there, watching the swirling mists and caring not a bit that rain began to drizzle from the low clouds; protected she was, with her mack turned up about her ears and her head covered in a scarf so even when the drizzle turned to a downpour, still she stood looking out over the water.

He thought about the three boxes of explosives and the thought made the blood pound in his head. Kill her! he'd said, and right he was, too . Now, with Wolfe gone, and Sheila, who was to stop him? Not Ben, not the weasel, Ben. Useful, he was, to get the boat, but in the end, a coward. He'd be no trouble at all, then, with fear to drive him, and his guts turned to water. And Kevin, he'd be down there eating, playing the fine Dublin gentleman, while, upstairs, the precious boxes would disappear and Sean with them. The pounding in his head was a steady roar, thunder filling his skull. This was when the thoughts flew in his head like a cave full of bats and anything, or everything, was possible.

He would go straightway to the boat-house and find them. They'd bloody damn well better agree when they saw what he had with him, or they would damn well be left there with her under the rock. Better, it would be, then, he alone, only to take credit for the final blow. "QUEEN DEAD IN BLAST! IRA LEADER, SEAN O'MALLEY -" Ah, it would be grand to see the papers. His face was hot and drops of sweat ran off it, but a chill ran down the bones of his back and his hands shook so that he put them in his pockets and leant against the wall, waiting, hearing the footsteps coming towards the door. He found his gun, and held it by the barrel. If the door opened and it wasn't Kevin he couldn't risk a shot; the butt of the pistol would drop the intruder, silence him until Kevin came.

"Hallo!" Kevin almost whispered, easing the door ever so gently open. "Are you here? I say, Sean -?"

"Shut the door, you bloody ass -" Sean hissed.

Carefully, Kevin undid the straps of his pack and lowered it onto the bed. "Jesus!" he said, "I'm glad to be shut of it. Sometimes I think I can feel the bloody thing getting ready to blast off -" He shrugged and stretched his neck and shoulders. "When do I leave it, for God's sake?" He peeled off the damp trousers and sweater; Sean's eyes were on the pack lying there on the bed. Why in sweet Jesus name didn't he hurry up? Fussing around with his clothes, wasting good time, he was. Ben and them could be alongside the mole now, waiting, ready; the blood pounded red behind his eyes and his mouth was dry with desire.

"You damn well take it as far as we tell you," he said. "And you bloody get yourself down to dinner, now, before they think about asking questions like."

Kevin stood by the door, defiant. "I'm taking a shower," he said. "You can do what you like - I never asked you to watch it, did I?" The door banged shut to shake the light bulb that hung from the ceiling. Bastard! Who the hell did he think he was, treating me like a bloody messenger boy? He imagined the door opening and Kevin would stand there outlined by the light from the hall and he would hold the gun in his hand and feel the trigger cold under his finger. When he pressed it Kevin's face would vanish in a blur of blood and scatter of brains and he would fall forward into the room and laughter would well up in Sean's throat.

Instead, he sat on the bed and held his head in his two shaking hands, holding it together before it exploded, keeping it from flying apart, bursting into a million bright pieces. He bloody well could wait.

At last Kevin was gone down and he could hear the others; doors opening and closing, water running, footsteps padding down the hall. He threw the bolt on the door; best to wait till they were all down there, eating and drinking, then down the back stairs and out into the sheltering dark. Ben would be waiting in the boat, the job done. Or not done. No matter now; blow up the whole bloody place if they hadn't got her.

He stood by the window, looking towards the lake. The blackness was thick with fog and mist; even the nearest lights, the ones in the courtyard, only showed as soft, glowing circles, and across the wall the darkness was opaque, impenetrable. The roaring in his head grew less and a pleasant quiet filled his mind; a power he'd never known was his, now. In his hands lay the future of his people, and for him, the glory and the honor -

He held the thing in his hands then and thought he could feel the pulse of it, straining to release its wild, unknowable destruction. He tucked it under his mack and started for the door. As his hand reached for the bolt he heard the footsteps. Someone was hurrying up from the room below. Then other steps running; whoever was by the door ran into the loo. Someone tried the door and called out, "Megan? You're missing the soup." It was the Yank. What the divil was he doing up here? He felt sweat run cold down his back and his hand gripped the gun until his knuckles showed white.

Then it was quiet in the hall until he heard Kevin's voice. Christ, they were standing there having a chat about the girl. The pounding in his head was a thousand hammers, now; he had to get out! Then Jamey's voice on the stairs - were they every blasted one of them going to stand outside there all the bloody night? An eternity passed and at last they were gone. Hunched over his precious box he ran down the back stairs, past the open kitchen door, and into the night.

The girl's eyes were round with wonder. "There it was, and the men in it, rowing off along the shore. I took me eyes from it a moment only and, sure, when I looked back it was gone, them and whatever it was they had in it -"

"Was it just the fog?" Charley asked. "You just lost it in the fog?"

"No," she whispered. "No. Close along the shore it was, by the rocks. One minute it was there and then it was just gone, under the rocks, like." Then he could feel the cold, slippery rocks and could see the girl, Megan, struggling beside him in the icy water there, while above them the two dogs howled and the man's curses rang out over the water. He remembered the tears of frustration, the treacherous hand-holds eluding his grasp and the bitter cold creeping through to his bones and numbing his hands. The wind had lashed the water into foamy waves there under the jutting rock and had buffeted the two children against the jagged stone. Then he had felt it, the smooth, mossy surface of the boards, and reaching blindly in the dark, he had found the heavy iron latch with the rusted lock hanging open from it. His hands were cut and bruised by the time he'd got it open; they had swum then into an open space where the water lapped more gently against thick pilings. Together, they had pulled themselves up onto a ledge above the pilings; they were on the dock inside a hidden boat house.

He remembered the terror of absolute dark, blackness so velvety it was a solid presence, more than the mere absence of light. It held them in its unforgiving grasp, and it was an effort simply to move. They had crawled on hands and knees, feeling around themselves, reaching out ahead for the rotting boards that held them. He felt that they were circling the edge of a cave built under the rock; they were in a prison, guarded by the gypsy and his dogs. Helpless, he leaned against the hard stones; he felt like crying. Megan shivered beside him, trembling with the cold. Then he had felt the opening in the wall. "Megan, there's a door! Feel it here -"

"It's Lady Dudley's secret!" Megan had whispered to him. Her teeth chattered with the cold, and her thin shoulders shook under the sodden sweater that clung to her. "There's a passage!" she said. "My Da has told me - but no-one ever knew where. For her luvver to come to her, it was." She had taken his arm in both her hands. "We'll find it," she said, "And be damned to the t-t-inkers and their b-b-loody dogs!"

He smiled, now, to remember the child laughing as she pulled him into the black hole, whispering to him the story of the bold gentleman who came across the water and found his lady waiting at the end of the lonely, dark passage. But the smile turned to a cold breath on him when he thought that she was there now, with the three men -

"Pegeen," he said. "How long since you saw it? Saw the

237

boat disappear?"

"A half hour since, sir - I took the wee muddy doggies to her majesty, straightway -" She covered her mouth with her hand and looked wide-eyed at him. "Took them to the lady, I mean, sir, the lady as brought them, you know -" Her face was crimson; her voice very small. She went on, "Then I was late and Mrs Anhouil had a right fit over it -" She giggled. "Half hour at least, sir."

"Thanks," he murmured. "You've been a great help -" He was half through the door while he spoke. The fog and the dark struck him like a force when he stepped into the courtyard. He ran back in, up the back stairs, fumbled in his bag for a flashlight and raced back down the stairs. Kevin and Jamey were still in the dining room. Before he could get to the door he heard Jamey's voice. "Find her, lad?"

He tried to sound reasonable when he spoke. "Just getting a light to go look by the lake - want to come?"

"Think I'll take a look about the road," Jamey said. "You do the lake and I'll do the road." He still didn't sound worried, not a little bit, just as though a daughter lost in the fog on a dreary, black night was an every day occurrence in his life.

The thin beam from the light hit the fog like a soft wall; a fuzzy circle of white traveled just ahead of him, showing him nothing. He ran, trying to remember the path, remember how to get around the end of the wall. It was one thing to work his way around it in broad daylight, to see where to step, how not to fall into the deep still water where the wall met the lake. Now, he felt his way like a blind man, stumbling and tripping as he ran. Branches caught at him, scratching his face and arms and once a

238

heavy limb struck him in the chest to knock the wind from him. The dank air was windless and, isolated by the fog, he felt alone in the stillness around him; he was the only person in the world. Thin and wild, the loon's crazy call floated through the blackness somewhere behind him. The damp air was cold in his lungs; he was breathless, as much with fear for her as from the effort of running over the rough track through the tangled trees. "The thing they had in the boat with them -" Pegeen had said. Megan!

At the wall he stopped, trying to see through the thick air that blunted the beam of light not two feet ahead of him. His foot slipped off the wet stones into the water and he had to throw himself against the wall to keep from falling in. The flashlight splashed when it hit the surface of the lake and he saw its light sinking through the water to settle on the rocky bottom. The water was as cold as he remembered it and deep; he plunged his arm in to the shoulder before he touched the still-burning light. When he stood up, the wet sweater clung to his arm like an icy embrace. But the light was still shining, waterproof as advertised!

By the time he had scrambled over the mole and splashed his way along the shore he was thoroughly soaked. Wet trees overhung the rocky ledges and much of the way he was splashing through shallow water. How far was the blasted thing? He couldn't see up over the bank to judge the distance; he glanced back towards the mole. At first he could barely make out where it was. Then the fog parted and he could see the shadowy shape of the old breakwater outlined against the lighter sky. And, bent over, a man ran along it, hurrying from the shore, half-way to the end of the mole. Then the fog closed down like a soft curtain; he

239

couldn't even see the shoreline beside him.

He stood still, listening. The water at his feet lapped gently, a little sighing sound, on the smooth, narrow shingle. Ahead, the sound changed and he knew he was almost at the ledge where the cliffy rocks plunged straight into deep water. He hung the flashlight from his belt and took off his shoes. He wrapped them in the sodden sweater and stuffed the miserable bundle into a crevice in the rock wall.

When the water closed over his head, surprisingly, it was less cold than the air had been on his wet body. He surfaced and swam parallel to the shore for a few yards. Reaching out in the dark he felt nothing but rough stone; he swam a few yards more and felt again. God, let me find it! He wished he was better at praying, had practiced more. Why should God help him, a perfect stranger for the last twenty years, why should he help him at all? But, God, listen, it's for Megan I'm asking You, not for me. Just let me find her, please!

It was clear to him that she would be there; the minute Pegeen told him of the vanishing boat he had known, known as surely as if he had seen her there, lying in the cold darkness, bound and helpless, alone. Of course he was a fool. He should have told Jamey, gotten him to come with him. Alone, he was helpless to see where the man had gone - to find the others, escape with them? Or come back after Megan?

Then his hand touched the slimy, mossy wood; solid and hard as iron, the ancient oak doors reverberated with the pounding of the gentle waves and the night was still but for the sound of the water against the unyielding wood. His hands, reaching for the latch, seemed to move of themselves. There it was, just where it had been then, but the lock that hung open in it was new, a heavy block of shiny steel run through the hasp, waiting to be locked.

He pushed up the latch; the door moved slowly through the resisting water. Forcing his way through, he felt for hand-holds along the side, trying to find the old pilings. "Megan!" he called. "Megan? Megan are you here? Oh, my love, are you here?"

CHAPTER TWENTY TWO

Inside, the darkness was a blanket, a suffocating presence.
He fought panic as he swam, feeling his way with one hand ahead
of him in the water. Twice he spoke her name and his voice
echoed in the watery hollowness under the rocks; it was the only
answer he got. Then his hand bumped against the slick surface of
a piling and above his head he felt the ancient planking of the
deck. He pulled himself up; his hands slipped on the mossy, slimy
wet wood and barnacles cut him where he gripped the pilings. At
last he sat, dripping, on the deck. "Megan?" he whispered and the
soft sound of the little waves answered him.

He took the flashlight from where it hung hooked to his

belt. He couldn't find the switch; his hands were shaking, with fear, he realized - fear that the light would show in truth what his mind had imagined. The beam of light slashed through the dark, bouncing from the rough walls and refracting through the still water. Unsteady, it moved around the space; he didn't know which dread was greater - that he wouldn't find her there, or that the light would show him her body, torn and bruised, lying on the deck. Slowly, he moved the ray of light along the surface of the deck beside him. Nothing. Across the dark water there were more pilings and another deck. He couldn't make out what lay there among the pieces of old rigging and the shell of a skiff, long rotted in disuse. He hooked the light back to his belt and slid into the water. Before he covered half the distance to the other side, with the beam of the light making crazy dances in the water as he swam, the sound of angry voices came unsteadily through the dark to him and he froze in the water.

Then the creak of an oar and the dull thud-bump of a boat against the oaken doors. He felt for the switch, desperate to cut the light off before the boat was through the doors. They could have seen it under the water already, glowing like some phosphorescent sea creature. Utter blackness surrounded him there in the water, then, and all sense of direction was gone from him. He heard the door swing open, slowly through the resisting water, and he dove, swimming, he hoped, back under the deck he had just left. When his hand scraped against a piling he reached up and found that he was in a space under the decking; there was about six inches between the surface of the water and the slimy, moss covered boards above.

Whoever it was in the skiff had ceased to argue. The only sound was the scraping of wood on wood, as the oars moved in their locks and the boat slid over the black water. His eyes were getting used to the dark and now he could see the paler black square of the open door and the shape of a large skiff, with three - or was it four - men in it. Then a light shot out from the boat to illuminate the opposite side of the boat-house. It probed along the wall, past the old, over-turned hull on the deck. It stopped and played slowly over an old tarpaulin lying crumpled by the edge of the deck.

"There she is." The harsh whisper from the boat echoed in the stillness under the rocks. Charley's spine stiffened and he clenched his teeth until they ached, trying to stop them from chattering. In the uncertain light, he could see two men get out of the boat and onto the deck. When they lifted the edge of the tarp, he almost cried out, "Megan!" She was tied, hands behind her back and tied to her bent legs. She was gagged and bound, and blood ran down over her eyes and soaked the scarf that covered her hair. The two men bent over her. He wanted to vomit.

The black-haired one roughly jerked the scarf from her head. She gave no sign of life. He pulled her face towards him and shined the light full on it. "Shit!" he yelled. "Who the f--- -?" He let her head fall, thudding back onto the deck. She didn't move, or try to cry out. God, she can't be dead, you can't let her be dead, God! Not now! He held onto the piling, gripping it until his hands were bleeding from the small, clinging sharpness of the barnacles and he didn't feel the hurt.

"You bloody fools!" the man shouted. "Look, you call this

her bleedin' majesty?" He nudged Megan towards the edge of the deck with his foot.

"Mother of God," whispered the other man on the deck. "Mother of God, you're right! It's a bloody girl -" The boat rocked when the other two jumped to the deck.

One of them spoke. Apology was in his voice, appeasement. "Ben told us it was her," he said. "The bloody fog - we couldn't see -" His voice was high-pitched and sounded to Charley, there in the cold, wet air, like the scream of bats flittering in their hollow caves.

The first man stood erect on the deck. He was tall, with shoulders built to fight; the others seemed to fear him. Then he threw his head back, and the sound from his throat filled the space and echoed from the water and from the ancient walls to make the hair rise on Charley's neck. It was the sound of an animal, some fierce and cruel animal, an animal that had learned to laugh, not the silly laugh of the hyena, but the laugh of a human, a human whose only pleasure is in the pain of others, and as he laughed, the others joined him until the cold, clammy space was loud with the sickness of the sound.

"Shut your bleedin' mouths!" The tall man's hand flashed out from him; the man nearest him fell to the deck. He struggled to his knees, and Charley saw that he was spitting teeth from his mouth. The laughter was over and the only sound, again, was the slow lapping of the water against the doors that moved back and forth, eery in the gentle waves. The man chuckled; satisfied, he seemed. "So, now we've no choice -" he said, low and deep in his throat. "We'll damn-all do what I wanted -"

"Blow it up, man!" one of the three whispered. "Blow them to hell, is it, Sean?"

"Right you, Paddy, the whole bloody damn lot -"

They were back in the skiff, now, and Charley willed them to go. One of them looked up on the deck to where Megan's body (?) lay close to the edge. "What'll we do with this one?" he asked. He gave her a little shove away from him. "Leave her?"

"Aye, leave her," Sean said. "She'll go nowhere, not now she won't -" The light was in the boat, and Charley could see it shining up on the face of the man, Sean. He was smiling. "Ta ta, love," he called out. "May you sleep the sleep of the angels!" And he was laughing as the boat slid past the doors and the insane echoes of his laughter were the last sounds Charley heard before the click of the heavy lock outside the door.

He shined the light full on her face; her skin was white as chalk and the blood, partly dry, looked black in the yellow light from his flash. She was alive. Her eyes were closed and he could see the pulse under the pale, transparent skin of her temple. "Oh, Megan," he whispered, "Oh, Megan, I love you-" He lifted her face to his and kissed her eyes. His hands found the sodden knots that held her gagged and he tore at them in a frenzy. The blood from his cut hands was fresh and red but he didn't see it, or feel the pain. When he finally got the knots loose her mouth fell open; she breathed in the cold, wet air with harsh, little gasps. He felt her body tense in his arms for a moment and he whispered her name.

247

Then he remembered the wires cutting into her wrists. He tried to turn her over; his foot grazed the flashlight, almost knocking it into the water. He lunged for it, leaning across Megan to reach it; without light he would be helpless to save her, here in the blackness of this hellish place. A little sound, a hurt cry, came from under him. He was hurting her, leaning across her bound body; she could feel his weight.

He fastened the light to his belt. It flopped about and didn't shine where he wanted it but, by its sporadic light, he was able to undo the wires and free Megan's hands and feet. Gentle, he held her then, straightened her cramped legs and laid her flat on the deck. She felt incredibly light in his arms; her white skin was colder than his, though the icy water still dripped from him and his wet tee-shirt clung like a thousand leeches to his back.

He lay beside her and held her to him, her body unresponsive; only the light breathing showed that she was alive. He sat up and held her in his arms; he rubbed her hands and kissed them and hot tears burned his cheeks. He tasted the salt on his tongue, the salt of his tears, and he remembered the taste of her tears when they lay in her bed in the morning and heard the first lark singing in the gray, early dawn. She was warm, then, and under the softness of her skin he had felt her strong body tensed with desire and she had laughed through her tears, because they were tears of joy for their happiness.

She had taken him by the hand and led him into her room out of the coldness of the early dawn. Softly she closed the door and he heard the bolt drop into place. Then she stood before him, shy, her eyes down and her hands at her sides. Her hair fell over her face and she threw it back with a defiant shake of her head. She looked up at him then and smiled, a child out of school. "I'm not good at this, you know," she whispered. "Sure, I've not tried it before - a man to my room, I mean." She bent her head again. "Sure, I don't know why I did it," she said, very small. "If you want back to your cell, you can go -"

Then she was in his arms and he felt her body (her warm, living body) pressed against him. They stood there, then, clinging to each other, drenched in love, while time stopped. At last she whispered, "There's the bed behind you, lad - we should be asleep this hour." And they fell laughing into it. It was too narrow and the mattress felt like corn husks. Under the white cotton shift her body was warm and her skin was smooth as silk. Her mouth was warm and soft and, as they kissed, she laughed again.

Desire made his throat go dry and he couldn't speak. "We should sleep," she whispered. "It's almost day." Then her mouth was on his again and their two bodies were one and the night was bright with unseen stars and all the longing in the world was over; for them the whole earth was new and it was theirs forever. Then the lark woke them and he kissed away her tears and held her, and it all started again.

In his arms, now, she lay cold and still and around them only the dank smell of ancient dirt and the chill of the under-earth and the gentle voice of the little waves.

> 'And then the wind came down from the North
> Chilling my Annabel Lee,
> Chilling and killing my Annabel Lee.'

He turned out the light; no need to waste it while they

weren't moving. When she woke up, they would have to find a way out. He had almost forgotten why they were here, or what he had to do. Those maniacs were on there way to blow up - what? Ussher? Who was it they wanted there? Had they got Kevin's little packet from him? "Megan," he whispered. "Megan, I love you. Wake up, love -"

Her arms tightened around him and she made a little sobbing noise. "Charley?" she whispered. "What is it, love?"

Her lips were swollen from the roughness of the gag, and she trembled with the cold, but their tears were warm, running together down their faces as they kissed. She pulled away from him. "It's dark, luv," she whispered. "Am I all right?"

"You're wonderful," he said. "I'll turn on my torch and you'll see -"

"I thought I'd gone blind, then," she said. "Mother of God, my head hurts!" He flicked the light on; she blinked and looked around her. "It's Lady Dudley's boat house!" she whispered. "Aye, we know all about that, don't we, lad?"

He was light-headed with relief. "I just sat here," he said, "And thought you would die." She laid her head on his shoulder and he held her. "I couldn't have lived, then, not without you."

She reached up and pulled his head down to her. "You'll not get rid of me that easy, lad," she said. "Just let's see if I can get up - Lord, they did a good job of it, tying me up like a wee pig to the market!" She got to her knees and stretched her back. Lithe, like a cat, she was. He helped her to her feet and saw the pain in her eyes. "I do believe they have broke my arm," she said. "Kicking me, they were -"

She held up her right arm, and he saw that the wrist was turned all wrong. "Oh, Megan, my poor Megan -" he breathed. "My love -"

"Tie it up," she said, "With a bit of wood next it. I'll live. Sure it's not the first bone I've had broke on me -"

While he splinted the bone he told her what he could of the men in the boat. "So we've got to get out," he said, "And see what they're up to."

"I know," said Megan, smug as a cat. "I know where they're going. You know why we aren't staying at Ussher itself? The bloody Queen is there - a secret, it is, but the lad told me. That's why all the help are staying in and that's who they're blowing up and we're in a bloody fix for stopping them, now, aren't we?" Her words came out all in a rush, breathless. He shined the light on her face; she was grinning.

The blood had dried on her face and her hair was matted with it. Good grief, he hadn't even looked at her head wounds! "Let's clean you up, love," he said, quiet, not to worry her. "You're a mess." He wet his handkerchief and washed the blood away. There was a nasty gash above her eye, and a big lump over her ear. She winced when he touched it, but smiled up at him. "They got me in a hard spot," she laughed. "My head. They've a bloody hard road to crack that -"

"Are you all right," he asked. "Your head?"

"Aye, it's nothing much," she smiled. "Just a thousand banshees screaming in it; pounding it with bloody hammers, too, they are." She shook her head to clear it and, above the smile, he saw her eyes go bright with pain.

"I'll find us a way out," he said, with far more confidence than he felt. He was certain the doors were locked; he'd heard the lock snap shut outside when they left. "Hold the light while I go for a little swim -"

The water looked blacker than ever and less inviting. She followed him with the ray of light until he reached the doors. Treading water, he paused and turned to look at her; she was very small, huddled there on the deck. Her hair was wet and she was getting a strikingly black eye under the jagged cut; she was the most beautiful woman on earth. "I'll give it a shove," he said. "And we'll soon be out. Can you swim? With your arm?" She nodded, a stiff little nod.

"Aye, I will," she whispered. "Just get it open, then -" Her jaw was firm; her teeth were clenched and she spoke between them but her voice shook and he was afraid for her. Maybe he was mistaken about the lock, maybe they could go right out into the lake. He reached up and gave a tentative shove. It moved a little; a small crack came between the doors. Just enough to tantalize him, make him think it would open. He heard the hasp slide a half inch, maybe, and then it stopped. Metal met metal and he knew the lock was in place. Small wonder Sean had so cheerfully left Megan there; dead or alive, she'd never get out.

He wondered how deep the water was here, and if the doors went all the way to the bottom. He kicked against them under water and felt the solid wood at least four feet down. Damn them! he'd have to dive and swim under. "I've got to dive under," he said. "I'll get help and come back."

Her face was white. The light in her hand cast an wild

252

glow upwards hiding her eyes in shadowed sockets. Her cheeks looked gaunt; only the smile was the same. "That you'll not," she said. "Think you I'd stay here and you gone outside having fun with those bloody bastards? Here, take the torch and have a look-see first." She held the light up in her hand. "Catch!" she said, and tossed it to him.

"OK," he said. "Here goes." .With the light in one hand he dived straight down alongside the door, feeling the unyielding wood beside him as he dove. He felt with his free hand for an edge. He shined the light on the boards and tried to see the bottom of them. His head began to feel light and he had to surface. The rush of oxygen to his lungs warmed his whole body for a moment and he shook the water from his eyes, looked for Megan. She sat with her legs in the water, ready to follow him. "It's too deep," he said. "Don't come. I've got to try again."

This time he went straight down as fast as he could. His hand, trailing down along the boards, came to an edge, buried in the muck of the bottom. He held the light in his teeth and felt with his other hand; maybe there were gaps, gaps big enough to swim through. Instead of a space under the wood, his hand touched something alive, something quick and smooth that flickered through his hand and was gone. He was forcing himself to stay down; his lungs cried for air and his body wanted to float up - then he felt it, something wrapping itself around his ankle, holding him there. With one hand, he took the light from his mouth and aimed its beam downward. A dozen gaping mouths were under him; the eel that was wrapped around his leg was slowly opening and closing its mouth, showing the complete circle of tiny, teeth, teeth that could sink into his flesh and could hold there until long after the head had been separated from its body.

There must have been a dozen of them, a whole nest of eels, angry at the interruption of their sleep. The muck on the bottom was stirred up by their twisting and turning; the water was clouded, now, and he could barely see them. The one on his leg was wrapped around his knee, it's head still probing, looking for a place to sink its mouthful of small, white teeth. Then the head darted upward; almost involuntarily his arm moved, reacting to its lightening strike. He shoved the flashlight into the gaping hole of its mouth. Startled, it relaxed its hold on his leg. He shot to the surface, his lungs crying out for air, his body shuddering with revulsion. He nearly choked on his own vomit as he gasped for air.

"Charley!" The sound of her voice oriented him in the darkness and he struggled, coughing and retching, to swim towards it. She reached down and he felt her thin, strong hand on his arm. She pulled him out of the water and he sat beside her, weak with the effort of breathing, his whole body still shaking.

"I'm - s-sorry, love." He choked out the words. "I can't - do it. I c-can't get us out."

"Just rest here a minute," she whispered. "Tell me."

"I've lost the light -" She held his head against her and he told her about the eels. "So there it is, crammed down his throat," he said.

The sound of her laughter echoed through the hollow space and then she was in his arms and the cold and the dark and the horror were gone and her kiss was warm on his lips. The waves lapped gentle outside their prison doors and from far off the loon called out his lonely answer in the night.

CHAPTER TWENTY THREE

Harry stared at the phone, his blue eyes clouded behind the thick glasses. He'd just hung up from talking with Gene. It was after nine and the only other light in the building was in Mossiter's office. He wondered if the Old Man ever slept.

"I gave him two hours," Gene had said. "Then I tried to raise him from here. Nothing. Dead silence. I don't like it."

"Where was he tonight?" Harry asked. "Still at Ussher?"

"Supposed to be. Supposed to be hound-dogging all the way to Oughterard. Keeping quiet - the carefree American, the brain-dead Yank."

"What do you get from Bill?"

"He was with him at Carna. They saw the landing, waited

all night and never picked up the transfer -"

"Bill heard from him since?"

"Nope. But last night he told me himself he knew who his pigeon was and he had the stuff with him. Charley said he could keep an eye on him." There was a pause on the line. "You knew the incident on the mountain?"

"Tell me -" A chill wind blew across the back of Harry's neck. Incident?

"He got crowded off the trail, had a bad fall over a cliff. Lots of apologies from the guy that did it. Said it was an accident. Could have been killed. Just one more thing I don't like. We've put this man into a lot of problems out there -" Gene's voice trailed off into a quiet growl. "I think there's something else going on -"

"Like what?" Harry leaned forward, staring at the blinking light on the phone; it was a recorded conversation. "What else -?"

"Bill's been out there a while," Gene said. "Knows the locals - who's who, who's on first. He's been seeing unknowns wandering on the loose near Ussher - could be relatives, oh God, do they have relatives! of an old girl he's had his eye on a while, does wash for them at Ussher. Just a guess, but if he's got mixed up with something else I wish we knew about it."

When an agent loses contact there are very few good answers. Harry didn't want to hear any of the more likely ones. Maybe Mossiter would hold his hand if he went in and spilled it to him, went in and told him they'd lost track of Charley out there in the cold. He took off his glasses and began cleaning them, a sure method of inducing productive thought. Where in hell *was*

Charley? Glasses in place again he lingered by his desk. A local tabloid lay there, a small headline jumping at him from the bottom of the front page. "FISHING IN CONNEMARA" it said.

He held it close to his short-sighted eyes to read it. 'The Duke of Edinborough is on holiday in Ireland, taking in two weeks of salmon fishing alone at a secluded resort in Connemara. The Duke is an enthusiastic sportsman ---' What was there about this bit of information that set him thinking? Of course it didn't say *what* secluded salmon fishing lodge he was staying at and it could just be a hunch. Of course it was just a hunch, and a mere coincidence that there had been no public appearance of the Queen for the last week. Suppose our friends to the north are having the same idea, he thought, and suppose they have sent some people down to check the fishing party out. Suppose these people are relatives or friends of the washerwoman of Ussher -?

His chubby body moved with surprising speed down the hall. He opened the door to Mossiter's room almost before he knocked. "Come in, lad," the Old Man said. "You're here late -"

"We've lost Charley," Harry said.   "I just talked with Gene."   The craggy brows shot up, questioning.

"When?"

"He didn't report tonight. Dead silence on his end." Harry waited, listening to the wheels turning in Mossiter's head, turning briskly, probing for answers, reasons why an agent on a fairly routine seek-and-follow could disappear overnight.

"Is Bill with him?"

"Not any more. Once he found the quarry he dropped out of Bill's territory. He just reported to Gene." The Old Man waited, listening between the lines. "Last night he was on schedule, the carrier identified and under surveillance. He lucked out there. Just the four of them staying at Ussher - the guide and his daughter, Charley and the carrier." Then he told Mossiter about Bill's people-watch. "He thinks there's more going on there," he said. "Strange northern types hanging around -"

"Tell me," Mossiter said. "I know you when you smell something."

The smile was warm and comforting. Nothing was all bad when the Old Man put his mind to it. "I may be wrong, there is that slight chance -"

"Not often," the Old Man interrupted. "Go on."

"I think the good Queen Bess is there and I think our friends know it." He showed him the paper. "Her appearances have been canceled for last week and this," he said.

Mossiter slammed the paper down on his desk. He picked up the phone and spoke rapidly into it. "Get me M15," he said. "Now."

The skiff pulled away from shore into the open water. Under the cover of the fog it could go straight across the water, around the end of the mole and be beached under the trees behind the lodge. The oars made only the faintest sound as they pushed through the water. Liam and his boat were as one, the oars an extension of his arms. The water had been his life and his livelihood; he and the skiff were always for hire. But never for a thing like this, he thought. Mother of God, I'd never of left that poor lass in there to die! One thing it was to carry off the Queen, to keep her safe and hid until bloody England was brought to her knees, and quite another to kill a girl they never even knew, by mistake, like, and then that madman to laugh in the face of her dying!

He wished to heaven he was out of it. Served Padric bloody right to lose his teeth; it was him got us into this. He bent his back to the oars and the boat sped around the point. The wind was rising now and soon the fog would clear. "Get along the shore, now! Get a f---ing move on you -" Sean's voice was a harsh whisper above the soughing of the wind. "We've not to be out here all the night." He leaned close to Liam's shoulder. "Under the trees, man and be quick if you know what's good for you."

No need to threaten him, there wasn't, now. He'd no more liking than the next man to be caught out here mucking about with their hands full of the bloody plastic - no, it was something new, they said, to blow up whole blocks with, it was. And they had it here in his skiff!

The boat nosed into shore, brushing under the wet leaves of an ash tree hanging low over the water. Paddy jumped ashore and pulled them up on the shingle. Now the man, Sean, was out and Ben with him. "Liam!" Sean hissed, "Get over here with you. Listen up, now -"

The four men huddled close under the trees and Sean gave them their orders. Ben would show them the way to the underground wine cellars. He'd been there once or twice when the fishing was out of season and he'd needed the work. Annie had got him a job delivering the stuff from the green grocer; she'd showed him the way to store it in the cool rooms under the kitchen. When they got there, they would leave one block of the explosive, set the detonator and then back to the boat. A good few hundred yards off-shore Sean would press the little black button and then -

"Aye," said Ben. "There's a door down at the back." He turned to Sean. "You can find it your own self," he volunteered. "No need we all come."

Liam agreed wholeheartedly. Let Sean take the bloody risks; it was his idea. "Better not all of us across the lawn," he said. "Just you, one man alone -"

"Shut your yellow face!" Sean snarled. "It's all of us go, all of us that are men -" he spat the words out in Liam's face. Padric was by his side.

"Best we go, Liam, and have done with it." His voice was quiet and had the effect of calming them all.

Ben was looking towards the back of the Ussher. Lights blazed from the windows. The dining room was still lit and they could see the party around the table. Elegant, they were, the candlelight flashing from the ladies' jewels, even, and the men all dressed in black and white. Here, at the Ussher! Over an hour since sunset; it was close to ten o'clock.

In the kitchen there were four people. Pierre and Marianne each occupied at the counter and the two serving girls listening near the door to the dining room, ready to scurry out and clear off when they were called. Sean joined Ben, studying the two groups through the lighted windows. He consulted Ben.

"Wait till they leave the dining room, eh? Have the girls busy cleaning up and them on their way to have their bloody drinks - upstairs to pee and pick their teeth -" He laughed. "For the last time, eh? For the last time!"

They sat down to wait, then, by the edge of the lawn where the trees overhung the grass. Liam looked through the windows as he sat, shivering, there on the damp ground. Lovely, it looked inside. Could these be the enemy? Holy Jesus! he was looking at the Queen herself. A good woman, she looked, somebody's Mum, passing the dessert plates around. Smiling. And in fifteen minutes, dead. Blown to bits. He'd give anything he had to be out of this.

He cramped the wheel into a tight curve; the tires squealed as he shot through the gate into the cobbled courtyard. The Rover skidded to a sudden stop by the carriage house door. Jamey rushed through the lounge, irrationally irritated to see Kevin lounging by the fire, smoking and sipping a dark brandy. He went straight through to the kitchen where Pegeen and her sister were still washing up. "Have they come back, then?" he asked her.

"Miss Megan, is it, you want?"

"Megan, Charley, both of them, lass. Have they come back?"

"Sure, he went through here like the wind itself," she said. "That excited he was." She looked at him with wide, green eyes. "What's to worry, sir? Here at Ussher there's no harm to come, now, is there?"

"Like as not you're right there, lass, and the Lord knows my Megan does as she pleases with herself." He smiled down at the girl.

"He's a luvly man," she whispered. "Having a walk-about by the lake, they may be -" She looked at her hands and her face went scarlet. "If you take my meaning, sir -" Jamey took her chin in his hand and turned her face up to look at him.

"Aye, he is a bonny lad, Pegeen," he chuckled, "And you may be sure my girl has seen it. Did he look like a man in love, or like a man afraid, then, when he ran through your kitchen? Tell me that, lass," he said, "And I'll give you a kiss for your troubles."

She ducked away, smiling. Then her face went serious, and the color left her cheeks. "Afraid," she whispered. "He was feared for her, he was."

"How long, then, since he ran through here, afraid?"

"La, I can't tell. Mary and I was that busy -"

Kevin looked up when he entered the room. "D'you find her?" he asked, casual, unperturbed. "Or him?" What was there about the lad that raised the hackles in his neck, Jamey wondered. He had spent two days convincing himself that the crash on the trail was really a mistake; murder attempts he had no need of on his ride, to be sure. Yet he wondered. Something there was about Kevin that wasn't true, something in his voice, it was, that didn't make sense.

"Nay," he said. "They've gone off together, it seems. It's

no fun, lad, being the father of a girl so luvly. You spend your nights wondering what they're up to and you look at every man as though he will take her from you without a by-your-leave. Lord, I wish the girl would marry and have a mickle of babies to keep her busy -" He sighed and sat opposite Kevin by the fire. He put his boots on the hearth rail and lit his pipe. He drew deeply on it and exhaled slowly; the smoke rose in a tiny cloud above his head. He leaned back, relaxed. No, he wasn't relaxed. A little mouse at the back of his head kept nibbling away at him.

However mad in love she might be, his lass never was one to miss a meal. To park the lorry only, she said; walk to the lake, he said. Three hours gone she was, three hours since he'd seen her. Blast the girl! Where had she got to?

"It's the only way left," she said. "Lady Dudley's tunnel."

"If we can find it," he said, "And if it goes anywhere."

"We were babies before," she whispered. "Now we won't be afraid." At least you won't, she thought. And somehow I'll get through it, too, even shut in under the earth where my heart turns to water and the terror in me becomes a scream caught in my throat, aching and unscreamed. Even thinking of it, the dark around her seemed heavy and the air too thick to breathe. Holy Mary, go with me, she prayed, take me by the hand and lead me!

She hadn't always been like this and she thought it a shameful weakness to fear it so. It came to her in dreams, even, and she would wake in a clammy sweat, crying and gasping for air. It was a mercy she had been knocked silly before they gagged her and wrapped her helpless in the tarp; she'd have lost her bloody mind in there, awake. In the dream, she was always back there, her face pressed into the mud and the weight of the horse on her back and her breath dying inside her.

She had been sixteen, and in America by herself, with Galway Laddie on the show circuit. Jamey had arranged for her to stay in Virginia, at Berryville, with friends, people who had bought two ponies from him the year before. He was hoping to sell Laddie in America as well, and had trusted her to make a good sale for him. She'd taken Champion at Upperville and had two good offers for the little stallion; Jamey was proud of her. For a treat, she was staying till opening meet of the hunt and her hosts had given her a big five-year-old thoroughbred gelding to take to the field.

The night before the meet a drenching rain fell from dark to dawn, turning the footing to muck, slippery and deep. But the day was clear and as the sun rose they started off across country to the meet. She never got there at all. A four board fence followed the edge of a ravine beside them. "We can get there in five minutes if you want to try the fence," her host had said. It looked like nothing for a big hunter to take. She rode him at it, laughing, flying over the ground.

She didn't ever see what made him lose his footing; he almost fell, then scrambled to his feet and threw his heart at the fence. Both forelegs hooked the top board and he somersaulted into the ravine. She felt his weight on her then, unmoving, dead weight and she lay there under him, the breath blown from her lungs and her face pushed into the muck at the edge of the stream.

266

She heard, dimly, the man's voice as he yelled at the animal to get up, until he realized its neck was broken and it was dead.

She was still conscious when he began to try to move the thousand pound creature from on top of her. She was able to think it was a good job the ground was soft; she was being pressed into it and it saved her from a broken back. Her chest ached from the effort to breathe and she began to pass in and out of a black terror where lights flashed pain and thunder was in her ears. And then fear had hold of her and she wanted to scream; she knew she was dying. Then it was only black and she was alone in nothingness.

Now she was holding Charley's hand in hers, squeezing hard enough to break the bones. "What is it, love? Are you OK?" he asked, close beside her. She threw her arms about him and clung to him a moment.

"I'll be all right," she whispered. "Just don't leave me alone there, promise you won't." She bit her lip. Beside his ear she spoke almost without a sound. "I don't like being closed in that much," she said. "Not much at all -"

He held her to him. She would be all right.

The unrelenting darkness began to seem normal. He helped her crawl along the deck to the back of the boat-house. "D'you remember where we found it?" he asked.

"You found it," she said, "By mistake."

He followed the wall with his hand, sliding over wet and slippery things; things he'd rather not identify. She was ahead of

267

him. "Don't move without feeling ahead to make sure there's something there," he said.

"Not to worry," she laughed. "We might as well be blind. How *do* they manage? Blind folk, I mean."

"They have dogs," he said. He wanted to keep her talking. The tunnel might be very long and it could be hell for her if she really had a problem with it. Talk about anything, keep her from thinking.

"Speaking of -" she said, "We had dogs enough last time we were here, eh?"

"We were babies," he said, "Remember, we aren't scared now -"

Then his hand felt it; the slimy stones gave way to smooth boards beside him and, as he ran his hand over it, the door swung inward. A cold breath drifted out over them. "We're here," he said. "Follow me."

"Give me a kiss, luv," she whispered, "And I'll follow you forever."

He took her in his arms and held her. He stroked her hair and felt her go all soft against him. "I love you," she said. "Let's go -" Something struck him on the arm, then another and another, flying from the tunnel. The air was thick with bats, their silent wings fluttering and their thin, wild cries filling the air. Megan screamed once, then hid her head on his shoulder. They flitted about, unseen, an invisible, yet palpable presence; the space seemed solid with their bodies. Then, the dark seemed unbearable to him; his eyes yearned for light, for the sight of anything. A roomful of bats unseen was more horrible by far than their visible presence would be. His flesh crawled and he felt Megan shudder in his arms.

At last the fluttering ceased and only a few cries pierced the dark. "They've gone back to sleep," he whispered. "Come with me love -"

"Hurry," she said. "We can beat the bloody fools if we hurry." He crawled through the low door into the new darkness. There was no sound in the tunnel, just Megan's soft breathing close behind him.

CHAPTER TWENTY FOUR

"Going to bed soon?" Kevin asked. He had been standing, his back to the fire, for the last five minutes. Now he moved towards the door, slowly, and in some pain, Jamey thought. He wondered why the man continued on the ride, now his American bird had deserted him. It was for her he said he was going; the saints knew he was no rider himself. He complained bitterly, hourly, as they rode - it was too cold, the horse tried to bump him off on a tree, his saddle was an instrument of torture. Now, five days into the ride he still walked as though he had a blackthorn bush up his britches. Something was wrong with the whole

271

picture.

From Dublin, he said he was, and he spoke like a Dubliner; you could tell them a mile off here in the West. Yet something else was in his voice; Jamey had tried all week to place it. A word here and there, a lift of the voice - had the man come from Belfast? Was there need to hide it, then? Jamey watched the smoke from his pipe curl up to the ceiling where the smoke of many turf fires had darkened the plaster between the beams far above their heads. He wished the lad would leave; he might take another look for his girl.

"Not yet, just," he said. "Don't bother yourself about me, now. It's a good night's sleep you need and a hot shower."

"Right, you," Kevin said. He slouched into the hall; he went up the stairs as one climbing a steep face of the Alps. Jamey could feel no pity in his heart. He plain didn't like the man. Small wonder the girl left him.

That was another thing, the girl disappearing like that. Got a lift along the road, Kevin told them. Sure, there *were* cars of tourists now and again down the road, and delivery vans and lorries, but Jamey knew this small world of Connemara and every cottage along the way. Funny a girl like her could go unnoticed, vanishing just like that and no one to see it. He'd asked a good few places about her and not even Mrs. Connery at the pub had heard of an American girl hitching rides, not to Oughterard nor back to Clifden, nowhere along the way.

It made him no easier about Megan, thinking like this. He leaned down to tap his pipe out on the hearth. Couldn't hurt to take another look down the road.

Kevin clattered back down the stairs and charged into the room "Is this the way you run your bloody ride?" he yelled. "You're responsible, you are! Someone's been in my room - they've taken my camera!" He was brandishing an open backpack in one hand, and empty it was, to be sure. His face was white with anger; the lad was in a right fidget, now, and ready to have Jamey's head for it.

"You're sure that's where you left it?" he asked. "Could be it fell out in the Rover. We can have a look -"

"You goddam well know that's where I kept it and if your people are sneaking around stealing -" He was almost incoherent; his voice was high and trembling. More afraid than mad, Jamey thought. There were blotches of red on his white face and a twitching muscle beside his nose drew the corner of his mouth up in a feeble sneer. He flung the pack on the floor. "You put us up in a lousy, bleeding barn, for Christ sake, where anyone can walk in your room -" Words failed him again; he stood there breathing like a mired ox, his nostrils dilating and his eyes burning red. The man has gone off his head, Jamey thought, the bloody man is mad. But why afraid? Feared of losing his camera? Not too likely, eh?

"Well," he said, smiling, "We've both lost something, then. You, your camera and me, my daughter. The lass has run off somewhere -"

Kevin whirled to face him, eyes wide with triumph. "She's done it! The bloody little bitch has got it!" He grabbed Jamey by the arm and held him with fingers like talons, strong, skinny talons. "You know where she is, damn you! I want her here, I'll bloody have her up for this -"

Jamey shook him off and held his arm in a grasp of iron, held him at arms length, where he squirmed and twisted to be free, like a hooked fish out of water. "Best watch what you say about my girl," he said. His voice was quiet and low; there was no mistaking his meaning. "If you've lost it for sure, we'll ring up the authorities, eh?"

Kevin's struggling stopped; he went limp where he stood. "P'raps you're right," he murmured. "Could be I've just lost it myself." A tortured smile showed on his face. "I'll have another look-about in my room, then -"

Jamey let him loose. "There's a good lad," he said. "Shall I come with you, now?"

"No. No, please don't. I'm quite all right - I'll just go up and look again." He turned and started for the stairs, walking with a curious hurried lope. Jamey went to the door and looked out on the dark courtyard. He turned his head, then, just in time to see Kevin disappear, not up the stairs, but through the door to the kitchen.

The serving girls were still washing up when he went through. Pegeen smiled at him, a shy, wordless smile, but the other never looked up. He felt the sweat going cold down his back; it was always like this, always had been, ever since he could remember. Something always went wrong and they always blamed him. It was Sean supposed to guard it, not him. But they'd make it his fault somehow, they would. Now his nose was running, too, and he wiped the back of his hand across his face.

He wasn't crying; it was just his nose. The air struck him cold when he went out the back, but the blessed dark wrapped him round and hid him.

He'd used to run out of the house whenever it happened. He couldn't remember his Dad, but his Mum was always after him; she'd never let him alone. He dreaded waking each morning, dreaded the cold wetness of the bed beneath him and dreaded most of all the sound of her voice when she found him shivering there in the shameful stinking damp of his sheets. "Filthy brat!" she'd bellow, as she came through the door. She was a huge woman, not fat, but built like a man, and strong as one, too. He often thought small wonder his Da had run off and left them; he must have feared her, too.

He would try and hide in the closet, then, in the shelter of the dark, but she would find him and pull him out. She'd put him face down on his bed, the wet, stinking bed, and beat him, then, beat him till the blood ran red onto the sheets. Then he would run, bawling, from the house and hide in the cool dark of the woodshed - it was always his fault, always.

Now he ran stiffly across the lawn towards the lake; blind panic drove him. He stumbled into the thicket. He'd missed the path. The path where Bettina was! Was she still covered over, or had she begun to rot and fester and come up through the earth? Is that what bodies did? She would, if she could, the bleeding bitch! He came to the wall between him and the Ussher and he was around the end of it, through the shallow water before he realized where he was going. Going to find Bettina, he was, and cover her over good. See what she looked like now, the whore.

Then he saw them under the trees. They'd heard him and were laying wait. A twig snapped behind him. Before he could turn, an arm like a band of steel was around his neck and a calloused hand covered his mouth. He felt the hot pee run down his leg and hot tears were running down his cheeks He wanted his Mum.

Liam was sitting far back under the tree, where the dull light of the night sky was blacked out. He wanted to go back to the boat, away from Sean and the black box that lay on the ground; innocent now, it was, but carrying death for who knew how many people. The light still shone from the open windows of Ussher, and glasses tinkled and laughter drifted out into the night. And dead they all were, every one of them, not her only, but everyone in that house, Marianne, Pierre, the girls - everyone. He heard the footsteps coming through the brush; they all listened, then Sean began snaking his way along the ground, hid under the trees, stalking like a panther, he went.

There was a dull sound, a scuffle on the ground, and then Sean signaled them to come. He held a man, choking him, and the man was sobbing. "Guess who?" Sean whispered. "Guess who was out here for a bit of a look." He turned the man's face to the open sky for them to see.

"Kevin." Ben said. "What do we do -?"

"I'll do it," Sean hissed. "Leave him for me -"

Liam moved forward. "What -?" he began. He stopped when Ben's elbow slammed into his gut. So he stood with the other two while Sean dragged the whimpering Kevin into the wood. The night was still and the sound of steel crushing bone came clear to them through the quiet air, and the gentle splash of a body rolling into the black waters of the lake. "We've no need of him," Sean said. He was tucking the forty-five back into his belt. His teeth gleamed white; Liam saw that he was smiling.

"Gene is going over to meet Bill," Harry said. "I've just talked to him -" He was back in Mossiter's office; the Old Man was demolishing a thick roast beef sandwich, washed down with a neat Scotch. It was 10:30. "They're going to have a look around Ussher," he said.

"M15 are curious," Mossiter said. "Have some?" He gestured towards the plate of sandwiches. His hand was bony and gnarled, the hand of an old man; it didn't match the sharp blue eyes that looked steadily from under wild, untrimmed brows. The old eagle was ready for the night if he had to stay there. Harry pounced, a starving man, on the food.

"Oh, thanks," he said, munching happily. "Are they sending someone?"

"Someone's already there, has been from the beginning. It seems you knew what you were talking about. The old girl really is there -" He looked pleased with himself. "They've laid on heavy duty all along. Feel better?"

"If you do," Harry said. "I do."

"Tell me what you heard from Gene -" Mossiter stared into his glass where the pale liquid glowed under the light from a

277

single lamp on his desk. "Well, he'd been in touch with Bill again - still nothing from Charley, by the way - and Bill had a problem." He took another bite of sandwich. "The thing is," he went on, "Bill was watching this group, the new ones, and they were making contact with two of them on the ride. He didn't know if Charley was onto that."

"Didn't he tell him?"

"Oh, he told him what he thought - told him to keep an eye open -" He paused. "But that wasn't all. The two on the ride, their friends, I guess, one of them is missing."

"How missing?" Mossiter said.

"Don't know. Gone. The day before yesterday."

"Who was he?"

"That's just it. Not him. Her. The girl from Boston, the one we tagged at the Embassy, the one getting the big dollars from Boston. Remember her? Bill heard it in the pub in Oughterard. Some of the ride people were in there night before last, talking about it."

Mossiter sat back in his chair. He spread the fingers of his two hands and pressed them together. He studied his hands, thinking. "You feel like a trip, Harry? Want to go to Connemara?"

"When?"

"How about, say, in five minutes. Find Charley. That's all." He held his glass up like a toast. "Good hunting, lad," he said. "And be careful." For once, the Old Man wasn't smiling.

Inside the tunnel, Charley tried to stand up. He was surprised to find that he could. The lover had done a good job with his tunnel and he prayed that it went on as it had begun. The cold air smelled of ancient earth and wood, but it felt clean and dry if you compared it to the boat house. He took Megan's hand. "Hang on to me," he said, and his voice echoed through the hollow chamber, whispering back to them -"on to me, on to me, to me, me" it said.   "Hey, we can stand up," Megan said. Her voice was firm, but he felt the coldness of her hand. It *was* awful here; the darkness made the closeness feel like suffocation. He thought it was like a mine shaft and then he remembered, from fourth grade, the story of the miner and the canary, and he thought he'd better not mention it to Megan. It had made him sad when he was eight years old, to think of all the poor canaries dying there underground to warn the miners and save their lives; now he wished he had one. *Was* there enough air for them in here?

The same thought had occurred to Megan. "I guess if the luver could get by on the air in here, so can we," she said.   In the dark, Charley nodded assent. "Right," he said. "Let's go -"

"Of course, the luver died," she whispered, "But maybe it wasn't here."

"Stabbed by her jealous husband -" Charley said.   He moved along, keeping against one wall. The stones of the wall were rough and wet, and every few feet a timber lay against them, supporting beams that crossed the ceiling. It was shored up like a mine shaft. The floor seemed fairly level; it might have been paved with brick or stone. Except for the aching void of the dark, it wasn't bad going.

Once he bumped his head on a beam lower than the others; it seemed firm enough, firm enough to hurt, in any event. Then he had to inch his way over a great pile of rubble that reached almost to the ceiling. He helped Megan over it. "This must be where we stopped that time," he whispered. Her hand in his was trembling. "Are you ok?" he said.

"Ok?" Megan's voice was small and sounded far off though she still held his hand and leaned against his shoulder. Their ears began to play tricks on them, then, deep in the middle of the earth.

"It sounds like water dripping," she said.

He stopped to listen, and he heard it. It was no trick. He could hear a definite "Plonk. Plonk. Plonk-plonk" "It can't be," he said, "We're ages away from the lake now." He went on a little further, still clinging to the wall on his right. Then his shoulder was grazing the rock on his left. It was getting narrower. And definitely wetter. His feet were in water, now, and he realized he was bent over. He had to be; the timbers couldn't be more than five feet above the floor.

Megan splashed along behind him. She was holding onto his belt, now; he needed both hands to feel his way. They were crawling over timbers lying at all angles on the floor and the water was over his knees. The sound of water was a steady gurgle; it was a running stream around their legs. There was a pull on his belt and a soft cry from Megan. "Charley, I can't -" she said. "I've got to get out, Charley - I c-c-can't -" She clung to him, her rigid body shaking, and she held herself against him, trembling, clinging to save her life.

So he held her close and stroked her hair.   "My own love," he whispered.   "My poor love -" He kissed her on the mouth and the trembling stopped. She laid her head on his shoulder.

"I'm sorry," she whispered. They were kneeling in water two feet deep, he judged; the roof beams were right over their heads.

"We must be almost there," he said, with more confidence than he felt. "It isn't more than two hundred yards -"

"It only seems like two hundred miles," she said. "Let's go - getting there is half the fun, like the adverts say." He could barely detect the quaver in her voice. "Hurry up, slowpoke - sure we're missing dinner." He loved her more than his life.

He gauged the height of the tunnel to be about four feet now. They were both soaked from crawling along in the icy stream and fear followed them like a dreadful beast through the darkness.   The timbers were all tangled now, like giant matchsticks and he had to work his way through them. Once he moved one and the rocks above them groaned and grumbled. He held his breath, afraid to move. A few pebbles splashed into the water beside him, then silence, with only the steady sound of the running stream.

Time had lost its meaning, only the cruel space mattered. Only to go forward - there was no going back - and find a hidden door, a way out. It seemed they had been always here; the real world was lost to them forever. "Megan?" he said, "Forgive me. No matter what happens, forgive me. I love you."

"I know," she said, small and low beside him. "I know -"

CHAPTER TWENTY FIVE

At last the light in the lounge was turned out; a flickering glow from the dying hearth-fire still shone from the windows. Upstairs lights came on and curtains were drawn. The kitchen had long been dark; the great house itself was quiet and everyone in it at peace. The little frogs chorused loudly from the shore and a nightingale filled the air with its elegant song. Under the trees the men waited for Sean to make his move. Even Ben held his silence; Padric shifted his weight nervously, standing by the yew tree a little distance off.

Liam crouched beside him. He wanted to talk, to suggest his plan to Paddy. They never meant to get into a bloody murder this night, not him and not Paddy. They were between Sean and the boat; they could edge further off until they were out of sight in the wood and then run for it. But if he caught them -

Paddy touched his shoulder. "Liam," he whispered, barely to be heard. "Liam, lad, we can run -" Liam got to his feet. No part of this they wanted. As one man they began to back off under the trees into the deep thicket. No word was needed between the two of them. They could see the burning end of Ben's cigarette where he stood with Sean on the edge of the grass. And then, of a sudden, Ben was standing alone; they couldn't see Sean anywhere at all. Liam broke into a run with Padric close behind him. They crashed through the thicket and be damned to the noise. He was almost to the shore when he heard it; a startled yelp that ended in a wet, bubbly sound, not human and not animal, a sound that raised the hair on his neck and made the gorge rise in his throat.

An arm was around his neck, then, and Sean's voice in his ear. "Forget it," the voice snarled. "Ye're f---ing staying here unless you want the same -" Sean slammed him against a tree and held him pinned there with a knife at his gut. His face was inches away and he was smiling, that fox's smile he had with him, and he whispered harshly, his breath hot on Liam's face. "No one runs out on this, not now. Ye're with us all the way or you stay here like him -" He kicked something on the ground. It was Paddy, with the hot blood still spurting from his neck. Even in the dark it showed black and Liam retched as he felt it warm against his leg.

"I'll come," he said, "I'll do it -" He walked ahead of Sean to where Ben waited. This is not me, he told himself. It is another man, not Liam O'Daugherty. Liam is dead, who was so brave not five minutes since. He will never live again, only this shell of him that I am. The last light still shone from the third floor; he saw it through a blur of tears.

Ben led them across the grass then; one at a time they went, each man waiting till the last one was out of sight. The steps went down a well behind the house; a door opened into a brick floored hallway. "Just here," Ben said. "The wine cellar first and then the storeroom." They followed him to the end of the hall, ducking under the low beams as they went. A door let them into an open room where shelves stocked with jars and bottles covered every wall. Bins of vegetables stood on a table in the middle of the room. A circle of wooden boards, perhaps the cover of a well, was set into the floor in the corner. Stubs of candles were on the table and on the stone steps leading up to the kitchen. Sean's light swept the room.

"It'll do," he murmured. "It'll do fine -"

Liam saw him take the black box from his pack. His dark face wore an expression of exultation; he caressed the box and turned it over in his hand. Like nothing it looked to Liam, like nothing to harm a babe. "Is that it?" Ben asked, incredulous. "That's bloody all?"

Sean was smiling now. "And this," he said. There was a wee thing in his hand, as you might have a pocket watch, it looked. "Like for the telly," he said. "Off in the skiff we press a number and here beneath the ground -" He paused and wiped the saliva from his chin with the sleeve of his jumper; his eyes were black and shifted from one man's face to the other's. He's mad, Liam thought, f---ing crazy. "Here," he went on, "Here, the bloody end of slavery comes, here Sean O'Malley gives his land her freedom -" He was breathing so heavy his chest was heaving and sweat stood on his face in great drops. Liam had to look away from him, so sick he was.

Sean positioned the box with loving hands. Twice he moved it to a more pleasing spot. Then he picked it up again; he held it to his lips and kissed it. Reverently he placed it back on the table. "Wait there, my luv," he whispered to it. "Wait there till I call ye!" He threw back his head and laughed, a laugh that crazy it turned Liam's bowels to water at the sound of it.

He looked back to the table as he turned to follow the two of them back into the night. Sean had left the detonator by the box.

The only sound, now, was the soft murmur of the water parting as he pushed his way through the narrow passage. They were on their hands and knees and he could hear, now and then, a small gasp of pain from Megan; her arm must be agony to her now, as she crept along behind him over the rough bed of the stream. Clearly, they were heading for a source of water, somewhere deep under the ground, hidden here for generations, slowly working to destroy the lover's tunnel, working in secret patience, eroding the rock and loosening the heavy timbers, seeping with sinuous fingers into every crevice, reclaiming the spaces of the deep earth for itself. It was so cold he couldn't feel the pain, though he knew his hands were bleeding. He felt blindly ahead and inched his body along. No use to think, just move, blind as a mole, moving forward into - what?

Megan was holding to his leg; he could feel the near panic in the grip of her hand. "Come on, love -" he whispered. He wanted to reach back and hold her in his arms; there wasn't room in the shaft, now, to even reach a hand back to her.

Then he felt her hold go weak and she was gone. He was alone in the black, airless hell and she was lost! "Megan!" he shouted. "Oh, Meg-" And his voice echoed dull in the airless confines of the earth. Its echo was the only sound above the whisper of the water.

So tightly he was wedged in between the crooked timbers and the stones that he couldn't turn. He wriggled backwards until his foot came against something yielding. "Megan?" he whispered, and the only answer was silence. He waited there, still, helpless, and the dark and the silence closed over and around him like a trap. Then he felt, more than heard, the quiet rasping of her breath; her face was out of the water, at least, and she could breathe.

If the tunnel opened up ahead, he could turn and come back for her. He shuddered to think of leaving her there, unconscious. What if she woke and found him gone and herself alone there in the deepness of the earth? He inched forward. "I'm coming back, love," he said. If only to stay here with you, he thought, until -

Not five feet further on, his hand struck a solid wall of stone! It was the end, the end of the tunnel, maybe the end of hope, as well.

Automatically he forced his hand to feel the entire surface of the wall. It went straight across from side to side of the tunnel, and as high as he could reach, and water ran down the face of it. He stretched his arm as high as he could from where he lay, half in and half out of the water. He was on his knees, now, and still reaching up. Then, laughing and crying, he got to his feet; the ceiling was far above him, here, and he could feel the top of the wall where the water ran over it. And far, far above him, there in the blackness, shined a narrow rim of light.

He fell to his knees, laughing and shouting, "Megan! we're there - we've found it!" He couldn't stop laughing; his sides hurt and hot tears ran down his cheeks. The opening of the tunnel behind him seemed impossibly small after his momentary freedom and its darkness even blacker after the tiny ray of light. He wedged himself in and crawled through the icy water until his hand touched her outstretched arm. It was limp and cold.

"Come, love," he whispered, and began to squirm backwards, pulling her by the arm. He heard her head splash into the water; then it was a struggle to keep her head in his arms as he worked to get her free of the tiny shaft. The few feet were like an endless mile in time; when he felt the open space above his head he stood and picked her up and held her to him; she felt dead in his arms, lifeless as a doll.

But there above him still glowed the tiny circle of light. What the hell, was this place? His head felt like a thousand bees were in it buzzing and his brain was fuzzed by the sound. Water, deep under the ground, had to mean something; why couldn't he think where he was? There was a wide ledge beside the wall, and he laid Megan there, gentle, not to hurt her arm.

He scooped some of the water up in his hand; God he was thirsty! It would save his life to have a drink. Lucky to be standing here in this well, wasn't it? The well! They could be right under the Ussher's kitchen. Hadn't he seen them bring the drinking water up in dripping wooden buckets into the kitchen, coming up on stone steps from the cellar? He bathed Megan's face with the water, and waited, quiet, beside her. He soaked his shirt and folded it and laid it over her forehead. "Megan, we're all right, love. We're there -" He kissed her on the lips and her arms came around his neck.

He pulled her to him and held her. "What is it?" she whispered. "What have I done, then?"

"You're ok," he said. "I think you fainted is all -"

"I never," she said. "I never fainted. I'll not believe the lying tongue in you -"

"Look, Megan, look -" he whispered. "Look up there." He turned her head so she could see the circle of unbelievable light shining like a tiny promise of hope for them, far above their heads.

The sweat stood out cold on her face and her shoulders ached. Before they got to the top her legs were lead and it was only for Charley putting them from rung to rung that she got up the ladder. Not really a ladder, it was, just metal bars stuck out from the walls of the well-shaft barely close enough to reach from one to the other, and her with the useless arm hanging at her side.

He must have been a tall one, that lover, to scramble up this forsaken way to get to his lady-love, tall and uncommon devoted into the bargain.

Only a few more feet and she'd be at the top. The light still shone, bright to their hurting eyes; her eyes did hurt, actually, from trying to see in the thick dark night of their underground prison, hurt to fall from her head, she thought, and the tiny warm light drew her to itself like a magnet draws filings of iron. "Can you reach it?" Charley called up to her. "I'll hold you -"

She felt his arms strong around her legs, and she let go the rung with her good hand. She leaned her body against the slippery wall, pressing it until it cleaved to the stones; she prayed not to think about falling. Very slowly, to keep her balance there, she raised her left hand until it was above her head. Mother of God! why did she think of it, even? Why think the cover might not lift? Suppose she couldn't move it. Weak as a hummingbird, she felt, and scarce dared put her hand to it.

It moved, ever so slight, she felt it move. "I can't lift it," she whispered. "Charley, I can't - can't lift -" Shamed, she was, of her weakness; she gave another shove and felt her balance going. She caught the rung with her right hand and pain seared through it, but she held on. "Just give me another shove," she said. Insane laughter was in her, then. "I'll put my head against it - it's hard enough, Dad always said."

Then it moved. Her eyes came level with the floor; she saw a rat scramble across the scrubbed stones of the storeroom, and somehow she pulled her body up to lie there, drinking in the light from the candle stubs that flickered and sputtered on the table above her, feeling her body bathed in the light that seemed a foreign thing after the hours of darkness and fear. Charley was beside her, and to look at him she began to laugh again. "A fine sight, you are, lad," she said through her laughter. So near to death, they were, that any life at all was pure joy, even the sight of Charley, his face white under the mud and streaks of blood, dragging himself to lie beside her, his breath coming in harsh gasps and his bare chest heaving to bring the air into his famished lungs. Poor lad, dragging a senseless woman through that muck and having to shove her miles up a madman's ladder -

And the blessed light from the candles flickered and glowed against the washed walls of stone; she couldn't take her eyes from them or cease from thanking God in her heart for the sight of them, for the sight of anything at all after the shattering, murderous dark of their tunnel under the earth. She was intoxicated by the gift of light, drunk on the extravagance of it; she blinked like an animal come out from hibernation, blinded by the light.

Charley leaned up on one elbow to look at her. He was grinning that crooked grin of his; to melt the heart inside a girl, it was. "Oh, Meg," he said, "Meg, love, we did it." Every bone in her hurt when he pulled her to her feet, and every muscle cried out in pain, but, her heart duly melted, she clung to him there while the breath came back in her and her eyes learned to see in the light again. Very gentle, his kiss was, then, and she thought for the love of him she would crawl through a thousand dark tunnels every day of her life until she died.

With Megan warm and safe in his arms like this, resentment boiled up in him. Where was it written that Charley Gibson alone must save the world? He thought of all the happy men who were holding their girls close and loving them, this very minute, no doubt, without having to know that the Queen was lying asleep over their heads, about to be blown to bits by a bunch of raving madmen. Happy men, who were not bound to leave their loves in a clammy cellar and trot about, looking, who knew where, or for what. He held her close against him, then; he could feel the beating of her heart, the thin, steady pulse in the hollow of her throat. God, oh, dear God, I love this woman! he said, almost aloud to be heard in the hard, still emptiness around them.

Then he saw it. Over the damp, tousled top of her head, halfway across the room, he saw the small, black box sitting, innocent as church, on the table, waiting he thought, patient, waiting to do its solitary, deadly task.

"What is it," Megan whispered. "What-"

He took her head in his two hands and turned it until she was facing where the box lay. "See that," he whispered. "We've found it." He saw her eyes widen. She drew in a little gasp of air. Her mouth opened as if she would speak, but there was only the silent, small sound of her breathing. "Stay here, love," he whispered. "I'll just have a look." His whole body seemed numb, seemed to belong to someone else, as he moved across the endless distance to where the box lay. It lay so harmless, there, doing absolutely nothing, while time was running, running crazy, faster and faster, and he moved as in slow motion towards it, heavy with knowing there was nothing he could do. He didn't even know what it was, what its method of destroying them would be. He listened for the ominous ticking that could be counting down their lives while he debated with himself what he could do; only silence answered him.

At his shoulder, Megan whispered, "Aren't there people who do this? Take the bloody things apart without blowing their own selves up?"

"Charley Gibson, instant demolition expert -" he said. He was surprised to see, when he took her hand in his, that he was not shaking anymore. He felt a kind of desperate calm settle in his gut. "Just watch," he said, "This won't hurt a bit." He was only a yard from it, on his knees, now, beside the table. There wasn't a sound in the room, only their breathing, while he reached his hand out to touch it.

In that silence, the sound of feet scuffling on the stones, coming down the stairs, pierced the clammy air like the heart-stopping shriek of a siren in the night.

CHAPTER TWENTY SIX

The wind in his face was like a cold shower; the damp air blowing across from the shore whipped around the wind-screen, howling like all the fiends of hell, Harry thought, and he wished there was time to stop and put the top up before pneumonia set in, or worse. He was doing roughly eighty miles an hour, here where the road was wide, almost wide enough to meet another car and stay out of the ditch at the same time. He kept trying to compute the wind-chill factor, hoping the unusual mathematical strain would keep him from thinking about Charley. The kinds of trouble he could imagine were none of them ones he wanted to dwell on.

The clock on the dash told him it was after one, less than half an hour since he had cleared the crooked streets of Galway, shifted into fifth gear and headed into the dark vastness of the Connemara night. He slowed to a modest sixty-five when the road suddenly narrowed. He was speeding between dense hedges that grew like walls beside the shoulderless road; it was very dark here and the rays of his headlights moved like gleaming blades cutting through the blackness. It was over thirty hours since anyone had contacted Charley.

He had left the coast, now, and the road twisted between outcroppings of rock and patches of scrubby trees. He picked up the phone from the seat beside him and, by the light from the dash, dialed five numbers. The receiver sputtered in his ear for a moment, then Gene's voice came clear to him.

"Harry?"

"Right."

"Where are you?"

"Wish I knew. Looks like a cow path -"

"Must be right, then," Gene laughed. Don't laugh, you ass, Harry thought; we've lost Charley.

He said, "Just get me there, Gene. The Old Man said you could-"

"You'll come to a church, one of those little stone ones. Three tenths of a mile after, look for a right between two stone walls -" The rest was easy; the scattered population of Connemara is connected by a road system of astonishing simplicity. There weren't any wrong turns. Then he saw it, the brooding silhouette of Ussher, rising black out of a grove of wind-swept trees. He flipped the lights off and let the car roll to a silent stop, hidden in the shadow of a great, spreading oak. The mysterious old building was dark, no single light showed from its windows. Here was where Charley ought to be - inside, safe and asleep.

Then he saw the twinkle of lights through the trees beyond the manor house. He could make out another building, beyond a high wall. He turned the key in the ignition; the lights flared on and the noise of the engine seemed enough to wake the dead. He let it idle along the road, then, past the sleeping Ussher, and he saw that adjoining it was an old stable, carriage house, whatever, and in it people were still awake, moving about on the ground floor.

Jamey was standing alone in the courtyard; Marianne and Pierre bustling about and worrying had put him in a right hissy. "The gendarmes," Pierre had said, "They must be notified -"

"Mais non!" Marianne, horrified, begged him. "Not now - what would *they* think?" She shrugged and nodded towards the lodge. "A scandal now? It would be of ruin to us, Pierre - you must not think it!"

"Ah, love," Jamey had said, "Sure it's not the first night I've waited for the girl and a young man -" In fact he didn't know why it bothered him at all, but it did. It was true, Megan had gone her own way when she pleased and a father learns when he should ask questions and when to keep peace. Yet, this night he *was* worried, and for no reason he could bring to mind. Could be the daft way the lad from Dublin was carrying on with him - that bloody fit over his camera and then rushing off into the night like an idjit. Sure, he'd plagued him the whole trip, had he not? That girl disappearing, running his horse into Charley, nothing but troubles from him there was, the whole time. He stayed there in the yard long after Marianne and Pierre had gone inside. Blast the girl! where was she? And why did it bother him so this night? A sensible man would be in bed, sleeping, a man with this lot of fools to get across the mountain on the morrow.

He saw the lights in the road before he heard the sound of the motor. It didn't occur to him that it wouldn't be Megan and Charley, getting a lift back from wherever the girl had taken them; dancing in Oughterard, they might have been, for all anyone knew. And him fashing himself the whole night over it! He stood in the shadow of the stableyard and waited; no need to look like keeping an eye on them, was there, now? Then the car door opened; one rather chubby individual jumped out and began to run across the cobbles towards the carriage house door. Not Charley, it wasn't, and no Megan with him, neither.

Before the door, the man stopped and stood, listening, was it? for voices; waiting, secret like, he seemed. Loose stones rattled on the cobbles when Jamey ran across the yard to him. Hearing him, the man turned from the door and peered into the dark, squinting through thick lenses. He moved with the grace and speed of a cat, this bear of a man.

"It's closed, can't you see?" Jamey said. "No need to ring, then."

Could be it was just a silly tourist, lost, here, in the night.

The man stood down from the stoop and took a step towards him. "Sorry to be so late," he said. "Are you the proprietor?"

"Nay," Jamey said. "A guest, only, out for a bit of air -" He held out his hand to the man. "Jamey Leary," he said.

"Harry Bedford," the man said. "Nice to know you -" He brushed the hair back from his forehead. His smile was warm, but Jamey could see the grey lines of exhaustion marking his face. "If you're looking for a bed, I'm afraid you're out of luck," he said. "The Ussher is full up, and only by the kindness of the landlady a few of us are staying here in the barn." He shrugged towards the carriage house; the last lights blinked out as they watched.

"Looking for a friend," Harry told him. "You wouldn't know anything about a bunch of people riding horses through here, would you?"

Jamey laughed. "Not bloody much," he said. "It's my people you're looking for, then, but most of the lot are staying other places. I told you Ussher was full -"

Harry interrupted him. "Did an American named Charley Gibson come along with you? A tall, thin guy?"

"Aye, he's along," Jamey nodded. "A good lad, he is, your friend. Would you be wanting to join us, now? We've a horse or two to spare -"

"Well, actually, no," Harry said. "No. Just had a message from home for Charley; nothing much, but I was near so I thought maybe I'd catch up with him here." The man seemed very happy at the thought, only, of being able to deliver a seemingly unimportant message to his friend, and in the small hours of the night it was, as well; something there was about the whole thing

Jamey didn't like.

"Well, sit you down and join me waiting for him then," Jamey said, "Sure, he's out with my girl, since before dinner - and she never saying a word of where they'd go." He tried a little laugh, but it dried up in his throat.

"Sounds like Charley," Harry said. He leaned closer to Jamey; his voice was serious, then. "Can we go inside to wait?"

"Aye," Jamey sighed, "Might as well have a pipe together, is it?"

"Actually, I need to talk with you," Harry said. "I think there's a problem-"

He saw Megan's eyes wide with fear; where could they hide? She pointed to the open well-cover, but he shook his head. There wasn't time. He searched the room with the beam of his flashlight. Behind them were three barrels, stood up close together; he seized Megan's hand and pulled her with him; they could hide there in the dark behind the barrels and wait. He could hear voices through the door, now. "--your bloody mouth shut. One of the two of ye could've picked it up --"

"It's *him*," Megan whispered. Inside the circle of his arm, he could feel her body shaking, trembling like a leaf moved by the early morning air; there, with nothing more than three wooden barrels of potatoes between them and death, he held her close to him, as though holding her would somehow keep them both from whatever disaster waited there in the dark cellar of Ussher.

The door to the stairs opened; a beam of light spread over

300

the floor. Almost to the edge of the barrels it came, then wavered back to the table not ten feet away. "There it is, where you bloody left it --" the smaller of the three men whispered. For a moment Charley felt hysterical laughter starting inside him. The idiots had gone off to blow up the Ussher and left the detonating device behind!

A dark, heavy-set man carried the torch. He shone it once around the room and then handed it to the little man. He ran to the table and picked up the thing that lay there. "Give us a light, damnit," he growled, and the two men leant close together, studying what he held in his hand. The third man hung back in the shadows. He was standing not a foot from the well. His foot struck the cover and he swore.

"Shut up, you fool," the first man hissed. "All of us killed, is it, you want?"

The light swung around to where the third man stood on the edge of the gaping, black hole. "What the bloody hell --?" the dark man said. He put the detonator down and snatched the light. He shined it down to see where the tell-tale water seeped across the stones. Through the space between the bottom of the barrels, Charley could see then, the light reflecting from the drying pools of water that left a dripping trail, from the edge of the well, across the floor, to where the men stood. From there, it led straight and treacherous over the cold stones of the floor to betray them where they crouched, trapped, behind the barrels. The beam of light followed the Judas signs and played around the barrels, a game of hide-and-seek, a game with very high stakes. He felt Megan's hand move in the sign of the cross; he held her very close.

"Bloody wet down here -- " The voice trailed off and the light moved away again. Charley began to breath again; Megan was still trembling in his arms. The man laid the light on the table top and reached once more for the detonator. Of course he needed to study it; this was the first lot of their new order, wasn't it? "Cum hold the damn light, ye idjit -- can I see in the dark, then?" the man growled. "Ye want us all blowed to hell and gone?"

"Sean," the other man began. "Sean, lad, stop and look you --"

"Shut up!" Sean snapped. "I've got the thing about figured, so just ye hold the light and keep your bloody mouth shut!" But his hands were shaking as he held the black thing in them; Charley thought he must fear its power, even as he was preparing himself to use it. Silence in the room echoed the fear. Charley prayed that Sean's friend was too gutless to defy him; his prayer appeared to him to be floating through the fetid air around them. He thought he could see it hanging there, an almost tangible presence. It didn't seem to surprise him that he could see this phenomenon, and there began to be a perception in the back of his mind that his head was lighter than air, and that he himself might float out there, a part of his visible prayer –

Megan's breathing beside him had almost stopped, and her weight against him seemed heavy. He remembered then why they were there and he heard his prayer unanswered, as the man holding the light spoke again. "There's summat behind the barrels, Sean. Look you ---"

The light made another sweep of the floor. It stopped at

the foot of the barrel in front of Charley.   "Summat must have cum out from the well --"

"You're daft, man. What creatur could be cummin' up from there –?"

There was a soft thud as Sean put the thing on the table. Steps came cautiously toward the row of barrels. "It's behind the potatoes, then." His voice was shaky now, but the light was steady, relentless, shooting prying fingers to one side and then the other of their pathetic barricade.

They were very close now. In one more second the light would shine over the top of the barrels and blind their dark-weakened eyes. They were trapped like giant rats in a virtually soundproof torture chamber, deep under the ancient walls of Ussher.

It wasn't conscious thought; it was animal instinct only that brought him to his feet. But it was a real rebel yell he gave, and it echoed from the cold stone walls and ricocheted from the low ceiling. He lunged forward, shoving the barrel over, with strength he didn't know he had. The man with the flashlight was sprawled across the floor and the light shone in crazy flashes around them. Potatoes rolled drunkenly everywhere.

The tall, sad man stood as if frozen, between the table and the open well. The dark one, Sean, hesitated a moment only, before Charley felt the searing pain of a fist against the side of his head. He was on his knees on the floor and one eye saw nothing but red, where the blood ran down over it. He was jerked to his feet, and from behind him an arm circled his throat.

The small man was up now, the flashlight abandoned on

the floor, its beam uselessly shining against the wall.   In the unsteady light of the candles, Charley saw that Megan was behind the man; in two more steps she would be close enough to shove him down the black hole in the floor.   And she would, Charley thought -- my God, she really would!

"Behind you, Ben!" Sean yelled. Ben turned, saw Megan and had her crushed against him before she could move.   Charley saw the color leave her face; her broken arm was twisted behind her back. The man was holding her not one foot from the edge of the well. A light fog rose from the black hole; its presence seemed a token of the evil that held them there in silence and in fear.

"Bitch!" the man hissed. "See how ye like the look of it yoursel." He shoved her to within an inch of the edge. The arm around Charley's throat tightened its grip; his lungs shouted for air. He tried to call to Megan and there was no sound. "I love you -" his lips moved to say and she smiled at him.

Then, behind her on the table, he saw it. It lay on the table, the detonator, innocent and quiet, looking like something that would change channels for you, or shut the set off; seeing it, it was hard to imagine that it had the power to ignite a holocaust of destruction, that everything around them could be reduced to ashes and dust by one touch on its sleek black side. Megan saw it, too. Their eyes met and he knew what she was telling him. As plain as speech, she told him to get it and - what? Throw it down the well, down to oblivion there in the fastness of the earth, to a forgotten grave under the ancient stones?

There were no clocks there; time was frozen and the air held silence heavy in it, filling the room with a poison he could almost smell. For an endless moment, no one moved. The arm across his throat was choking him, and a grip like a vise held his hands behind him. He tried to nod to Megan and the arm tightened; he couldn't breathe. The third man still stood alone, just at the edge of the light; alone, as though to separate himself from the scene, remove himself from the cast of characters that stood frozen in the yellow light.

The room seemed to be getting darker; he was going to black out. He felt his body go limp, and Sean let him slide to the floor. He looked up and saw the gun stuck in Sean's belt, and his hand reaching for it. If only he could move, Charley knew he would get the gun, save Megan and destroy the detonator, but his arms and legs refused any suggestion of motion. It was as if his body belonged to another person.

But if Sean had a gun, he could shoot Megan! Gotta get that gun, gotta stop him -- His body seemed to unroll in slow motion; in an agony of slowness he pulled himself up on the edge of the table. His eye came level with the little black detonator. Better get it first; what good to have the gun and then all be blown to bits with that bloody thing? As his hand, seemingly of its own volition, stretched out to get it, his mind waited quietly for the dead, dull shock of a bullet in his back. He almost had his hand on the thing when the butt of the gun smashed into his shoulder and, through the flash of pain, he saw a dark hand reach past him toward where the instrument lay on the table. The screaming pain reminded him that he was alive; they hadn't shot him.

Of course, they wouldn't shoot him and they wouldn't shoot Megan either; they couldn't afford to be heard above the stairs. However casual security was, a gunshot would have them here, running.

The small, heavy-set man grinned. "Let me get rid of her, and we run for it, eh, Sean?" he said. "And him?" he nodded in Charley's direction. When he spoke, Charley focused on him and saw that he had the gun now, pressed against Megan's temple. His eyes were bright and glittered from under heavy brows. His arm was clutching Megan to him; his hand was on her breast. She wasn't struggling now; she could feel the cold steel against her head.

Sean stopped in mid-reach. The detonator still lay on the table. He took a step towards the man. "Ye'll bloody wait till I tell you what, Ben Shane," he snarled. He reached out again towards the thing on the table. It was so quick Charley almost didn't see it. Twisting in the man's grasp, Megan's foot shot out as Sean stepped past the well-opening. He lost balance and almost fell, then stepped back, back into nothing, and they heard his scream of rage echoing up through the damp, miasmic air of the well-hole. Over the sound of him, over the thin, hoarse sound of his scream, they heard a dull, splashy thud. The scream became a string of curses --

Then the curses turned to a wild shriek; it sounded like a woman in travail. They stood transfixed by the horror of it; the terrible cry from deep in the earth echoed round the little room and chilled their blood as they heard it. Ben glared at Charley. "Get him out," he finally yelled. "Get him bleedin' out of it, you bloody bastard!"

Now the sound was only a little whimper; then it ended,

leaving the memory of it hanging all around them in the fetid air of the room. Ben moved back from the well, pulling Megan with him. "Liam," he hissed. "Get the bloody thing -- I'll get rid of these two --" His breath was heavy with fear. Command was new to him, and he was sweating with the weight of responsibility, sweating here in the cold cellar. Charley held his breath; there was no reason in the man, now. He'd fire the gun when he damn well pleased. And it was still at Megan's head. He could see the pulse in her temple; it fluttered like a bird's wing beside the muzzle of the gun.

Their eyes met. He saw, then, the determined little girl's face, going to meet Lady Dudley, fear or not, and his heart froze. Dear God, don't let her try anything. The man will shoot you, love -- he wanted to shout it to her -- don't try it! He began to pull himself up again by the side of the table. The man's voice was pitched high with fear. "Git down! I'll f---ing kill her --" he screamed. "Liam! where the hell --?"

The hammer came from nowhere. It smashed the man's skull as if it were a clay pot full of geraniums. The gun went off, wild, unaimed, and Charley felt the sting of the ricocheting bullet on his leg. Megan wrenched free of Ben's grasp before he fell, heavy, to the ground. Beside her, the man, Liam, stood holding the bloody hammer in his two hands.

Even under the cast, the flesh of her arm crawled when she thought of it, how the body looked when they finally got it out of the well. She'd bit clean through her lip, trying not to scream, and

307

after, outside on the cool grass, she'd been sick, gasping and retching till she was so weak from it she couldn't stand. Charley held her close, then, and took her back into the kitchen, where Daddy was, with that short-sighted teddy bear of a man who'd come bursting down the stairs after the shot.

When she'd tripped the bloody bastard and sent him down the hole, she'd only just had time to think jolly good riddance to bad rubbish, before, all at once she heard the sound of crushing bone, the yelp of surprised pain and the crack of the gun beside her head. Then she was free and in Charley's arms. A tall, gaunt man stood beside them, his face as grey as ashes, his eyes staring at nothing. Then he leaned over and picked up the tiny black thing that still lay on the table. Gravely, he offered it to Charley. The hand that held it shook; the rough, boatman's hand, shaking like the fragile birch leaves by the lake, and Charley took it from him. Wordless, he held it, then, and nodded a polite thank-you. Frozen, they were, like characters in a play; they couldn't remember what the next lines should be.

Then the door burst open and Daddy had come running down the stairs, with a man looking like a teddy bear in glasses behind him. Two Englishmen were right behind them; she saw the guns in their hands as they pushed past Daddy and the teddy bear. A right mess she and Charley must have looked; sure her Dad went white when he saw them. The two men with guns had seized poor Liam and taken his hammer from him. He stood dumb as a sheep while they did it; they had him handcuffed, then and shoved him down on a stool between them.

"No," she whispered. "No, don't. Daddy, it's him that

saved us --"

Then Jamey had her in his arms; her and Charley both, and he was laughing and crying at once, and his arms so strong around them she felt faint with the effort of breathing, even.

Charley looked at the teddy bear and he laughed. "Toad, by God, they let you out!" It seemed a great joke to Harry, and they both laughed. Her head went light and the room swam about her, so she sat on the floor. No one seemed to notice Ben, stretched out like a shorn and bloody fleece on the stones. The men had let Liam go and when he found his tongue he said, "Hadn't we ought to get Sean up from there?" He motioned to the black hole in the floor.

So they sent for block and tackle and the lad from upstairs to help. They winched him up on the block; his body swung against the side of the well, bumping along. Once it caught on something -- "One of the rungs," Megan said -- and they had to fiddle with the rope. She was watching as the body came sliding over the edge of the hole. "Mother of God!" Jamey gasped. "Oh, Holy Mother of God --" Thick, slimy bodies writhed and turned, covering most of the thing they had brought up into the light. Blood oozed from where the eels' heads were fastened, holding to the death, seized onto the belly and the legs of it; the face was concealed under the deadly kiss of a monstrous eel as thick as a man's leg, it was, and wrapped about the neck and chest of what had once been Sean O'Malley, murderer of tyrants, savior of his people.

She couldn't stop looking; she heard a small, thin scream far away and didn't know it came from her own throat.

Now, sitting in the bright great-room beside the kitchen, clean and plastered and stitched, she looked across the table at Charley. "They must have been there all along," she said. "A good job we didn't wake them --"

She'd have to stop thinking about it now. Breakfast was on its way, Charley was smiling at her, and she was hungry, hungry as a starved cat, and it was a new day and she loved Charley until she thought her heart would burst inside her. Pegeen came in, very gentle, with a smile for them, and plates of eggs benedict steaming on her tray.

The doctors had made a right mess of Charley. His head was in a great plaster and there was a row of stitches like a centipede crawling across his nose. They'd wrapped his leg in yards of white bandage where the bullet had creased him; one eye was black and nearly shut. "Have you seen a mirror, lad?" she said.

"Don't have to," he said. "I can just look at you." He was watching her with a look to melt a stone, and she reached her cast across the table to touch his hand. He held the plaster in both his hands, then. "Megan Leary," he said, "When will you marry me?"

"Not before tonight," she said, and when the words were out of her mouth, her head drooped and she fell asleep, there on the table with her face resting on a plate full of Marianne's best eggs benedict. The next she knew, it was dark and she was in bed and all the devils in hell were bashing about in her head. Her arm blazed with pain, and her swollen lip was cracked and bleeding. One eye was swelled shut and her mouth tasted of something vile. She could see Charley, where he slept sitting up in the chair by her bed. She reached over and touched his hand. Every bone in her body screamed in pain. "Tomorrow, my love," she whispered, "Tomorrow it is we'll marry, I promise --"

She closed her eyes again and through the open window came the song of a night bird, floating across the quiet air. Next door, in an upstairs bedroom, the two corgis woke and listened to the singing of the bird. They stood a moment, with stiffened hair, by the window. Then, satisfied that their mistress was safe in a peaceful world, they lay down by the foot of her bed and slept.

EPILOGUE

Spring often comes late in the west of Ireland. The sky hangs low over the mountains and thick fog washes in from the sea. This year was no exception, but there wasn't another place in the world where they wanted to go. So Charley brought Megan to Ussher House for their wedding night. All night the cool, soft air blew in the open windows of their room, smelling of gentle growing things and bringing them, at dawn, the song of a lark, distant and clear; they woke in each other's arms.

They hadn't married the next day, after all. It had been almost a year until Charley could get free of the agency for a month's leave, and Megan had had a time finding someone to take her place with Jamey. No one ever could, he told her, but then the lad, Timmy, found that horses were more to his liking than primroses, and he began to follow Megan about like a shadow until Jamey said the two of them were driving him mad, and why in the name of the Holy Virgin didn't Megan run off and get herself married?

Marianne was like a mother hen preparing a nest, so excited she was over the honeymoon. A suite was prepared with the best linens and fresh flowers; Marianne found the new girl a wonderful help getting these things ready. She loved Sheila; she could never forget the day she found the poor child on her doorstep, starving and cold, begging for a job, any job, to keep her until her baby should be born. A poor little mouse of a girl she was; her eyes set in dark circles and no light in them at all, only a sadness to break the heart. Impossible to turn her away!

It was almost a year ago, just after the terrible affair of the bomb. Now the baby was here, a perfect little boy; a wonder he was, so loving and good. Wolfe, the girl called him, and while she worked, he lay in a basket by her side and she sang to him as she trotted back and forth between the rooms; songs of love and longing she sang, old songs she sang to him, and never he cried, only smiled and laughed the whole day long.

*With gratitude to the dear critic on my hearth,
my husband Gene, without whose enthusiastic
support this book would never have come to be*

Nancy Bradley

*N.B. The lines of poetry that go through Charley's head in
times of crisis are from 'Annabel Lee', Edgar Allen Poe's
chilling account of terror and of fear and of love long lost*